To Tony

From Jacklee

July 2 '04

Max Blake, Federal Marshal

The
Killing Trail

Best Wishes
and
Happy Trails
Florence
June 2004

Max Blake, Federal Marshal

The
Killing Trail

William Florence

Dally Press

Dally Press
12822 E Rialto, Sanger CA 93657
On the internet at
www.dallypress.com
email: editor@dallypress.com

ISBN 0-9718511-2-3

Max Blake, Federal Marshal
The Killing Trail
© 2004 William Florence

Cover: artwork by Jack Lee; design by Ben Protasio

ACKNOWLEDGMENTS:
*Many people helped bring Max Blake to life. Among those who
require special thanks from the author: Steve Jackson, Joe Howry,
and Mike McClinton, for early support and assistance; Bob LeRoy,
for an excellent critique; Jack Lee and Ben Protasio, for the cover
concept; Len Wilcox, for great catches ... and for taking a chance;
Bernie Knab, for support and encouragement and friendship; Dick
Thien, for being the finest newspaper editor in America; William
E. Florence, whose appreciation for antique firearms cast a
decades-wide net; and most of all Linda, Will, and Erin, for
constant encouragement and their love of the American West.*

Max Blake, Federal Marshal

The Killing Trail

Contents

For my mother, Susanna Bauer Drouillard,
who always shared her love of literature ...
and who knows how to tell great stories

Chapter One
Four Doors, Three Girls

The feeling was always the same.

But what would you expect when someone was trying to kill you again?

There was a tightness – almost a knot – deep inside of him. Yet he was somehow relaxed, even confident. His eyes burned with an intense fire that directed and focused his energy. And all of his senses seemed to spring to his hands and move on to his fingers, which instinctively curled in and out, in and out, near the gun that was carefully strapped to his side.

Max Blake waited, wordlessly. His eyes picked up every movement around him. His fingers continued to flex, and his grim stare drilled holes in the man who stood no more than 15 feet away in the middle of the only saloon in the dusty town of Pueblo Springs, population 72.

"You're a no-account bastard, Blake," the man shouted. "Everybody in this flea-bitten place'll thank me when I've shot you sure dead. This town'll owe me. Everybody'll owe me."

Max Blake said nothing. He continued to stare at the man who cursed him, all the while flexing the fingers of his right hand, held just inches from his holstered Colt revolver.

"What's the matter, Blake? Nothing to say before you die?" the man called out from across the room.

His voice was filled with bluster, but he was growing nervous when he received no answer to his taunts. He swayed a little as he spoke: perhaps because of the thick heat in the saloon, perhaps because of the tequila that he had been drinking throughout the day. Or maybe it was his nerves that caused his body to rock noticeably from side to side – that and the slow realization that he was facing down a man infamous in the territory for fast draws and faster kills.

With his hat pushed back to expose an unruly crop of greasy black hair, a heavy stubble that indicated a distinct distaste for a razor, and clothes that looked as if he hadn't taken them off in days, it was tough to figure why anyone would lay claim to a man with so little charm – and seemingly so little time to live. But even a wild animal has its admirers.

"Sit down and don't say no more, Johnny Dole," one of the saloon girls said softly, pleadingly, from a far corner of the room. "Sit down before it's too late. Please. You've bit off more than you can chew up this time."

"Shut up yerself," the man called Johnny hissed back at the girl. He steadied himself a bit. "I can handle this hombre all right. He's a no-account bastard. I just want to see him squirm some 'fore I kill him."

Max Blake had used this time to quickly take in the rest of the saloon. When the shooting started, and he knew that it would, he didn't want any innocent people to get in the way of a stray slug. He also didn't want to be surprised by any of Johnny's friends.

Johnny Dole now turned again and called out loudly: "How 'bout it, Blake? You gonna squirm some?"

There was still no answer – only the grim stare and the burning eyes.

"Come on. Say something, Blake," Johnny called out. "You've kilt your last man, mister. You're nothing, Blake. Nothing at all. You'd best make your final peace with whatever God..."

And with that, Johnny Dole went for the gun at his side.

But his hand had just grasped the wooden handles of his battered six-gun when the shot from Max Blake's Colt .45 exploded through the saloon, echoing off the walls and the windows and the batwing doors and the bottles of rye and tequila and the shiny mirror behind the long counter.

Johnny's body jerked violently backward, crashing into the crudely painted wood that served as the edge of the bar. It then tilted sideways and finally slammed into a table before pitching onto the dirty, beer-stained sawdust floor.

Johnny was dead before he hit the ground.

His gun never cleared the holster, which had been slung low at his side.

The eerie echoes of the single gunshot continued to linger as the dozen or so bar patrons tried to grasp exactly what had happened.

"Did you see that?" one of the cowboys asked at last, directing the question to no one in particular. The saloon girl who had spoken only seconds before tried to stifle a single sob, but she made no movement at all.

No one moved.

"Someone had better go fetch the sheriff," the bartender said at last.

"Deke, you run out and fetch Sheriff Todd. Get him now, ya hear? And tell him that Johnny Dole looks to be rock-hard dead."

Deke, a bald-headed man with a heavy brushy beard, backed out of the saloon, his wide eyes never leaving Max Blake's until he stumbled on the loosely nailed wooden planks outside. Deke then cursed and headed for the sheriff's office. "Tell me what I miss," he called over his shoulder.

Max Blake, federal marshal, walked cautiously up to the body that was lying grotesquely and misshapen on the floor, the arms outstretched and the legs twisted and arched at the knees. He bent and looked hard at the dead man for a moment. Then he stood up, holstered his gun with an effortless flick of his wrist, and slowly put his back to the bar.

He took in the room around him once again – his eyes still hard, still focused, still searching. He remained wary; a man in the killing business learns quickly never to let his guard down. And Max Blake knew from years of experience that the dead man might have a friend somewhere – another hot-headed cowboy with a belly full of cheap liquor, a six-gun strapped to his side, and not much in the way of brains to help him along in life.

"Nice shootin', mister," one of the men at the card tables said in a nervous effort to break through the awkward silence. "Mighty glad to see that man dead – and we all are, I'd say."

The saloon girl who had tried to talk Johnny Dole out of his pursuit of a quick death sat down in a heap at one of the card tables and began softly crying, but no one seemed to pay her any notice.

"That's right, Mr. Blake," the bartender said. "Johnny Dole was an ornery cuss, always picking fights and trouble and such. But he sure as hell shouldn't have picked a quarrel with you, no sir. Only a plum loco fool would do that – meaning no disrespect, of course.

"Here, let me get you a drink, Mister, ah, I mean Marshal Blake."

The bartender quickly poured a shot of tequila into a clean glass, and Max accepted it without comment, taking the drink with his left hand so that he could keep his gun hand free. He tasted the tequila and then put the glass down on the bar, his eyes never leaving the dozen or so men and the three saloon girls who were still waiting around as though they all were expecting something else to happen.

The batwing doors to the saloon suddenly flew open, and the town's sheriff, Neil Todd, walked quickly inside with Deke Wilson a couple of steps behind.

"It's just like I told ya, sheriff," Deke said. "You can see old Johnny right there. It all happened so sudden-like."

"I see him, Deke. You take it easy now. Someone tell me what happened here," the sheriff said as he slowly circled the dead man. He glanced down at the body of Johnny Dole once or twice, but his eyes traveled around the room, looking at all of the faces that in turn were staring not at him but at the man at the bar just a few feet away.

"Well, it was a fair fight, sheriff – if you can call something like this fair," the bartender said.

"What do you mean by that, Mike?" Sheriff Todd asked the bartender.

"Well, there's no doubt that Johnny braced this man here," he said, gesturing toward Max. "Mister Blake – I mean Marshal Blake – was minding his own business here at the bar when Johnny came up and kinda pushed him aside. The marshal looked at him but never said a word and even moved a couple of feet away. But then Johnny came over and pushed him again, hard this time. And he swore at him and told Marshal Blake that he was a no-account bastard who needed to die."

"What got into Johnny this time – other than a belly full of lead?" the sheriff asked; the irony was missed by most everyone in the saloon.

"He was full of tequila," the bartender said. "And he was always looking to make a name for himself when he was drinking hard like that. Word had spread around the bar like a Texas twister that Marshal Blake had come on in; and Johnny started pushing at him, trying to start something, right away. Old Johnny was looking for the chance to make himself famous, I guess."

"But what'd you mean when you said something about a fair fight?" Sheriff Todd asked the bartender, who was now absent-mindedly polishing the top of the dirty bar with a damp dirty cloth.

"Hell, sheriff, Johnny went for his gun first after trying to prod Marshal Blake here, the way he always did when he picked a gunfight. But Johnny no more'n got his hand down to his holster when Mister – I mean Marshal – Blake's gun was out and spittin' lead. Johnny moved first, all right. But it sure as hell weren't no fair fight, if you get my meaning, sheriff. Johnny Dole never had a chance. The stupid bastard never had a chance."

The sheriff looked at Max Blake for the first time. "You ever see this man before?" he asked.

Max shook his head but didn't answer.

"You have any idea why Johnny Dole would try to pick a fight with you?" he asked.

"I'd say the man was a fool, sheriff."

These were the first words that Max had spoken since he arrived in the town, and they sounded odd even to his ears. He had been on the trail for days without having talked to a living thing outside of his horse, and he had been hot and thirsty when he walked into the saloon with the mind to ask a couple of questions and instead had run headfirst into the disagreeable Johnny Dole.

He didn't like to talk much anyway, and so he had only motioned for a beer when the trouble started. But Johnny Dole had pushed the issue before Max had been able to get the drink, and well before he could offer so much as a thanks for getting it.

All that Max Blake could do was to see that no one else died in the gunfight that ensued.

"Is that the way it happened then, like Mike here says it did?" the sheriff asked.

"That's the way it happened," Max agreed without adding more.

The sheriff nodded his head for a second or two and then motioned to two men to cart away the body. "You'd better take him down to Doc Jones before the heat starts eatin' away at him," the sheriff said. He pulled a soiled bandana from his back pocket and wiped down the back of his neck.

Max watched closely as two men struggled with the dead weight of the body, knocking over a chair as they lurched across the room and out the door. He reached for the glass of tequila on the bar, took another small sip, and then noticed what he was drinking for the first time. "I'll take that beer now," he said to the bartender.

"Right, Marshal Blake. Right away, sir."

"What brings you to Pueblo Springs?" the sheriff asked. "I trust that you are just passing through?"

"Hard to say."

The sheriff studied Max for a few seconds and then tried a different approach. "You might not want to say why you're here, marshal. But I run a quiet, peaceable town, and I want to know when people aim to disturb that peace – no matter what side of the law they ride on."

Max took the glass of beer that the bartender offered him, pulled a coin from his shirt pocket and slid it across the bar, and then took a long draw from the glass. He wiped his mouth with the back of his hand and looked hard at the sheriff.

"I'm looking for a man," he said. "Been on his trail for the better part of a week. He's called Tom Culpepper."

"I know that name," the bartender interrupted. "Most everybody here-'bouts does, too."

"Mike's right," the sheriff said. "There's a lot of paper on Culpepper – for robbery, rape, murder and such. A big, ugly man, he's supposed to be, with a deep scar on his left cheek from a knife fight, as I've heard it. Never seen the man myself, though; just the picture on the wanted posters. And I've got some of his in my office."

Max looked around the bar and then said in a quiet but steely voice that commanded attention, "Anyone here see this man Culpepper in this town?"

"Tom Culpepper's a right dangerous man," Sheriff Todd said. "I'm glad to say he hasn't been seen in Pueblo Springs or in these parts, so far as I know of."

"You might want to keep your eyes open then because his trail led into this saloon," Max said as he watched the sheriff blanch at the words.

"What are you saying exactly, marshal?" the sheriff managed to blurt out after a moment.

Max shrugged. "The trail looked fresh to me – hours old, if that. Not many places where a man can hide in this town. Are there, sheriff?"

Neil Todd's eyes darted nervously about the saloon. He looked carefully around the room and up and down the stairs that led to the four bedrooms over the bar; they were used by the saloon girls and the drunks and cowpokes and the drifters who were looking for a little fun while passing through.

"You boys seen any strangers about?" he asked, his voice more than a touch on the testy side.

"God, but that would be too much to hope for," Mike the bartender said. "Tom Culpepper and Max Blake in this very town on the very same day. What would you pay to see that?"

"You'd better think twice about it," the sheriff said. "There's been enough killing around here for one day – and maybe even enough for a full week or more.

"How 'bout it?" he called out. "Anybody seen any sign of a stranger in town? Anyone of you girls?"

"I think I'd recognize a big man with an ugly scar, sheriff," one of the saloon girls said. "This man here" – she pointed at Max – "is the only fresh face I've seen all day. Maybe one of the other girls..."

"Just the same, you'd all best be on the lookout," the sheriff interrupted, intently studying every face in the room. "Tom Culpepper is no man to mess with, I can assure you all of that. There's enough wallpaper on Culpepper in my office to torch up this town, if anyone cared to take a match to it."

The doors to the saloon suddenly flew open again, and a frantic man carrying a black bag bustled inside. Doc Jones was grizzled and in his mid-sixties, with a ragged beard of white and gray hairs that sprung out in odd directions around his face. He made his way directly to the bar and called for a double whiskey. He knocked it down with a gulp, asked for another, and then looked up and curiously eyed Max Blake, whose attention was now directed toward the top of the stairs above the bar.

Max had noticed that there were four doors upstairs, and three of them were open; there also were three saloon girls in the bar. The fourth door had remained closed, even after the shooting, but now it was open just a crack.

"That was some piece of shootin', mister," Doc Jones said, momentarily interrupting the deathly silence. "You plugged old Johnny Dole once through the pump – dead center and make no mistake. That's not a bad way to go if it's your time, I'd say."

He downed the second whiskey and looked at Max again.

"You might be good for business," he said, "but I hope you ain't staying around town long. I'm not sure I can stand all this excitement at my age. It's not good for the heart."

Max never heard what was said. The words had barely cleared the Doc's mouth when Max spun to his right and crouched low along the edge of the bar. Before anyone realized what was happening, he pulled his gun in an effortless motion and fired two quick shots toward the top of the stairs. The sharp report of a rifle cracked at the same time, and the whine of a rifle bullet could be heard as it double-thumped into one of the bar tables and finally lodged itself in a distant wall.

Then, slowly and with a steady thump-thump-thump, a body pitched forward and slid down the stairs, head-first and face down, following the clattering of what looked like a well-used Winchester lever-action rifle.

The body slumped into a heap at the bottom of the stairs and didn't move. A growing pool of blood stained the floor beneath the chest.

Max Blake cautiously rose from his crouch. "Anybody hit by that stray bullet?" he asked. Getting no reply, he mumbled an almost inaudible "good" and then slowly moved toward the body.

"Unless I miss my guess, that's Tom Culpepper," Max said.

For the second time in the space of but a few minutes, he bent down, took a long look, and made sure that a man he had shot was stone dead. Standing upright again, he broke open the cylinder on his Colt and quickly shucked three fresh .45 cartridges into the gun while keeping a wary eye on the others in the saloon.

A man needs some backup in a situation like this, Max thought. *I just might want to pick up a second gun one of these days.*

A surprised Sheriff Todd, who hadn't moved from his place at the bar during the shooting, finally collected himself somewhat and walked slowly toward the body of the dead man. He knelt down and looked hard into the man's face.

"There's a big scar here," he said. "This has got to be Tom Culpepper, all right. Now how in hell do you account for that?"

"He must have come up the outside stairs and through one of the open windows," Mike the bartender said. "He sure didn't come in the front door."

"Marshal Blake?" the sheriff asked.

Max turned to the man and said easily, "Four doors upstairs, three girls downstairs. Culpepper was behind the fourth door."

"But you ain't been here long enough to notice that," the sheriff protested.

Max shook his head. "I stay alive because I notice those things."

"But..."

"He likely heard the shooting and enough afterward to know why I was here. He just wanted to settle things without more talk."

"But how did you see him up there?" the sheriff asked. "I had a direct line up those stairs from where I was standing, and I didn't hear him or see him – or anything else 'cepting the Doc here ... and you."

Max said nothing. Doc Jones, meanwhile, moved over to do a fast examination of the body. He shook his head and stood up after a minute. "A single shot to the heart, clean enough," he said. "The second shot must have missed."

"You'd best look again, Sawbones," Max said as he moved back toward the bar and picked up his half-finished beer.

Doc bent over the body again. "No, there's only a single wound here," he said. "There's a big bullet hole right dead center in the man's heart.

"No. No, wait just a damned minute: That hole's too big for a single bullet."

He cursed softly under his breath and turned around to look at Max. "You hit him twice in damn near the exact same spot, didn't you?" Doc asked, unable to disguise the awe in his voice. "There's two bullet holes there, all right — one right on top of the other. Well I'll be a go-to-hell."

Deke Wilson, who had been quiet in the corner, broke for the doors to spread the latest news to the handful of people who had gathered on the street outside the saloon.

Sheriff Todd could only shake his head and look at Max Blake. "Marshal," he started to say; but then he stopped, shook his head again, and turned to leave the saloon.

"Any paper on this Johnny Dole?" Max asked as Sheriff Todd started to walk away.

"Hell no there ain't," the sheriff said, turning around again. "If there was, I'd 'ave had him in my jail a long time ago. I'm an honest man, by God. What do you ask for, anyway?"

"Seems a shame to kill a man and not have any paper on him," Max said. "Judge Radford back in Twin Forks won't look kindly on that."

The sheriff looked hard at Max for a second. He started to say something but once more thought better of it; even so, Max could spot the look of distrust – perhaps fear was a better word – in the man's eyes.

"Don't worry, sheriff," Max said. "I'll move on as soon as you get Judge Radford's stamp to collect the reward on Culpepper. There's three-hundred dollars offered, dead or alive."

Sheriff Todd looked squarely at Max Blake. "That shouldn't take long – an hour or two at the most," he said. "I expect that you can leave this town well before sundown. And frankly, I'd be obliged if you did, federal marshal or no."

He motioned to two cowboys as he turned and walked toward the door. "You boys get that body the hell out of here."

"Imagine that," Mike the bartender said as the doors swung shut behind the sheriff. "Max Blake and Tom Culpepper in my bar at the same time on the same day, and Max Blake and me both live to tell about it.

"Drink up! Drink up, boys – and there's a drink on the house for you, Marshal."

"I'm not a drinking man," Max said as he finished his beer. "I came in because of the tracks."

He started to leave and then turned toward Doc Jones. "Sorry about causing the run on your time," he said. "But killing's a tough business on everybody."

With that, Max Blake walked assuredly through the saloon and pushed past the doors and into the fading sunlight. An old, tired mongrel looked up from his lounging spot on the wooden porch; the dog rolled his eyes open as Max approached and started to get up to slink away. Max stopped for a brief moment, reached down, and scratched around the dog's ears a bit.

"Stay where you are, old fella," he said softly. "No need to move on my account." Then he headed on down the street toward the sheriff's office.

He could feel the eyes of every person in town boring into his back. And every face on the street followed his every step.

Chapter Two
An Old Score To Settle

Max Blake was used to having people stare at him. His tough, weathered features and the confident manner in which he moved were certain signs that he was a man to be reckoned with – constantly.

Max was young in years, but his time on the trail with a six-gun in his hand made him seem far older. He was an even six feet tall, a lean and muscular 180 pounds, with skin roughened and darkened and weathered by the sun. His face was evenly chiseled, although handsome was not a term that first came to mind when people described Federal Marshal Max Blake.

What people remembered most were his eyes: coal black, almost emotionless – frightening in a way.

"His eyes have a way of burning holes right through you," Mike the bartender was telling anyone who would listen to him – and there were plenty of people who would – soon after Max left the lone saloon in Pueblo Springs, where the population had been reduced by two shortly after he rode into town.

Most everywhere he went, in fact, people with any sense at all gave Max Blake a wide berth. Only fools or drunks, the ones like Johnny Dole, picked a quarrel with him.

When Max Blake turned his attention to someone, killing was often sure to follow. He was as quick, and surely as deadly, as a mountain cat.

Max had learned to shoot when he was 10 years old. His father and mother were killed in 1862 in a raid by renegade Confederate soldiers outside of their small Missouri home, and Max was packed off to his Uncle Edward's ranch in Wyoming. His father's brother

20

was a fair man and a good man, and he treated Max as if he were his own son. His Aunt Emily also took kindly to Max and did her best to provide him with a good book education and to instill what she called decent Christian values into the boy.

But Edward Blake hired hard men to work the cattle on his ranch, and Max was an apt student of everything he heard and saw and was allowed to do – from riding to roping, from mending fence to tracking strays, from dealing with hard-bitten men to shooting guns.

Especially shooting.

Max took to the feel of a gun naturally. He was gifted; he knew it. And everyone around him who saw him handle a Colt Peacemaker or a big-bore Sharps rifle could only marvel at the youngster's skill. He always considered that a six-gun was an extension of his arm and his hand – a natural thing. He understood it: how it worked, how it felt, how it reacted in different weather and in different situations or circumstances.

By the time he was 12, there wasn't a man on the ranch who could shoot straighter or quicker, and there were a number of men on Edward Blake's spread who could handle a gun.

By the time he was 15, there wasn't a man in the county who could hold a match to young Max Blake's skills with a gun of any kind.

"Course, you ain't any good and proved yerself till you've kilt a man," an old ranch hand named Pops McCoy told Max one afternoon after watching him destroy with deadly, rapid-fire accuracy a row of whiskey bottles along a split rail fence. Pops had spent his life in the West and years working with Max as a teacher first and friend second.

"That's just the trouble," Max's uncle broke in. "Being good with a gun only guarantees killing in one form or another. I don't hold much truck for men who use a gun for that purpose, or for any reason other than putting meat on the table and defending themselves and their family."

"But the boy has a knack, a gift," Pops said. "This boy could surely make his way in the world with a gun."

Max kept quiet. His uncle reflected on Pop's remark for a time and then finally answered.

"You can earn a living with a gun if you want to, son," he said to Max. "But I've been around for a lot of years now, and I've seen enough in this life to know that I hope you don't head down the killing trail. There are too many fellas out there aiming to make a name for themselves. Once you get caught up in that kind of life, there's no turning back. And them fellas who are out looking for a name – they won't ever stop until they've killed you."

"Or till they git kilt tryin'," old Pops was quick to add.

Max had thought hard about what his uncle said that day and decided that he was right. But a few short months later, Max's life would become forever tied to the gun, and in a way that his uncle, at least, would never live to see.

Three of the ranch hands – all nail-hard cases who had been hired only days earlier – crept into the big house in an attempt to make off with the cowhands' payroll. Edward Blake surprised them before they reached his study, but two of them pulled their guns and shot him dead. One of the men – a surly, cock-sure, disagreeable wrangler named Piker Holladay – then walked calmly and coldly up to Edward Blake and without hesitation fired two more bullets into the prone body.

Max had been asleep when he was jolted awake by the explosive boom of gunfire. He raced downstairs in time to see the three ranch hands running toward their waiting horses in the courtyard outside.

Max ran first to his uncle's bedroom; not finding him there, he hurried into the study and saw the lifeless body crumpled on the floor. His aunt, sobbing softly, was kneeling at her husband's side. Some of the other ranch hands who also heard the shots ran into the house and found the two of them: Emily clutching her dead husband's blood-soaked body, while Max stood off to one side with a look of fiery hatred etched across his face. Some of the men later said that it was a frightening look to behold on anyone so young.

"I saw Piker Holladay and that fellow Smith bolt out of here as I came down the stairs," Max said coolly as he collected himself. "The other new man, Reyelts: He was with them, too."

"You just take it easy now, son, and help with your uncle," one of the ranch hands said.

Max just shook his head. "There's not much I can do about my uncle; nothing I can do for him now. There's little enough to be said about it. But there's something to be done about the rest of it."

Then he left the room quietly to gather up his gear.

Max and a few of Edward Blake's longtime hands who refused to stay out of the hunt left the ranch within a half-hour of the shooting.

"You can come along. I can't stop you," Max said simply as they started out. "But those three are mine. Understand?"

And then he added, "I don't expect we'll be gone long, either."

With that, the men followed Max into the night, galloping away on a grim and deadly chase.

As it turned out, they were gone a mere three days.

Old Pops McCoy served as the lead tracker and followed the trail of Holladay, Smith, and Reyelts into a horseshoe canyon twelve miles or so east of Edward Blake's main spread. They stayed on the trail through the night and didn't stop until they saw the smoke from a small fire near daybreak. Pops thought it best to wait until it was light enough to see clearly before moving in, and he said so.

"You wait here, then," Max told him. "I'm going down to settle this now."

"You're good, Max — mighty good with that gun," Pops said. "But shootin' a man ain't exactly like shootin' whiskey bottles off'n a fence, no sir. That man Holladay down there is a tough, mean hombre. He'll kill you as soon as look at you, just like he's prob'ly the one kilt your uncle stone dead."

"No time to argue," Max said. "I'm going down there now – with or without the lot of you."

"Then you're goin' down there with me," Pops said. "Your uncle would never forgive me if I let you git into that canyon by yerself. And I've known poor Emily too long to have to take you home strapped over a horse."

Pops looked around. "The rest of you boys wait here," he said. "Make sure no one gets out. We'll just have to do this quiet."

Pops had to scramble hard to follow Max down the narrow trail into the steep canyon below. Max's steady, sure-footed strides made it clear that he was dead set on what he was about to do: a piece of grisly business that would mark his soul and way of life forever.

That was a long time back, Max thought to himself as he walked down the middle of the dusty street in Pueblo Springs, headed toward the sheriff office. He noticed that a group of men moved quickly out of his way as he approached them, all of them careful to avoid eye contact, and he could hear them whispering among themselves as he passed.

Max would have liked to stop and listen in for a moment or two, in the same way that he had with the ranch hands on his uncle's Wyoming spread. But those days were gone, he knew: Few men wanted to get anywhere near Max Blake, let alone talk with him. The kind of life that he led now didn't much allow for friendships or casual conversations. It was a thing that he regretted but couldn't control. And so he shrugged the thought off, although he made sure that the men kept their hands away from their guns as he passed.

Sheriff Todd was seated behind a small desk, cleaning a rifle, when Max strode through the open door. The sheriff nodded as Max came in but didn't look up again for several minutes as he wiped the Winchester clean, using a rag that had long since turned brown from repeated applications of a light gun oil.

Max studied the sheriff's movements closely for a time and then took in the rest of the office. He noted the rack of rifles behind the desk with the single empty notch and the door off to the left that led into a room with two small jail cells.

He walked over to look through a tiny window in the door, checking to see whether the cells were empty. He turned and noticed that some wanted posters were stacked on the sheriff's desk; a few more were hung haphazardly with small brads on the wall to the right of the front door; one of these advertised the ugly face of the late Tom Culpepper. A single chair was lined up directly in front of the desk.

Neither man spoke a word.

Sheriff Todd finished with the Winchester and then turned and placed it back in the rack behind his desk, careful to keep his fingerprints off the metal on the barrel. He reached for another lever-action model and started wiping it down with the same cleaning rag.

"Well, I wired your judge back in Twin Forks like you asked me to," he said at last. "I expect to hear something shortly from the telegraph office, provided the line stays open between here and there in the meantime – a just god and the U.S. Cavalry both cooperating."

Max nodded but didn't speak.

"I would've suggested that you have a drink in the saloon while you wait, but there's been killing enough in there this day. You might just as well wait in here with me, though I'm not much on company and don't intend to change my ways none now – not even for the famous Max Blake."

"Suits me fine, sheriff. I'm not much for conversation myself," Max said.

"The less said, then, the better," Sheriff Todd replied after a moment. "You've got a long reputation, yes sir. And you already raised enough hell in my town to put it on the map back East, which is something I don't much appreciate a'tall. I only hope no newspapers get wind of what happened here today."

Max said nothing, so the sheriff continued talking out of nervousness.

"I respect the fact that you are a federal marshal and that you hold no truck with fear or messing with the likes of a Johnny Dole – and especially with the likes of an outlaw like Tom Culpepper.

"But I'm duty-bound to tell you that your reputation far outweighs your marshal's badge in my eyes; I'll say nothing 'bout the things that I hear – like you're little more'n a hired gun for that judge in Twin Forks or that you like to make a profit on the killings. No sir, I'm not sure that a U.S. marshal should..."

"Should what, sheriff?" Max broke in, suddenly riled by the man's words. "I'm a lawman, same as you."

There were a lot of things that Max wanted to say: He wanted to ask the sheriff if he knew how little a federal marshal was paid. He wanted to ask whether a federal marshal shouldn't care about putting food on his table, or treating himself to a beer from time to time, or maybe even putting a little money away for the time when he wasn't young enough – or fast enough, or good enough – to stay alive on the job.

"You shouldn't listen to loose talk, sheriff – about me or about Judge Radford," Max said at last. "You know better than the next man that wearing a badge doesn't guarantee a man much, nor does it keep people's tongues from wagging. I work for the law and stay within the law. I do what I have to do. That includes sometimes collecting on a dead man's things.

"And I expect that you do the same, Sheriff, after your own fashion."

Sheriff Todd reflected on Max's words for a minute but said nothing. He was uncomfortable with Max Blake. He wanted to tell him that he thought Max's methods were shocking and that he didn't like him or the way that he had disrupted his town. He wanted to tell him that he thought Max enjoyed his work a little too much: After all, killing was the kind of work that made most men uneasy, no matter what side of the law it was done on.

But he decided that he had already said enough.

The sheriff turned behind him, replaced the lever-action he had been cleaning, and pulled yet another rifle from the rack – this one a .50-caliber Sharps – and picked up the cleaning rag once more. He slowly stroked the barrel of the rifle up and down, rubbing a smudge here and there as he worked, paying more attention to the job than was necessary.

Max pulled out the chair in front of the sheriff's desk and turned it so that his back was toward the wall, giving him a clear view of the lone door leading out to the street. Then he sat down and put his boots up on the desk.

"This Johnny Dole," Max said after a minute. "Did he have a family?"

"Not so far's anyone knew around here," the sheriff said. "But that's a strange question for you to be asking of me."

"There's two good reasons I ask it," Max replied. "If he had family, there's often a man among them who'll be wanting to come looking for me; sometimes a woman, too. That's a thing I tend to keep an eye on."

The sheriff nodded thoughtfully.

"And the second reason?"

Max paused for a moment and then said: "I'm all for giving this Johnny a decent burying, and that'll need to be paid for, of course. But whatever's left over, I'd like you to sell and wire the money along to Twin Forks in care of the judge: Dole's guns; his horse – I suspect that he had one – and anything else he might have owned. He didn't have land hereabouts worth anything, did he?"

The sheriff shook his head at the question, and then shook it again at the thought of selling Johnny's things and sending the money on.

"Johnny had a girl back at the saloon," the sheriff said. "She might want to stake a claim to something."

"She'll have to pick a horse once I'm gone from the stable, sheriff. But you give her whatever you think is fair; that's all right by me. Still, she lost most of her claim when her man picked a fight with me."

The sheriff was quiet for another minute before breaking the uneasy silence again. "I heard that you shot a man named Jonathan Grant a few weeks back – a couple of counties over, in Jefferson."

"That's right," Max said. "He tried to shoot me in the back when I went to bring him in. There was a lot of paper on the man."

"That's the way I heard it, all right," the sheriff said. "But what you said earlier, about family? You know that there are other Grants around these parts. One of the brothers is especially spiteful, as I understand it. A mean, hateful man – might be even worse than the brother you killed off. Damned if I can remember his first name, though. I hear tell he's mighty handy with a gun, too."

"I had heard something like that myself," Max said, nodding. His reply hung in the air for a moment, as though the sheriff had issued a warning without identifying it as such. But Max let it go, well aware of the possibility of revenge.

"About Tom Culpepper, sheriff," Max continued. "I'll pack his horse and guns and such with me back to Twin Forks, seeing as there's no claim to them here. The judge, of course, will want to see that your undertaker..."

"That'll be Doc Jones..."

"...that Doc Jones gets his due for the burying. There's no reason for me to tote that body back in this heat. So long as you certified to Judge Radford that Culpepper is dead and that his death was the result of a necessary fight, then the judge will have no great quarrel with me, even though he'd rather see Culpepper hang."

"I wired the judge and told it the way it happened," Sheriff Todd said. "I didn't tell more'n what happened – nor less, comes to that. Fact of the matter is, there wasn't a lot to tell. You shot the man dead, and you shot him fairly.

"I've got to tell you, though," the sheriff continued, "that even though I was right there and saw it, I didn't see more'n a flash of movement from you and the crash of Tom Culpepper's body come bouncin' down the stairs. And I heard it, of course – heard the shots, all right. It's just hard for me to believe that it happened.

"But it happened, all right, didn't it? Just as sure as Tom Culpepper died sudden-like to prove it, it happened."

Max didn't say anything. He just stared out the window, his eyes taking on a hard, grim look – as if he were remembering something unpleasant.

The man named Piker Holladay died sudden-like, too – back in the horseshoe canyon where Pops McCoy had tracked the killers of Max's uncle so many years ago.

Old Pops was several hundred yards back up the trail, trying to keep up with Max as best he could, when Holladay, who was loudly urinating behind a large boulder, turned to see the grim face of young Max Blake looking directly at him. He noticed that the youth was flexing the fingers of his right hand, which was held but inches away from a holstered Colt revolver.

But what he noticed most of all were the boy's eyes: black and cold and deadly.

"Well, well," Holladay said, calling for his partners as he finished. "Hey! Smith, Reyelts – look'it what we got ourselves here: the old man's brat has come to git hisself kilt, too.

"You ought to know, boy, before you die, that I kilt that old man and then shot him twice after, jest for fun. I think I'll do for you the same damned thing."

Piker Holladay bellowed out an evil laugh and went for his gun.

Pops came into view just as Holladay made his move. Pops saw that Holladay was fast, all right – faster than anyone he had ever seen, save one. For Max Blake cleared leather and pumped two shots into Holladay's chest before the startled man could level his own gun. The brutal smile on the outlaw's face twisted up into a quizzical look, and then he pitched forward and fell headlong into the rocks that were strewn about the ground at his feet.

"You do what you think you have to do," Max said softly as he looked at the body of the dead man sprawled across the rocks.

Alerted by the gunfire, the man named Smith lunged from behind a tree, holding a rifle, and started to take aim at Max. Pops shot at the same time that Max turned in a crouch and fired, and both guns found their mark. Smith's body twisted in different directions as the bullets hit him from cross angles, and he managed to squeeze off a single round that whined harmlessly through the trees before he, too, plunged to the ground.

At the same time, Max and Pops could hear the thudding sounds of a horse galloping away; this was likely the third outlaw, Reyelts, making a break for it out of the horseshoe canyon.

Max looked around at Pops, nodded to him in thanks, and then walked carefully up to where Piker Holladay was sprawled on the ground. He stood there for a moment, taking a long look at the body with his Colt cocked and ready, before slowly returning the revolver to his holster.

"Yer uncle would be proud of you today, though I don't think the same would be true of yer aunt," Pops said. "I never saw a quicker pull of a hogleg, boy – not in all my life, no sir. You made it seem almost easy, Max. And killin' a man, even saddle tramps like these two here, ain't supposed to be easy."

"It was easy enough though, Pops," Max said. "And it's strange, but I don't seem to feel anything for it. It's just something that had to be done."

Max, in fact, had thought a great deal about it afterward. He didn't feel good about killing the two men, nor did he experience regret. The truth of it was that he didn't even feel one way or another about his uncle, and he wasn't quite sure what to make of it all. It was almost as though he had finished a job that he set out to do, and there was no more to it than that.

"I know one thing, though," he told Pops as he looked down at Piker Holladay. "I need to get on after Reyelts right now."

"If the boys up top don't get him, Reyelts'll have to wait," Pops said. "We need to put your uncle into the ground and give him a decent buryin'. You need to stand with yer aunt at the service, Max."

Pops looked long and hard at Max then. "You were gonna shoot him again," he said, pointing at Holladay – "even though you knew he was as dead as dust when he pitched into those rocks. You had just that in mind, didn't you?"

"He said he shot my uncle twice after he was dead; said he was going to do the same thing to me. I just thought for a minute that I might return the favor."

Pops frowned. "It might be that killing a man once is enough, especially fer a young pup your age."

Max paused for a moment, looking once more at Holladay's body sprawled in the dirt and rocks, and then he said to Pops: "I don't figure they're going to get Reyelts up top; we'd have heard something by now. But I'll go back with you. I won't let my aunt face that chore alone.

"But you need to know that at some point, Pops, I'll be lighting out to settle up with Reyelts. And it'll come sooner than later."

Max returned to the ranch and helped his aunt put things in order after a few awkward weeks had passed. But he had changed; and his aunt, along with Pops and the rest of the regular hands, knew that Max wouldn't remain for long. The thought of the outlaw Reyelts, moving about wild and free, fueled a fire in him.

"I don't suppose I can hold you here much longer," his aunt said to him one day when she saw that restless look in his eyes.

"There's a man out there I need to settle up with," Max replied.

"There's a lot of things you need to learn in this world, Max, but I suppose that you can't learn them all on this ranch," his aunt said.

Max nodded but said nothing.

"I know that I can't hold you here; I know you have to leave because it's eating at your very soul. But you'll always have a place here – a spot to come home to," she said simply.

And even now, after a lot of hard trail, Max Blake took comfort in his aunt's words. He hadn't been near the ranch in Wyoming for almost 10 years, and he had no idea whether his aunt was even still alive.

I don't reckon that she would take kindly to my way of life, he thought. *But it doesn't matter much now, anyway.*

The man from the telegraph line, who hurried into the sheriff's office and handed Neil Todd a written note, interrupted Max's thoughts. All the while he looked nervously at Max as the marshal with the reputation tipped back in the chair by the desk. The man nodded gingerly at Max and then turned his attention back toward the sheriff.

"It's all agreed to, Neil," the man said. "The judge back in Twin Forks says you are to pay Marshal Blake the three-hundred dollars reward money and bill to his court the cost of the burial here. Judge Radford, from over in Twin Forks; that's what he wrote here, all right. It's all right there in the..."

"I can read it now, Harry, but thanks," the sheriff said. Turning to Max, he said, "If you want to follow me over to the bank, I'll see that you get your money. Let's just get this business settled and send you on your way."

"Still hankering to see me go, sheriff?" Max asked, a slight smile wrinkling his eyes. "I thought that the two of us were getting on right neighborly by now."

The sheriff looked at Max and allowed the smallest trace of a cautious grin to pass across his face. Then he got up and extended his arm toward the door leading out of his office.

"After you, Marshal Blake."

"I never let a man carrying a gun move behind me, so long as I can help it," Max said. "But I'll walk on over there next to you."

And the two men passed through the door together.

Chapter Three
A New Assignment

U.S. marshals were a common sight on the main streets of Twin Forks. But the sight of Max Blake leading a riderless horse – a horse that only a few days before belonged to a notorious killer like Tom Culpepper – gave many citizens of the town pause; and they stopped what they were doing for a minute and silently watched him pass.

He got off his horse outside the stables and nodded, even smiling a bit, at Joey Gray, who ran out when he saw Max. Joey's was the only wide grin that Max had seen on the street that morning. The stable boy, who was 14 or so but tall for his age, was one of the few friends that Max could count in the town of Twin Forks – or most anywhere, for that matter.

It wasn't that Max Blake didn't want friends. But the deadly pursuit of his profession, and his intensity in pursuing that profession, made him a difficult friend to have.

"Hi ya, Max. Good hunting?"

"Hi, yourself, Joey."

"That's some horse you've got there – besides old Buck, I mean," Joey said. "Where'd you get him, Max?"

Max swung down and handed the reins of Buck, his big chestnut gelding, to Joey. He walked back toward the second horse and said to the boy, "This horse belonged to a man who was wanted by Judge Radford's court."

"Which one, Max? Which man?"

"Tom Culpepper," Max said simply.

"Tom Culpepper? Himself?"

32

"One and the same."

"And you had to kill him, Max?"

Max nodded without comment.

"Was he fast? Was he fast on the draw, just like they said he was?" Joey asked.

"Just take care of old Buck here," Max said. "When you finish, give this other horse a going-over, too, Joey. I'll want him looking his best."

"I'll get right at it, Max. But I want to hear about the shootin' later," Joey said.

Max frowned, dug into his pocket and pulled out a couple of coins, and then tossed them to the boy one at a time.

"You don't want to dwell too much on gun play, Joey," Max said. "There's not much of a future in it. You'd be likely to end up the way Tom Culpepper did over in Pueblo Springs."

"I still want to hear all about it, Max.

"Hey. Ma says I shouldn't bother you, but why don't you come over for dinner tonight? You can tell me just what happened then."

"I thought your mother didn't approve of me," Max said.

"I think it's what you do that she doesn't like, Max. But never mind that. Can't you come by for dinner? Please?"

"We'll see, Joey. You've got work to do now, and I've got to go and see the judge. He may have something to say about all this."

Max gave Joey a wink and then moved along toward the town courthouse.

Joey is a good kid, Max thought as he walked down the middle of the street, cautiously avoiding the wooden planks on either side out of long habit – because they clattered and attracted attention. Max considered that Joey was a lot like him in some ways: It was just that he didn't know quite yet that a man who makes his way in the world with the business end of a Colt .45 is a marked man – with no time for family, or for friends, or even much for friendships.

Like Max, Joey didn't have a father to help out with the things that a boy needed to learn to grow into a man. Max knew that the man in Joey's life had died in a bar fight a few years before; he hadn't started the brawl, but he had been killed just the same.

Even though Max liked Joey, the boy's mother didn't seem to appreciate or share Joey's fondness for Max. The few times that he had spoken with her, always in Joey's presence, Rebecca Gray exhibited a distinct dislike for him, Max considered. It wasn't what she said, necessarily; she was always polite, and she had raised Joey to be the same. It was more the way she looked at him.

That's a pity, Max thought: *Joey's mother is a pretty woman: If a man like me had a ranch instead of a marshal's badge...*

Max put aside all thoughts of Rebecca and Joey Gray as he entered the back door of Judge Thomas Raymond Radford's courthouse, a large wooden building that dominated the center of town, and carefully climbed the stairs to the second floor. Max was steeling himself to see the judge again. He always was a little uncomfortable talking with the judge, recognizing better than most that there was something forbidding about the man.

Judge Radford was an imposing figure: six-feet, five inches tall and weighing more than 270 pounds on a muscular frame that belied his age of 54 well-kept years. He sported a bushy salt-and-pepper beard that matched his ever-present gray suspenders.

He was a vain man: proud of his beard, his dress, his manner, his bearing, and the fact that he was a prosperous businessman in Twin Forks as well as a judge. At the same time, he was a fair man who ran a disciplined, iron-tough court.

Thomas Radford had been educated at Eastern law schools and spoke with a crisp distinction that was seldom heard elsewhere in the region – and certainly not within the confines of his courtroom unless the judge himself was talking.

The judge also owned the hotel in town, with meals and drinks served in a spacious dining room on the ground floor. As long as the business of hanging people was good, the hotel was full, hungry and thirsty people would spend their money – and the judge was a happy man.

As much as any person in the town, Judge Radford knew that it was in everyone's best interest that the hanging business was good in Twin Forks.

The judge's office and courtroom were almost new, a sign of the progress that Twin Forks had experienced during the past five years or so. The judge liked to think that his courtroom was the primary cause for much of that progress, in fact; but not every citizen in the town agreed, even if the frequent hangings helped the other merchants prosper.

Progress that resulted from hanging men in a town square was not necessarily a healthy thing for any community or any person to be proud of, some of the judge's more vocal critics were inclined to say. But few of them were willing to express their opinions too loudly, for fear that their comments might be overheard by the judge himself and that they themselves might be subjected to a stern lecture on the importance of the law, and particularly of his court. Worse, some of them feared that if their views were widely known, they might become the object of his powerful right hand.

When Judge Radford walked down the streets of Twin Forks, he drew the same kind of cautious awe that normally was reserved for the federal marshals who worked for him.

But it wasn't quite the same as when Max Blake was in town.

That was a different thing entirely, and even Judge Radford recognized that simple fact.

In many ways, the judge and Max were alike: They were men to be reckoned with, and everybody in Twin Forks knew it.

Max knew that if the court was not in session, he would find the judge on the balcony outside of his office, which overlooked the town square. The judge liked to sit in a large padded chair of black leather and fan himself while reading from his law books. It was a perch not unlike his bench in the courtroom.

The seat also gave the judge the best view in town of every hanging that took place in Twin Forks. And Thomas Radford was a man who made sure that the hangman, just like the three marshals who did his bidding, was busy the year round.

Max ducked his head into the courtroom, saw that no one was there, and then swung around and knocked on the door of the judge's office before entering.

"I am out here, Marshal Blake," the judge called out as Max entered. He beckoned Max to join him on the balcony, never taking his eyes off the book he was reading.

Judge Radford read for another moment before finishing a page. He marked his place in the book carefully and then looked up at Max, continuing to fan himself all the while.

"I understand that you have assured us of the demise of Mr. Tom Culpepper, although the good citizens of Twin Forks and the neighboring communities are being deprived of the sight of his rightful hanging," he said.

35

"If you are asking whether Culpepper is dead, the answer is yes," Max replied. "I would have preferred to bring him to trial, sir. He just didn't leave me much choice in the matter."

The judge frowned. "I am disappointed, of course, Marshal Blake – greatly disappointed. Mr. Culpepper deserved a fair trial before he was hung. That's only the way of justice. Besides, hanging a man with the late Mr. Culpepper's reputation would have been good for business, as you full well know."

Max said nothing, but the judge's words angered him.

"I am also told that you dispatched a no-account individual named Johnny Dole at the same time that you visited Pueblo Springs," the judge said after a time.

"That's right, sir."

"Was there any particular reason for that act, Marshal Blake?"

"He was anxious to die, I guess," Max said, the expression on his face unchanged.

The judge nodded slowly again and then gave Max a small smile that curled and hung off the edge of his mouth.

"Here was yet another opportunity to dispense justice immediately in this circuit, Marshal Blake," he said. "This man Dole wasn't well-known, not like the late Mr. Culpepper at least, but he would have been a good hanging companion for the man with the wider reputation. You recognize that this procedure is good for the laws of the land and the territory and the citizens of Twin Forks, I trust?"

"To say nothing about it being good for the saloon and hotel business," Max said, the annoyance beginning to burn in his voice while his face betrayed no sign of emotion at all.

"Indeed – to say nothing about it, and we'll say nothing more," the judge responded evenly. "As long as I run this court, Marshal Blake, we'll do it my way and my way only."

Cautious of the tension, Judge Radford waited a moment for Max to respond, carefully watching his face. But Max said nothing and held the judge's look with a steady gaze.

The judge involuntarily shuddered inwardly. *There is no need to push a man like Max Blake*, he thought. *Even for a powerful man like myself, that's not a healthy idea – most definitely not good for business.*

"Good enough, Marshal; good enough, indeed," the judge said at last, breaking the stalemate and forcing a small smile.

Max touched his left hand to the bill of his Stetson but said nothing.

"I suppose you are interested in your next assignment, then?"

"The thought crossed my mind a time or two on the way back," Max said carefully.

"Indeed. A man needs to keep busy," Judge Radford replied. "Especially a man in your business; isn't that right, Marshal?"

The judge ran the fingers of his right hand slowly over the leather-bound edge of his law book and then glanced back up at Max again, a decidedly uncomfortable look upon his face.

He looks sad, almost uncomfortable, Max thought – emotions that he had never seen in the judge before; or at least he couldn't remember seeing them.

Maybe it's just that the judge is tired today, he thought. *Maybe he didn't like our little exchange much, either – it's hard to tell.*

"Have you ever heard of a disagreeable alley cat named Foster Johnson?" the judge asked, interrupting Max's thoughts.

"Yes, sir. He hails from Texas or close by," Max said, nodding. "They call him Hoss Johnson – or maybe it's Boss."

"That's right. You are quite right again, Marshal," Judge Radford said. "He doesn't like the name of Foster, so he goes by the undistinguished moniker of Hoss.

"As a matter of fact, our Mr. Johnson doesn't like a great many things. But the things he does enjoy – like murder, rape, armed robbery, mail theft, and just plain general disagreement with the law – have brought him to the attention of this court."

The judge paused a moment. When Max said nothing, he continued:

"It seems that our Mr. Johnson has been busy south of here. Five days ago, he was identified as the leader of a group of three men who held up a bank in Twisted Junction. They made away with one-thousand dollars and change. The bank president and his wife, who happened to be in the bank with her husband at the time, poor woman – well, both were killed. The wire I received from the sheriff in Twisted Junction said that Mr. Hoss Johnson shot the old man out of just plain meanness – he actually said that he didn't open the safe fast enough for him, if you can comprehend that – and then shot the poor man's wife because he didn't like hearing her cry."

"Nice fellow," Max said dryly. But he thought to himself that the judge's long-winded, flowery oratory was a lot like taking a long trail to go a short ways.

Judge Radford paused for moment, leaning back in his chair while stretching his arms over his head. Then he set out again, fanning himself as he talked:

"Two days later – three days ago now – our same Hoss Johnson returned to the same town of Twisted Junction and robbed the same bank all over again. This time, he and his men killed a teller in the bank and then shot two men dead in the street as they were riding out of town.

"The pity of it was that he only managed to withdraw two-hundred dollars or so in this second robbery; the sheriff said that people had been nervous about putting their money back into the bank after the easy success of Mr. Johnson's first effort."

"Any idea of who is working with him?" Max asked.

"At this point, no. But the sheriff in Twisted Junction – a man you well know, as I recall – might know something that he didn't send in his wire," the judge replied.

"This is a most unseemly man that we are dealing with here. During the course of several years, our Mr. Johnson has cut a large trail of lawlessness across the otherwise pristine face of the great Southwest. He does what he wants to do, he goes where he wants to go – and he kills because he likes to kill, apparently. As you well know, good citizens of the territory frown on this sort of thing, as do I.

"The day that he hangs will be a great day for this territory, not to mention an economic enrichment the likes of which this fair community has seldom seen.

"There was little reason to pay him much mind when he was in Texas or Mexico, where he also spends his time. But now he has come into my sights by breaking the law in this judicial circuit. And as you fully know, Marshal Blake, I don't take kindly to that. I am certain that you do not as well."

"I take it you'd like me to have a talk with the man," Max said.

"By all means, Marshal Blake," the judge said. "By all means seek Mr. Foster Johnson out and return him to the pleasure of this court by whatever means you deem necessary and by whatever fashion you can accomplish said mission. It will be my privilege to try him in this courthouse and then hang him by the neck until he is short on breath and long on death."

The judge chuckled a bit at his turn of phrase and worked his fan a little faster.

"I trust you won't mind if I look after a little business in town first," Max said.

"So long as it doesn't take more than a couple of hours, Marshal. Twisted Junction is a good four-day ride from here, and there's no telling what kind of trouble our Mr. Johnson can stir up in the meantime."

Max nodded to the judge and turned to leave.

"It's always a pleasure to see you, your honor," he said as he walked through the balcony door and back into the judge's office on his way out of the courthouse.

"And you, Marshal Blake," the judge called back. "It is always a pleasure to converse with such an effective officer of this court.

"Be cautious of Mr. Johnson, Marshal Blake. But do bring him back here to hang."

Max, however, failed to hear the judge's caution. He already was thinking of Foster Johnson and the tough trail that stretched between Twin Forks and the far-away outpost of Twisted Junction.

Max returned to the stable after checking his room at the hotel and picking up a few supplies at the general store: two new boxes of cartridges for his Colt, some jerky, a sack full of hard crackers made of ground corn – corn biscuits, he called them – and some other odds and ends that he would need, including a sharp new straight razor that had just arrived from St. Louis.

Joey Gray was rubbing down Tom Culpepper's horse when Max arrived.

"Hey, Max. Did you come back already to tell me how you got old Tom Culpepper?"

"Not exactly, Joey."

"Well, you can come to dinner tonight, right?"

"The judge has got another job for me to do. What kind of shape is old Buck in, do you reckon?" Max asked. And although he was fully aware of the condition of his horse, Max liked to include Joey in such an important consideration.

Joey was disappointed about the dinner invitation; but he knew better than to show his feelings to Max Blake when he was about to set out on the trail, and he was proud that Max had asked his opinion about Buck.

"Another day of rest wouldn't do Buck a bit of harm, but I suppose he's fit enough if you don't ride him crazy-like. Where you heading, anyway?"

"Twisted Junction – if Buck is up to it, that is."

"Who you huntin' this time, Max?"

"An outlaw called Hoss Johnson, Joey."

Joey had followed Max inside to look after Buck. "Hoss Johnson? Hoss is kind of a funny name, isn't it, Max? I don't think that I've ever heard that name before. What's he done, this Hoss Johnson, anyway? Why does the judge want him here? And is he fast on the draw, Max, like Tom Culpepper was?"

"He's likely faster than Tom Culpepper was, Joey," Max said. "Tom Culpepper's dead, and Hoss Johnson's still out there causing a ruckus."

"Well, I know one thing," Joey said as Max took a good look at his horse, rubbing his hands up and down the length of old Buck's legs. "This Hoss Johnson character has met his match in you, Max." Lon Barbers, who ran the livery stable in Twin Forks, walked over to where Max and Joey were talking and nodded at Max in a cautiously friendly manner. "Good day to you, Marshal," he said.

Max looked up and nodded. "Lon, I'd like you and Joey to look after that other horse I brought in today till I get back. Thought I'd take care of some business today, but I won't have a chance for some time."

Max rose from his kneeling position and patted Buck a couple of times on the horse's huge neck. "I'll be gone a couple of weeks, maybe longer. Hard to tell."

Barbers nodded in agreement and said: "Joey told me about Tom Culpepper. That was a right good job, Marshal. If ever a man needed killing, it was Culpepper."

Max tossed his saddle up on Buck's broad back but said nothing.

Joey started to help with the cinching, but Max finished the job himself and led the big horse out of the stables.

"Joey, you take care of yourself and your mother – and mind that other horse for me now. I'll see you again when I get back. All right?"

Max smiled at Joey, nodded toward Lon Barbers, and then climbed aboard Buck and turned the horse south on the dusty road leading out of town.

"You take care of yourself, Max," Joey called after him. "And you watch out for this Hoss Johnson fella."

"Did you say Hoss Johnson?" Barbers asked Joey as Max rode away.

"That's right," Joey said. "Max is chasing after a man named Hoss Johnson; least ways, that's what he said. Funny kind of name, Hoss – don't you think?"

Lon Barbers looked grim, and he shook his head as he watched Max Blake turn slowly smaller in the distance.

"A whiskey drummer stopped by this way a year ago or so and talked about this fella your marshal friend is after – this Hoss Johnson character. From what the drummer said back then, this Hoss Johnson is no man to mess with," Barbers said to Joey. "Tom Culpepper was a mean enough man, but he wasn't a patch next to Hoss Johnson, from what I hear tell."

Barbers started to head into the stables and then called out without turning around: "Joey, come on in here and start cleaning out these box stalls. You'll need to make room for the marshal's other horse. Let's get crackin' now."

Max decided to move easy that first day. The morning was gone anyway, and he wanted Buck to be fresh when the time came. So he let the horse lope along at a steady pace on the trail that wound its way through the wooded hills toward Twisted Junction. Regretting only momentarily his forced early departure from home in Twin Forks – an event that he was used to, given the nature of his job and Judge Radford's hurried disposition to dispense justice

41

– Max spent the time thinking about what he knew of the Twisted Junction sheriff and of Hoss Johnson himself.

Ned Clark was a good man who ran a law-abiding town. Max had run into Clark a time or two during his pursuit of some train robbers a few months earlier in the Twisted Junction area, and he had liked the cut of the man and the way he did business.

Ned Clark won't take well to what's happened in his town, Max thought. *It'll be interesting to hear what he has to say about all this.*

He rode along a bit farther and then started talking aloud to Buck.

"This Johnson fella will be an interesting case for us, Buck," Max said to his horse, a habit he had acquired from long periods spent alone on the trail. "He's a dangerous man, all right. And he's likely to be even more dangerous depending on who he's running with."

Max recalled when he had first heard the name of Hoss Johnson; it had been two, or maybe it was three, years before. He had been on the trail of some outlaws who were robbing banks along the Arizona-Mexico border and kept scooting across to the Mexican side to hide. He recalled a conversation with a lawman in one of the towns outside of Tucson who had brought up the name of Hoss Johnson as someone to avoid.

"He's just plain Texas mean," the lawman had said. "And he's kind of crazy, too. There's no telling what he'll say or do. He shot up my town a few months back for no good reason at all, and then he killed one of my deputies who tried to bring him down for it. I tracked him for nigh on two weeks or more but finally lost him up in the mountains outside the border. I knew the skunk had crossed over, and there was nothin' I could do but turn around for home at that point.

"If you come across Hoss Johnson, don't do anything but shoot him fast and shoot him dead. I lost a damn good man on account of that no-good snake."

Max never did come across Hoss Johnson on that trip, although he was able settle up with the border outlaws. But he remembered the name all the same.

I wonder if Paul Reyelts is keeping company with Mr. Hoss Johnson these days, Max thought to himself, turning his attention once more to the death of his Uncle Edward so long ago and of the one man who had yet to pay for that crime.

Wouldn't that be interesting now?

Chapter Four
Evil Has A Face

A hard day's ride away, and just a few miles outside the little village of Indian Wells, Hoss Johnson was forking a plate of lukewarm beans and some scattered bits of bacon and jerky into his cavernous and decidedly ugly mouth. He finished the contents on the battered tin plate and then began licking at it with his long tongue.

"Hungry tonight, Hoss?" Freeman Morgan asked with a laugh, his own mouth full as he spit out the words along with some tiny chunks of unchewed food.

"What do you think there, Weasel? You think ol' Hoss is some hungry tonight?"

"Yeah, good ol' Hoss looks like my old hound used to when he was goin' at it hard after a night a'runnin' down some critter or other. Ha ha ha. Ol' Hoss looks nigh on to hungry tonight, I'd say."

Weasel Morgan, Freeman's brother and the third member of Hoss Johnson's rough-hewn band of seasoned outlaws, flashed a yellow-toothed grin at Hoss and started to say something else when he was cut short by Johnson's glare.

"Why don't the two of you jest shut the hell up," Hoss said — a command more than a question. "God a'mighty, but you boys can drive a man crazy. Hand me that bottle, dammit. Now!"

Weasel gave Hoss a near-full jug and said, "Hell, Hoss, we don't mean nothin' by it. We was jest – well, you know – jest havin' some fun's all."

"Have yer fun with somebody else," Hoss snapped. "If you ain't learned nothin' by now 'bout me, you both ought to know that I don't like bein' made fun of and bothered with. Not now. Not never."

He wiped his mouth on his grubby shirt sleeve and the inside of his huge hands and wiped them in turn on his dusty pants. Then he hoisted the jug to his mouth and took a long pull of rot-gut whiskey.

"We been two days out here now, Hoss," Freeman Morgan said, at the same time shaking his head at his brother to keep him quiet. "It's 'bout time we pulled out and found us some action again – don't you think?"

"Yeah, I think," Hoss said. "I think for all of us. I say when we go and when we come and when we stay and where we stay. The two of you" – he took another pull on the whiskey jug before finishing his thought, smacking his lips together when he had his fill – "the two of you need to jest keep yer damned mouths shut and do what I tell you to do and nothin' more.

"And Weasel, why in hell don't you learn to cook?"

"What's wrong with the way I cook?" Weasel complained, a look of hurt forming on his narrow, pinched face. "You ain't never griped 'bout the way I cooked before. You didn't look much like you couldn't stand my cookin' a minute ago, the way you was jest shovelin' in that meal there. You can't..."

"You call that a meal?" Hoss interrupted as he stood up and threw his plate on the ground at Weasel's feet. "That weren't no meal; that weren't no better'n slop. You been servin' up worse than snake meat all this time, and I only jest figured it out tonight."

Hoss threw back his head and laughed as Weasel's face screwed itself up into another look of disappointment and anguish. He started to protest again when his brother kicked him hard in the leg. "Jest shut up and git these plates and such packed up, Weasel," Freeman Morgan said. "Jest shut up and git to it and let it go with old Hoss here."

Freeman walked over to where Hoss was looking out across the mesquite-strewn landscape and said: "Don't pay no attention to Weasel there, Hoss. He ain't too bright, but he's good in a fight and don't mean no harm. And he done his best with that grub tonight. It's jest that we don't have much to work with out here. We need supplies. We need to get us some things."

"Don't you think I know that already?" Hoss snapped. "I'm fixin' to settle that soon anyhow. There's a town nearby that might be jest the right size for us to put some good food in our mouths for a change – and maybe even some money in our pockets."

"I'm all fer some action, Hoss," Freeman said. "But if'n you're thinkin' 'bout Indian Wells, well, it really ain't much of a town. It's more a crossroads, really, filled up with a bunch of Indians and 'breeds and Mexicans and such. Don't have no bank, so far'n I know. Can't be much there worth stealin' a'tall."

"It's got a cantina, ain't it?" Hoss asked. "If it's got a waterin' hole, then we can git something to eat and something to drink. And there might jest be enough pocket change in the place to make it worth our while to pay a visit.

"Might pick up a card game while we're at it. Might even be a woman or two there." Hoss smiled at the thought, his large, weathered face breaking into a wide grin that showed large gaps in what remained of his yellowed teeth.

"Anyway, that's the way I got it figured. You and Weasel don't like that plan, then go yer own way now. Jest don't git in my way. Clear?"

"Yeah, that sounds fine to me, Hoss. That'll be jest fine with the Weasel, too. When we figurin' to move?"

"Why hell, Free Morgan: You think I want to spend another minute out on this hard-pan and scrub-brush patch of nothing? There can't be a living man from Twisted Junction still fool enough to be tracking us now. And Indian Wells can't be more'n a hour's ride from here. I'm figurin' to saddle up right this here minute. You got any problem with that?"

"Not me, Hoss. I'm ready to go. Yes sir — right now."

"What about that idiot brother of yers? You think you can get him ready to go?"

"Jest ... jest let me go help him with the grub and the tins and such. The Weasel'll be more'n happy to get the hell out of here, too, I expect. The prospect of a woman might cheer him some considerable."

"Then let's quit jawin' about it and git a move on," Hoss said, already throwing the saddle onto the back of his large black horse. "The night ain't gettin' no younger, and we sure as hell ain't, neither."

Indian Wells was as out-of-the-way a spot as could be found in the territory. It was tucked up in the forward slope of the foothills, a meeting place for a couple of dusty trails that didn't lead from or to anywhere special.

In addition to a single saloon, the village contained a small livery stable, a blacksmith shop next to the livery, a tiny church with a cemetery in the back but no preacher, and a general store that did its best to cater to the handful of homesteads that were sprinkled around. The little trickle of a natural spring that bubbled up in the middle of the main street, just to the north of the saloon, gave the place its name and a reason to exist.

The handful of inhabitants of Indian Wells did their best to coax a meager living by raising sheep and the few crops that the thin soil of the foothills would support. The fact that there was a steady supply of water was as much of an invitation as anyone needed to remain there – that and the fact that most people tended to leave Indian Wells, and the folks who lived there, alone.

Hoss Johnson thought all of that would work to his advantage as he and the two Morgan brothers rode into the sleepy community. A handful of tiny stars were just starting to poke through the wisp of clouds in the night sky when the three men climbed off their mounts and strolled through the battered batwing doors of the Indian Wells cantina.

"I'm mighty thirsty," Hoss called out. "A beer sounds jest about right. And a card game, too."

The bartender, a middle-aged man with a narrow face and gaunt features, nodded grimly at the three outlaws, recognizing trouble when he saw it. He pulled a beer and gingerly placed it down on the long bar in front of Hoss Johnson. "And for the other two gentlemen?" he asked in a thin, nervous voice.

"Tequila. Make it a double," Freeman Morgan said.

"Gimme a shot of yer best whiskey – no cheap bar stuff, neither – and a beer," Weasel said. "Make it a tall shot and a taller beer."

"Si." The bartender nodded and turned his back to get the drinks as Hoss surveyed the place. Four other men were in the saloon: three Mexicans in their mid-thirties who sat at a table off to his left, and a dark-complexioned man of undetermined age who stood at the bar nursing a small glass of what looked like plain water.

The man at the bar wore a poncho that was cut from a colorful Indian blanket. A large, dusty sombrero hung on his back, attached to a thin rawhide tie that was strapped around his neck.

Hoss took a long drink of beer, emptying half the dirty glass, and then poked Freeman's arm and pointed toward the man at the bar.

"What do you think, now, Weasel? Is that a Mex or a damn Indian we got here? Or maybe it's a 'breed? Or jest what in hell is it, anyway?" he asked loudly.

Weasel grinned and moved a couple of feet over toward the solitary figure at the bar, sizing him up. He saw immediately that the man was not carrying a gun, and that increased his boldness.

"Sure beats the hell out of me, Hoss. He might be a Mex, all right. But that blanket he's wearin' might well make him an Indian at that. What say we jest ups and asks 'im?"

Weasel turned to the man and said: "How 'bout it, pardner? Would you be a Mex, or an Indian maybe, or maybe something else entirely?"

The man turned; he looked blankly at the three strangers who were staring back at him and then shrugged his shoulders. "No comprende," he said simply and turned again to face the mirror behind the bar.

"Sounds to me like he's a Mex," Weasel said, turning back toward Hoss with the trace of an evil smile on his face.

"Most of us here are Mexicans," the bartender said as he set Freeman's and Weasel's drinks down. "There are Apaches who trade with us, sometimes other Indians, and some of them have settled nearby. But this is mostly a Mexican settlement of good Christian people.

"If you don't mind, sirs, that will be one dollar for the drinks, por favor."

"Well, now. As a matter of fact, I do mind."

Hoss pulled out his revolver and placed it on top of the bar near his glass. "I don't think you should try to collect any money for the watered-down beer you're servin' up here.

"In fact, the way I see it," Hoss continued, "I think you ought to pay us for drinking at your bar. How much you figure you ought to pay us?"

The bartender nervously shrugged his shoulders. "I don't know. How about I pay you the one dollar instead?"

"How about you pay me every dollar you got instead?" Hoss snapped. "How about you jest put every stinking dollar and every stinking piece of silver you got right down here on the bar, right now? Let's jest see what kind of business we can do here, amigo."

The bartender turned nervously toward the counter again and reached for a small wooden box. The three men who sat at the table, fully noticing the trouble, started to get up to leave; but Weasel Morgan pulled out his gun and motioned for them to sit back down again.

"No tricks, now, old man," Hoss said, his fingers curling around the gun on the bar.

"Si. No tricks, of course," the bartender said. He turned with the box and placed it in front of Hoss. It contained three one-dollar bills and a handful of change, mostly Mexican pesos.

"That's it?" Hoss demanded. "That's all of it?"

"Si. That is all the money I have."

"Well, it ain't near enough, old man," Hoss said. "Empty yer pockets. And tell these four here" — pointing in the direction of the other men in the saloon – "to do the same. Let's jest see if we can up the ante anything much a'tall."

The bartender spoke a few words of Spanish to the others, and the four of them dug into their pockets – the younger man dropping a single coin on the bar, while the other three scattered a handful of coins on the table where they were seated. Weasel Morgan went over to the table and picked up the little bit of money that had been offered, all the while waving his gun about in his right hand.

"Darn'n hell, Hoss," he said. "There ain't hardly anything a'tall here, and most of it ain't even real money. It's just Mexican or somethin'."

Hoss shook his head.

"This is a damned sorry sight," he said slowly as he fingered his revolver, looking at the bartender all the while. Then he casually turned and pumped two slugs into the startled man at the bar, only an arm's length away, which sent him crashing noisily to the floor.

The three men who were seated at the table started to run from the saloon, but Weasel Morgan quickly had his gun on them and fired three rapid shots, hitting all of them in the back from no more than ten feet away. They pitched forward, two of them slamming into a small table, the other man simply sprawling across the floor with a deadly rush.

The four men were dead in less than ten seconds, and Hoss had his eye and his gun on the horrified bartender but said nothing to the man.

Weasel creased his face with a huge grin. "Got 'em fer you, Hoss. No trouble with them three a'tall." He then walked over and fired three more times, hitting each man on the floor in the back of the head.

Hoss Johnson turned away from the bartender and looked pleased with himself and with the Morgan brothers, especially Weasel. He nodded in his direction and then looked at Freeman, who had pulled his gun but hadn't fired a shot.

"We didn't scare you none there, did we Free?" he asked.

"You're jest too quick for me, that's all," Freeman said. He returned his gun to his holster and looked over at his brother, who continued grinning and waving his own revolver about, talking to himself the whole time. "That was good shootin', Hoss. Good shootin' there, Weasel. Mighty sudden, it was. Mighty good work."

Hoss looked up and down the bar as though he owned it and then turned to where Weasel was standing.

"Tell you what, Weasel," he said. "You stand by that door for a spell and see if all this noise here brings anyone else a'runnin' in this fleabag of a town. In the meantime, Free and me is gonna sit down and have us a drink and maybe play us a few hands of poker."

"Hell, Hoss, poker ain't much fun with jest two of us playin'," Freeman protested.

"Well, take a look around, Free. Everyone else here 'cepting the barkeep and yer brother is just plain dead. Weasel's gotta keep watch. The barkeep here's gotta serve us drinks. And dead men ain't much use to play poker with."

Hoss reached across the top of the counter and grabbed the bartender by the shirt. "I'll take a bottle of tequila," he said. "I'll also take me a deck of playin' cards. And while yer at it, you kin find me another bottle of somethin' good. You understand me, amigo?"

The bartender nodded, and Hoss let him go. "You remember what you saw here tonight," he said simply. Then he moved across the cantina to one of the rickety wooden tables that were spread casually around the room.

"Bring them bottles on over, Free," he said. "This table here is close enough to the light so's I won't have to squint at the cards."

Hoss turned toward Weasel and called out: "You keep a watch out there and see if anything starts to stirrin'. I don't want to have my card game interrupted on account of someone getting fired up because we shot us a few Mexicans here. You get my meanin'?"

Weasel Morgan, still grinning broadly and waving his gun about wildly, nodded back to where Hoss had seated himself at the table.

"Anything you say, Hoss," he yelled back. "Jest let me know when I can get cut in. And I sure could use a bottle'a somethin' over here. That's all right, ain't it?

"Wait. Hey, something's movin' out here, Hoss. I kin see it some over there a'ways."

Hoss got up quickly and walked across the room to the door, stepping over the body of one of the dead men on the floor without paying it any attention. Freeman Morgan followed him cautiously.

"See it? See it there?" Weasel asked excitedly, pointing out into the blackness with his gun hand. "There something movin' out there in the night, Hoss – sure as hell."

"Why hell, it ain't nothing but a damn dog, Weasel," Hoss said after peering out into the street. "You got me up from my table 'cause of a dog? What the hell is wrong with you anyways? Between you and yer brother, well, I just don't know."

Hoss pulled out his gun and fired a single shot into the darkness. The surprised squeal of the animal put an immediate smile on his face, and he turned and ambled back to the table.

"Think I'll play me some poker now," Hoss said as he sat back down. "But ol' Free is right: Poker ain't much fun with jest two. We need us another player or two."

Hoss turned to where the bartender was standing.

"Hey, amigo," he said casually, "listen carefully. I want you to prop up a couple of these dead Mexican boys here at the table and then stick some cards in their hands. But jest you be careful that you don't give 'em too good'a hand now.

"And be careful they don't get no blood on the cards, neither. I'd hate to have to shoot 'em again for messin' up the deck."

Hoss threw back his head and laughed deep and hard.

He stopped as quickly as he had started, however, and looked again at the quivering bartender: "You do get my meanin' here, amigo. Am I right?"

Fifty miles away, a strange chill ran through Max Blake's spine, and he shifted closer to the small fire that he had built. He didn't like the feeling; but he didn't know what had caused it, either, and that bothered him even more.

Max looked over to where Buck was standing to see if the animal was troubled by any movement or sounds drifting in on the night air. But the horse stood quietly and disinterestedly by, casually swishing its tail, the ears still and unmoving, the eyes closed.

Max listened closely again, shifting his head this way and that, but he detected nothing save the slight chill wind that blew softly down from the nearby hills.

He took a small juniper branch that he had gathered earlier and carefully placed it onto the small fire, though he was careful not to look directly into the flames.

"There's something ... something not quite right," he muttered.

He said it half aloud, then shook his head and silently moved his crumpled bedroll off into the distance, well away from the fire at the base of a large cluster of boulders. He set it down and walked quietly over to where Buck stood, took a second bedroll from the horse's back, and spread this one out near the edge of the fire, close to where he had been sitting a moment before.

Max pulled out the blanket that was stuffed inside, unrolled it lengthwise, and placed it down on the center of the bedroll. He folded the bedroll over once, removed his Stetson and placed it at the top, and then quickly slipped away to the pile of boulders. He slid into his own bedroll there and positioned himself so that his back was against the rocks and his face was turned sideways from the fire.

Then he pulled out his Colt, set it on his lap, and rested cautiously to await the morning.

He thought for a time about his aunt and uncle and their Wyoming ranch.

He thought about the man named Paul Reyelts – a man he had looked for in vain for 10 years now. He wondered how Reyelts could have simply vanished, as though he had disappeared from the face of the earth.

Maybe he left the West entirely, Max thought. *Maybe he went East – to New York or someplace far away, a place you can only read about in books.*

Maybe he just changed his name. Or maybe he's working in a job you'd never suspect – like a preacher, or maybe even a sheriff or some other type of lawman. Maybe he's just dead and buried in some shallow grave in the middle of nowhere.

Not a day went by that Max Blake didn't think of Paul Reyelts.

After a time, Max's mind returned to Hoss Johnson. *The judge has stuck me with a mean one this time*, he thought. *But he's out there somewhere. He's even close – close enough to feel now.*

The wind picked up a little more, and Max pulled his bedroll tighter around his chest and closed his eyes before drifting off into a light, nervous sleep.

For a short time that night, Max Blake dreamed. He was facing three men in the dusty main street of a town he didn't recognize. They were veteran saddle tramps with hard miles on them. They stared grimly at him, and he returned their stare, his right hand slowly flexing near the black holster that held his Colt. Max wondered about the men: Who they were and why they were bracing him in the middle of a cow town he couldn't place, or even understand why he was there.

As he considered his situation, all three of the men suddenly made their move, instantly pulling their revolvers, and Max realized for a split second as he reached for his own gun that they were fast for cowboys – mighty fast, in fact.

But he reacted as he always did, with deadly speed, and –

He awoke with a start then, his hand already clutching his finely tooled .45. Max immediately saw Buck look up at him for a second, then lower his massive head to the ground once more.

Nothing, he thought. *Nothing there. Just a dream.*

But he knew that he would sleep no more this night.

Chapter Five
Some Added Protection

Three uneventful days later, Max Blake arrived in the bustling town of Twisted Junction and stopped at the livery stables, which was located on the western edge of the tidy settlement. He dismounted from Buck and walked the big horse inside the stables, where a man was hammering square nails into a door on one of the stalls.

Max stood quietly by, rubbing the horse's broad head, until the man looked up in surprise.

"Sorry, mister. Didn't hear you come in," he said.

"I'd like you to water and brush down my horse, and give him some of your best feed – oats if you got it," Max said. "He could stand some quiet, too, if you're done with all that banging."

"Sure thing, mister," he said. "Sorry again I didn't see you right at first. Name's Weller. Tim Weller. I run the stables here. And you?"

"The horse's name is Buck," Max said as he turned to walk away. "My name's Blake."

"Blake? Hey, you wouldn't be Max Blake, would you?" Weller called out.

Max turned around, his right hand already hovering near his Colt.

"That's right," he said. "Why do you ask?"

"The sheriff told me to keep a watch out for you," Weller said. "He's been expecting you – starting since about yesterday, I'd guess. He's waiting for you over at the jail, I expect. Sheriff Clark's his name. Ned Clark."

Max nodded and said, "What's the fastest way to the jail?"

"Just follow the street up there to the left," Weller said. "You'll run into the jail just a ways down on your right – can't miss the place. It's got a sign on it, if you can read."

"I'm obliged," Max said and turned away again. Then he stopped and turned slowly, looking back over his shoulder. "You'll take good care of my horse, right?"

"Anything you say, Mr. Blake," the stable man agreed. "Anything you need, you just ask old Tim Weller here and I'm your man. You just ask Sheriff Clark, Mr. Blake. Better yet, ask his deputy – a good friend of mine. They'll both tell you that I'm all right, that you can sure count on me..."

But Max was already moving down the street.

Twisted Junction was large enough to support two saloons and a rambling house situated between the two that catered to rough-and-tumble cowboys and young girls, mostly of Mexican heritage. The general store was large and carried a sign proclaiming goods from as far east as New York City. Max thought to himself that a man couldn't get much farther east than that and still stay on dry land, and he had to suppress a slight smile as he recalled his aunt's weekly geography lessons.

That was a long time ago, he thought.

He walked past a sturdy adobe building on his left that must have been the bank, although he didn't see a sign beyond the one on the front door that read "Closed For Now" in hastily scrawled hand-lettering. There were bullet holes in two of the windows in the front, and the door also looked as though at least one bullet has recently passed through it.

The sheriff's office was just past the hotel on the same side of the street. It was next to a gun shop that offered smithing services as well as new and used items for sale, and Max made a mental note to check the store out before he quietly moved up the steps to Ned Clark's comfortable office.

Max knocked softly a couple of times and then entered. A man in his mid-twenties, wearing a tin star and a big smile that was somewhere between being cocky and annoying, gave him a thorough once-over as he entered. The man was seated behind one of two desks in the office; his large boots, spurs still attached, were crossed over one another on top of the desk as he leaned back in his chair. It was a good trick, considering the length of the spurs and the height of the desk.

Max nodded a slight greeting and said, "I'm looking for Sheriff Clark."

"The sheriff's not in right now. Something I can help you with, mister?"

"You can tell me where I can find Ned Clark," Max said simply.

"Like I said, the sheriff ain't here."

The deputy continued to wear his toothy smile, and he looked at Max as though the matter was settled and there was nothing more to say. Max walked around and stood a couple of feet away from where the man was seated, waiting.

"You got a name?" Max asked after a moment of staring intently at the man and watching him smile back.

"Tom Bolton," the deputy grinned. "What can I help you with, mister, ah ... I didn't get your name now, did I?"

"No, you didn't," Max said as he suddenly used his left hand to knock Bolton's feet off the desk. "You didn't ask, and I didn't offer."

Bolton looked surprised, but he stayed in his chair with the same smile still attached to his face. His eyes were wider now, however; he wasn't sure about the situation he suddenly found himself in, but he knew for certain that he didn't like it.

"Now tell me," Max said, looming over the deputy, "where I can find Ned Clark."

"He's making his rounds around the town," Bolton said, a trace of nervousness creeping into his voice. "He's probably in one of the two saloons now; that's where the action comes in town – when there is any action. But the sheriff doesn't drink; don't get me wrong."

Max turned to leave when the deputy called out, "Hey, Mister – I still didn't get your name. I'd like to tell the sheriff in case you don't find him..."

"The name's Blake," Max answered without turning around, pushing his way through the still-open door and walking briskly out into the street.

The deputy's face lost its grin for the first time. "Now that ain't exactly getting off to a good start, is it?" he muttered aloud after Max left. Then he shrugged, put his feet back up on the desk, and pulled out his smile again. If the world could be set right with an unquestioning smile, then Tom Bolton would be at the front of the line.

Max walked out to the middle of the street, mindful of a passing horse-and-buggy and a couple of riders on stocky horses, and started back toward the saloons. Moving his eyes warily about, he walked the block or so to the first saloon and eased his way through the doors. A few men turned to look, and one of them nodded in recognition and poked the man seated next to him to whisper what he knew.

Max looked carefully around and, not spotting Ned Clark, slowly backed out before heading up the street again to the next saloon. As he passed the brothel, one of the girls – pretty with long, coal-black hair and delicate features – called to him through the large open picture window that was facing the street.

"How 'bout it, cowboy?" she sighed, her dark eyes fluttering slightly. "Want to show a girl a good time?"

Max smiled slightly and tipped the brim of his Stetson, but he neither spoke nor broke his stride.

He found Ned Clark in the next saloon, seated at a table with two other men. Clark had a small cigar in his mouth and was nursing what appeared to be a bottle of soda. He looked up as Max entered, said a couple of words to his friends, and then stood up and hailed Max, walking over to the door.

"Marshal Blake. It's good to see you again," Clark said, holding out his hand.

"And you, sheriff," Max replied, firmly gripping the man's hand in return.

"Come on, let's go across to my office; we can talk there," Clark said as he held the door for Max. "I got a wire from Judge Radford that said he was sending you over this way. You had a good ride, I trust? See any action along the way? Any sign of Hoss Johnson?"

"Nothing to report," Max replied. "But I'm anxious to hear what you can tell me about Johnson and his sidekicks."

"Well, Johnson raised all kinds of hell here," the sheriff said as the two of them started to walk down the dusty street. "He's a big, powerful man – an ugly man. And he's as crazy as a coyote that's been feeding at the loco weed patch."

Clark paused and shook his head. "What he did here just ain't right.

"The first time he came in town, I was out to one of the nearby ranches trying to settle a fence dispute. Left my deputy in charge – a good kid named Tom Bolton – but he's young, and he didn't hear or see anything until it was all over."

"I met your deputy a little while ago," Max said dryly.

"Anyway, Johnson is moving about with two brothers named Morgan..."

"One named Freeman, the other called Weasel?" Max interrupted.

"Those are the ones, all right," Sheriff Clark said. "You know 'em?"

"Know of them is more like it," Max said. "A couple of tough hombres, the way I hear it, and both of them not quite right in the head."

"They would both as soon shoot you as talk to you – and they'd forget the talk soon afterward anyways," the sheriff said as they came up to his office, and he opened the door and motioned for Max to enter.

"You first, sheriff," Max said, and Ned Clark walked into his office and pulled up a chair by his desk. "Here, have a seat. You already know my deputy, I understand?"

Max sat down and nodded again at young Tom Bolton, who had removed his boots from the desk when his boss entered but continued to grin widely, disarmingly, at both men.

"Anyway," the sheriff said, starting to chew on his cigar while he spoke, "the three of them slipped into the bank and ended up shooting both Bill Stryke and his wife, Mary Ellen. She was just in the wrong place at the wrong time, poor woman. She brought ol' Bill's lunch over to him and happened to be there when the damn shootin' started.

"You probably heard what I wired the judge: that Johnson shot the two of them out of meanness. He plugged ol' Bill because he didn't get the safe open fast enough to suit him, and then he shot poor Mary Ellen because she started to carryin' on after Bill got shot.

"At least, that's the way the teller at the counter told it after it was over. And he's lucky he didn't get shot hisself, although he'll tell you that he'll never set foot in that bank again."

"Did you go after them?" Max asked.

"Sure we did," Sheriff Clark answered. "We saddled a posse of 12 men, myself included, and were on the trail east of here no more than two hours after it all happened – right quick after I got back into town.

"But the bastards must have doubled back on us by moving in and out across the hard-pan that forms by the streams coming out of the foothills, and a day later they were back in town robbing the same damned bank while we were still out trying to pick up their trail in the hills and the scrabble.

"It's the price you pay for not having a good tracker in town. As it stands now, I'm it – and I ain't near as good at it as I should be. Too old, I guess.

"Anyways, this time it was the Morgans who did most of the shooting, although Hoss Johnson did kill one man that we know of for sure. Bolton here" – the sheriff motioned to his deputy – "was in the office when the shooting broke out on the street, and he managed to get off a couple of shots. But it was too late; they were already headed out of town."

Bolton shut his smile down for a minute. "There wasn't much I could do except to send a man out to tell the sheriff what had happened all over again right back here," he said.

Max eased forward in his chair a little. "That wasn't a bad idea on Johnson's part," he said after a minute. "Pretty smart, in fact."

"Actually, I'd call it a damn good idea," the sheriff said. "I had never heard that Hoss Johnson or the Morgan brothers had much in the way of smarts or good sense – tough killers, surely, though not smart – but they sure played us for damn fools."

The sheriff turned in his chair and kicked the inside of his desk. He was nearing 50, but he was tough and lean and didn't like the fact that he had been bested by outlaws. He looked at Bolton, who was smiling broadly again, and then back at Max.

The sheriff chewed hard on the cigar now as his anger kicked up with the recollection of recent events.

"I wired Judge Radford at that point," he said at last. "I wasn't going to get my posse to chase after those three killers again. My people were mad as hell when they heard what had happened to

Bill and Mary Ellen; but they are family men, too, and they were already tired and mostly worn out. Besides, they didn't want to chase out again and likely as not even get themselves shot doing it."

"Well, you did the right thing, sheriff," Max said. "You did all a man could do under the circumstances."

"I don't know that I agree with you there, Marshal. I wish to hell that I had been here to stop them. But there's more to tell you.

"Word came to us through one of the girls over in the Red Palace that three tough bastards shot up the saloon down in a little village called Indian Wells; it's a good day's ride from here, south and east," Sheriff Clark said, his voice weary now.

"It happened two days ago. Four men were shot dead in the cantina there. Not one of them was packing so much as a gun, or even a knife. Three of them were shot in the back; another was shot in the face at close range – close enough, in fact, for powder burns to show on his skin. Or at least that's what we've heard through the girl."

"What makes you think it was Johnson and the Morgans?" Max asked.

"Just a damn good hunch, I guess," the sheriff said. "That's a Mexican and Apache village – a peaceful, tight-knit group of sheep farmers, mostly. One of the villagers saw three men ride into town at night and then ride out again early the next morning. This fellow remembered that one of the men was big and that he rode a big horse. But it was dark and windy, and nobody apparently saw or heard much of anything else."

"That's all?" Max asked.

"Except for the fact that the men were heading east and back into the foothills when they rode out of Indian Wells; that's all of it," Sheriff Clark said. "It's not a lot of help, I know. But it's all I got."

"Well, I've picked up a day, anyway," Max said as he stood up to leave. "I'd best get started and not lose any more time."

"Listen, Marshal Blake," Clark said. "I'd like to go along with you and help settle this thing. Bill and Mary Ellen Stryke were friends of mine, as were the others in my town who were killed by these bastards. A couple of them boys I played cards with – good fellas, all. I've got a stake in this, and I can help you."

"I'm sure that you can, sheriff, and I appreciate the offer," Max said. "But I work alone.

"Besides, you've got your hands full looking after your deputy – not to mention the rest of the folks in your town."

Max smiled and held out his hand to Ned Clark. "Any town that has two saloons, a brothel, a closed-up bank, and a deputy who keeps his feet up on the desk all day long needs a full-time sheriff," he said with a slight chuckle.

Bolton started to say something and then thought better of it, his grin fluctuating between mild anger and a some-things-are-just-better-left-alone expression.

"I really would like to come along, Blake," the sheriff said. "Besides, I'm not sure that you can stop me."

"Well, you might be right about that," Max said. "But look at it this way: I like you well enough, sheriff, but I don't know a thing about the way you work. I'm not used to watching out for anybody else. And I'm not anxious to tangle with the likes of Hoss Johnson and the Morgans while I'm wondering about where you are and what you might be doing."

"You wouldn't have to worry about me none," the sheriff said.

"You're probably right there, too," Max said. "But let's just agree that I'd like to take this thing on alone for now. If it gets to a point where I need some help, I'll send for you."

"Fair enough, Marshal," Clark said after a moment's pause. "Can't say I didn't offer or try."

"Can't and won't. I'll be going then," Max said. He reached for the door handle and then stopped. "The gun shop next door – an honest place?"

"Yes. A good man named Jackson runs it," Clark said. "He knows most everything there is to know about a gun. If you're thinking of stopping by, just tell him that I sent you."

"I'm obliged again, sheriff. Good day to you."

As Max headed out the door, Tom Bolton absently put his feet back up on the desk and grinned at Ned Clark. "That's a dumb stupid man that don't want no help chasing after Hoss Johnson and the Morgan brothers," he said. "And I can't believe you offered to go along, sheriff. The man's likely to get hisself all shot up to hell before this thing is over."

"Shut up, Tom," the sheriff said. "And get your damned feet off that desk before I shoot 'em off."

Max walked into Jackson's Gun Shop and immediately went up to a glassed case of revolvers.

A man in his late fifties, clearly the proprietor, walked in from the back room and nodded while wiping his hands on an oily rag. "Something I can help you with, mister?" he asked.

"The sheriff said you ran a good shop," Max said. "I need a small sidearm that I can tuck away in my belt or boot – something not too big, but with kick enough to let a man know that he ought to take notice."

"A little life insurance, is it? Yes sir, I think I can help you with that, all right. My name is Jackson, Steven Jackson; I own the place."

"A pleasure," Max said simply. "What have you got?"

"Let's see. We've got this nice Merwin and Bray here." He pulled the gun up and placed it on the counter top, paused for second or two, and then tried again when Max showed no interest. "Here's a pepperbox that'll fit down in your boot, but it might be a bit too clumsy. Yes, I suspect that it would be, comes to that.

"Now this might be just the thing — a .41 caliber Remington derringer with striking pearl handles. It's sturdy and damn near foolproof – not that you look like a fool, sir, not at all..."

Max pointed at an odd-shaped gun in a corner of the case and said to Jackson, "Let me see the Knuckleduster."

"My, yes," Jackson said, "a nice little gun: J. Reid's `My Friend' Knuckleduster, made at Mr. Reid's factory in Catskill, New York, and patented in 1863. We have seven shots here, .30-caliber rim-fire, solid brass for long wear, a variety of engravings on the handles. It doesn't have as much firepower as the Remington derringer, mind you, but it'll give you five more shots, and it's almost as small. Plus, it acts as a little club to strike someone over the head with as well. You just slip your fingers through the hole there and..."

"I'm familiar with the gun," Max said, picking up the Knuckleduster as Jackson set it on the counter in front of him. He carefully slipped his ring and little fingers through the hole in the handle, wrapping the other two fingers around the frame – his index finger finding the trigger nicely. He slowly cocked the hammer and held the gun close to his ear as he did so, listening to the metallic clicks as the Knuckleduster's inner mechanisms fell into place.

Max eased the hammer down with his thumb, repeated the process a half-dozen or so times, and then looked up at Jackson. "Apaches are known to like these things, you know. How much?"

"For a friend of Sheriff Clark's, ten dollars. With a box of shells thrown in for good measure, of course."

"I'll take it," Max said. "And make it two boxes of shells – I'll pay the difference. A gun like this one might just come in handy somewhere along the trail."

"You would like me to box it up then?" Jackson asked.

"That's all right," Max said, loading the Knuckleduster before sticking it into his belt. "I'll take it just like this."

"Mind if I take a look at your sidearm, sir?" Jackson asked admiringly as Max paid him with a gold coin. "It looks like a fairly nice piece, even sitting there in your holster."

Max effortlessly pulled the Colt, turned it around in his hand so that the butt of the gun was extended toward Jackson, and then carefully set it on the counter. At the same time, his right hand drifted down to the newly loaded Knuckleduster in his belt.

"Oh, a dandy," Jackson said as he carefully picked up the Colt. "I'm sure I don't have as fine a sample anywhere in my store, and that's saying something.

"My, yes," he continued, "Sam Colt's famous Peacemaker model in .45-caliber, as fine a gun as has ever been made anywhere. Single-action, six shots, five-and-a-half-inch barrel, pearl grips, stylish engravings – beautiful workmanship overall. Some people call this gun the Cavalry Artillery model, you know, but I like the sound of 'Peacemaker' better – don't you?"

Jackson took a gun cloth and wiped the Colt down before handing it back to Max.

"A most beautiful and reliable weapon, sir. I salute your taste," he said.

Max took the gun and flicked it back into his holster with a deft movement of his right hand that made Jackson arch his eyebrows.

"You'd be Max Blake now, wouldn't you?" Jackson asked, although he already knew the answer.

Max touched his hat and headed for the door. "At your service," he said before walking out into the street.

Jackson's murmured response – "Well I'll be a no good go-to-hell" – was lost in the clatter of activity along the main street of Twisted Junction.

Chapter Six
Don't Forget The Name

Two days after Max Blake left Ned Clark's town in the pursuit of Hoss Johnson and the two Morgan brothers, a solitary figure rode into Twin Forks and began asking questions about the whereabouts of a certain federal marshal.

The stranger – a tall, willowy man in his mid-forties with a leathery face and long, dark sideburns — carried two matching Remington percussion-fired revolvers, clumsy but reliable remnants of the Civil War. His clothing was dusty, and the rough stubble on his face indicated that he had spent some hard days without a lot of rest on the trail.

"Hey boy," he called sharply to Joey Gray as he rode up to the stables and slowly dismounted. "If'n you help me find a fellow hereabouts in town, I'll consider making it worth your while."

Joey, who was brushing down one of the stable horses, stopped and looked at the man; he immediately noticed the two huge Remingtons and thought to himself that such big pistols wouldn't be of much use in a gunfight unless the man who carried them was especially strong and quick.

"Who is it you're looking for, mister?" Joey asked.

"A federal marshal who hails by the name of Max Blake," the man said, spitting out the name like it was a curse. "I'm told that he lives in this town or around these parts."

"Sure, everybody in town knows Max, ah, Marshal Blake. And I'd like to help you, mister, but Max ain't here right now. He's out working for the judge, chasing after some outlaw named Hoss Johnson."

"Where exactly did he go, boy?" the man asked. "And when?"

"I'm not rightly sure," Joey answered, "except that he left town heading south a couple of days ago. But you should go over and ask Judge Radford at the courthouse. He'll know right where Max went."

"And this Johnson fellow: Any idea of who he is or what he's done?" the man asked, a sense of danger lurking in his reedy voice that even Joey detected.

"He sounds like a right bad fella to me, mister," Joey said, starting to get a little edgy because of the persistence of the questions and the man's constant sneer. "But I don't know much more'n what I've already told you. The judge keeps track of all that kind of stuff, though – over at the courthouse."

"You'll take care of my horse for a while, boy?"

"Sure thing, mister. The courthouse is over that way," Joey said, pointing out the direction.

"And the saloon, boy? Which way to the saloon?" he asked. Joey pointed down the street again in the direction of the saloon and then said, "What's your name, mister – so we know who the horse belongs to?"

"Name's Grant," the man with the Remingtons said without turning around as he walked quickly away.

Lon Barbers came out of the stables a few minutes after Grant had left, and he walked up to where Joey was rubbing down the tall stranger's horse with a soft, wide brush.

"Thought I heard voices out here a bit ago," he said. "Who belongs to the horse?"

"A tall, skinny fella named Grant – carrying two big old revolvers near as long as my arm," Joey said. "He didn't tell me his first name, unless maybe his first name is Grant. He was looking for Max, so I sent him over to see the judge.

"He was kinda scary though, Lon. He had a mean look to him, like he was used to hurtin' people. And he was acting, well, odd, I guess is the best way to put it."

"What do you mean odd, Joey?"

66

"Well, like he was going to explode at any minute," Joey said after thinking about it for a time. "He looked like he was ready to hit somebody the whole time he was here.

"It seemed kinda strange, looking at him, that he wanted to see Max. There was a big streak of meanness in the man, all right. I can tell you that much about him."

"Well, a man had best know what he's doing, searching after the likes of Max Blake," Barbers said. "He didn't say what he wanted, did he, Joey?"

Joey shook his head. "Only that he was looking for the marshal and that he would make it worth my while to help him find Max.

"Why do you ask, Lon? You don't think that Max is in any trouble, do you?"

Lon Barbers smiled a little and patted Joey on the boy's shoulder. "Your friend Marshal Blake is always sniffin' around trouble," he said. "The thing of it is, it's the other fellow who needs to be careful.

"You just take good care of that man's horse. A man who carries big pistols like you described – well, we don't want him to start looking for us."

The man named Grant turned his back to the counter in the saloon after ordering a beer and called out to the dozen or so men inside: "I'm looking for a man who goes by the name of Max Blake. He's a federal marshal."

A few of them looked up but didn't say a word. The handful of others paid him no mind at all; they were engaged in a game of cards at a far table.

"Most everybody in Twin Forks knows of Max Blake," the bartender said after an uncomfortable moment, "though I wouldn't say that anybody really knows him well, except maybe for Judge Radford and the boy who works at the livery stable."

Grant turned around and looked at the man. "Keep talking," he said.

"Well, the marshal's on the trail a lot, doing the judge's bidding, and he keeps pretty much to himself during the little bit of time that he's in town – which ain't that often anyway."

"You got a name, barkeep?"

"Carson's my name, mister. Clem Carson. Yours?"

"Grant," the big man said; he had turned halfway around so that he could watch the bartender but also keep an eye on the rest of the men in the saloon. "The boy over at the stables told me that Blake's not in town. That true?"

"Can't say one way or the other," Carson said, "though the stable boy knows him better'n most. I do know that Marshal Blake was here two or three days ago – can't remember which, exactly. He rode in with the outlaw Tom Culpepper's horse and guns to return to the judge. A meaner man never existed in these parts than Tom Culpepper, and the marshal was only gone a week or so before he came back in packing the man's horse."

"So Blake is good, is he?" Grant asked, although he already appeared to know the answer.

"Max Blake is a good man to steer far clear of, Mister Grant," Carson said. "You better hope that you are on friendly terms with him.

"What did you say you wanted with the marshal, anyway?"

Grant smiled through thin lips, exposing a couple of missing teeth. "Let's just say that I need to conduct some overdue business with him," he said.

"Well, I suggest that you go over to the courthouse and talk with Judge Radford," Carson said. "He can tell you where Marshal Blake is, or at least where he's gone to."

Grant finished his beer and started to leave.

"That'll be two bits for the beer, Mister Grant – before you get to see the judge or find Max Blake," Carson said.

Grant turned slowly and pulled a silver coin from his pocket. He tossed it on the bar and then looked at Carson. "I don't feel at home in a courthouse any more'n I do a jail cell – or in this saloon, for that matter," he said. "But I'll find Max Blake, all right – one way or another."

He turned fully around once more, stretching his arms out far and back on either side of the edge of the bar, and again called out: "How 'bout it? Any of you know where Max Blake has gone?"

But Grant's question was met only by indifference and a handful of empty stares; and so he moved away from the bar and pushed through the narrow doors of the saloon and walked out onto the street, heading again toward the livery.

When he reached the stables and Joey Gray again, Grant was in a foul mood that made Joey back away a bit after looking up and seeing the man's face.

"You done with my horse, boy?" Grant snarled.

"Sure am, mister," Joey said as he watched the stranger pull his tall frame up into the saddle. "Did you get over to see the judge?"

"What's that to you, boy? Don't you push it with me, else I'll pull out my quirt and whack you a time or two."

"I meant no harm, mister," Joey said. "It's just –"

"Never mind. You watch what you say to me, boy," Grant said, looking down menacingly from his horse. "You said Max Blake was heading south when he left town?"

"That's right."

Grant nodded and sat quiet for a few seconds, looking hard at Joey. "You won't forget my name now, boy – will you? It's Grant. You remember that now, you understand?"

Joey shook his head up and down with puzzled eyes and a frightened look on his face.

"Say it now, so you don't forget."

"Sure, mister. Your name is Grant."

And with that, the tall man turned his horse south, heading quickly out of Twin Forks in pursuit of Max Blake.

"What do you suppose that was all about?" Joey asked Lon Barbers when he saw the stable owner around the back of the box stalls shortly after the man named Grant had left.

"What'd he say his name was again, Joey?"

"He said his name was Grant; he told me to remember it – to remember the name, like it would mean something to me."

Barbers shook his head and thought for a minute.

"The man the marshal shot and killed a few weeks back, over in Jefferson County: Wasn't that man's name Grant – or Granite or Grady or something like that?" Barbers asked, talking to himself as much as he was to Joey.

"I don't think I ever heard," Joey replied. "I know the man wasn't famous like Tom Culpepper was. I don't know that it ever came up. You know how Max doesn't like to talk about that sort of thing."

"Well, I don't rightly remember, neither," Barbers said. "But this is something we'd best let Judge Radford know about. You run over to the courthouse right now, Joey, and see the judge. You tell him I sent you and tell him what happened."

"You don't suppose..."

"I don't know, Joey. I don't suppose nothin'. But I'm not a gambling man, and I don't think that we should take a chance.

"You run over to the courthouse now and tell the judge what you saw and heard. Go on, now – git goin' quick-like."

But Joey Gray was already running hard down the dusty street.

Chapter Seven

A Smaller Camp Fire

Max Blake rode into Indian Wells a day after the mass burial of the four murdered villagers. He had pushed Buck hard after leaving Twisted Junction, and they both needed some rest when they arrived.

He didn't take time along the way to search for signs of the three outlaws he was chasing. There was little reason for Hoss Johnson and the two Morgan brothers to hang around between Twisted Junction and Indian Wells, Max reasoned. More than likely, they already were heading for the Mexican border and one of the many towns that sprawled out in succession along the bottom of Arizona.

These were tough towns filled with tough men, Max knew; and Hoss Johnson and the two Morgan boys would be right at home among them.

Max went directly to the stables to check his horse over thoroughly and to ask a few questions; he wanted to find the Indian Wells *jeffe* and learn what he could about the bloody killings in the saloon. Although the big horse had chewed up the miles without showing any signs of tiring, Max knew that his very life depended on how well he treated Buck – and on how well the animal performed when it counted.

"You look all right, old boy," Max said softly into Buck's ear after he ran his hands up and down the big chestnut's legs, checking for any sign of the trembles. Then he ordered up some grain from the stable boy, tossed him a coin, and followed the boy's directions down the little street several hundred yards to the home of Pedro Ruiz, who served as mayor, village spokesman, and respected elder in Indian Wells.

71

"This is a bad time for the people in my village," Ruiz said sadly as he came to the door and Max had introduced himself. He was a frail man who was in his mid-sixties, but he looked much older because of the toll that the long years of back-breaking farm work and sheep ranching had taken. His eyes were sad, his weathered face was creased with deep lines, and his shoulders were stooped.

Despite his sorrow at the loss of his friends, Ruiz was gracious and hospitable as he received Max into his two-room adobe house.

"There aren't enough men for the women we have here in this village and the work that must be done," he said after bidding Max to sit on a small wooden chair. "And now we are four less.

"Perhaps you know of some good young men who would like to come here and work and stay and live in this village?"

The old man didn't sound hopeful, but he felt that it was his duty to ask. When Max said nothing, he continued: "Perhaps you would like to stay yourself? Or perhaps you would come back when you have found these men? A man such as you could live very well in such a place as this."

Max smiled, shaking his head a little at the thought of spending the rest of his days in Indian Wells.

"What happened here? What can you tell me?" he asked after a long pause.

"Only that they took the little money from the saloon, plus some bottles of tequila, and robbed the men they killed. And poor Tomas Hernandez, the bartender: They beat him senseless – *loco* – before they left. He is only now starting to get well again, with the help of the saints and our many prayers."

"Go on," Max said.

"Gregorio Martinez was up early, working outside of his hut, and he saw three hombres leave the village; they were heading east into the mountains. They must have been the ones who did this thing; they were the only strangers anyone saw in our village for days."

"No one heard the sound of gunfire?" Max asked.

"That is true, I am sorry to say," the old man said. "No one in the village heard a thing that night. It was a windy night. But I think that might have been good – a blessing. If anyone else had heard the sounds of the shooting and gone to see what it was, they would be dead now, too, I think."

"Is there anything else you can tell me?" Max asked.

"Beyond that, well, I can offer nothing – other than my sadness for the families of the four dead men and for you, who must chase after these killers. What kind of men are they, who could do this thing?"

Max only shook his head.

There were no simple answers; he knew that much, at least.

Three hours later, at an elevation that Max estimated to be at least 3,000 feet, judging by where the timberline broke above him, he picked up the trail of three men who were moving east and south – and who seemed to be traveling in a hurry. He could tell at a glance that one of the horses was a large animal and that it must have been carrying either a big man or a heavy load – or perhaps both.

"I think, old boy, that we are on the right track," Max said aloud to Buck as he swung the horse off to the right and followed the tracks along a narrow game trail.

The path wound its way across the rim of a broad sweep of progressively higher and higher hills that far off in the distance became grim, jagged, snow-capped peaks.

"From here on, Buck, we've got nothing but hard work and little rest ahead of us," Max said.

And a minute later he added as an afterthought: "I'm sorry, old friend, but that's just the way it is. The judge has served us a bucketful of spiders this time."

The horse confidently picked his way over the narrow trail, carefully avoiding the loose rocks. Skimpy scrub pine, gnarled and twisted from years in the wind and harsh weather, sprouted here and there along the landscape. For every bush and pine tree and warped juniper that poked its way up through the rocky ground, Max had the feeling that nature had gained a small triumph in this rugged land.

For as far as he could see, the earth rose and fell in shades of dull browns and reds and rocky grays, peppered by the occasional dull and dusty green of a beaten pine or a skimpy growth of equally beaten mesquite.

Max stayed at all times on or close to the trail that he suspected had been used by Hoss Johnson and the two Morgans only a day or so before. But he was careful not to show himself against the skyline and provide an easy target for any man below him with a steady hand, a good eye, and a long-barreled Winchester or Sharps carbine. He moved Buck carefully this way and that, watching the slope of the hills above while keeping a relentless eye for any activity that might occur in the swales and ridges that fell off before him.

A biting cold that swept down on the wind from the barren peaks overhead forced Max to pull his buckskin jacket close around his neck. Tight-fitting leather gloves kept his hands warm, but he was always uncomfortable wearing them because they gave him less control of his gun – and he knew that his life depended as much on his Colt Peacemaker and his Winchester lever-action rifle as it did on old Buck.

A wet snow started falling just as the trail began to sink down the southern slope of the foothills. But within another half-hour or so, he was out of the damp dusting and the stark wind and was winding his way through taller pines and thick shocks of scrub brush and scattered mesquite and prairie grass. The sky was a gray pall above him now, and he knew that the snow would be sticking on the ground in the upper elevations he had just passed.

The trail picked up a small stream that had started as a trickle of water from the mountains and was now rushing across the hard-pan of rocks and smaller boulders that by summer would be baking with the rest of the region in the arid heat of the high desert.

But summer was still more than three months off, and Max stopped for a moment and allowed Buck to amble into the stream to drink, although he was careful not to let the animal gulp the water too fast and become quickly bloated. He got down from the big horse and knelt on one knee, cupping his hands together to taste the icy, snow-fed water. He went back to where Buck was standing, removed the two wooden canteens that were looped around the saddle horn, and then emptied them out before refilling them with the fresh, sweet water from the stream.

Max returned the canteens to the horse, scouted around for any sign of fresh tracks again, and pulled himself back on Buck, following the northern edge of the stream for another five miles or so.

He pulled out the Winchester that he carried in a sleek buckskin scabbard and placed it across the pommel of his saddle, expecting trouble.

It was growing dark, and Max picked up the distant scent of wood smoke, probably from a campfire that had been hastily or carelessly made, he thought. He rode another quarter-mile or so before the light of the fire – almost a bonfire by trail standards, he considered – came into view through the thin trees in the distance.

Max quickly got off Buck, tied the horse to a nearby pine, and moved silently forward to scout the activity around the fire.

He crept within voice range and saw immediately that the fire had been built by pilgrims – people not used to the trail or to traveling in such rough country – because sparks were now firing high into the air, and large branches and other pieces of wood had been gathered and were waiting to be added to the already massive flames.

No wonder I picked up the scent from so far away, Max thought. *These folks are hanging out a shingle to die.*

He could plainly see three figures near the fire: a man who looked to be in his mid-thirties, a woman who appeared to be slightly younger, and a small boy of 7 or 8 years or so. In a moment another boy, this one somewhat older – 10 or 12 years, Max guessed – returned from what looked like a wagon off in the darkness and sat down on a nearby branch. The older boy broke a long length of wood into small pieces and tossed each one into the hungry flames.

Max could see from the way they were dressed that the trail had been hard on this family. The two young boys were in loose-fitting pants that had large, flannel patches on the knees and seat and in dusty flannel shirts. The man wore frequently patched overalls that were at least two sizes too large. And the woman, although she still cut a fine figure, wore a gray, threadbare dress and a blue- and white-striped bonnet that fit loosely over her short-cropped blonde hair.

75

Max shook his head a bit at the sight, returned to collect Buck, and then walked the horse back toward the camp, approaching with caution.

"Hello, the fire!" he called out loudly.

"Hullo yerself," the voice of a man called back after a pause, a surprised, wary edge to it. "Sing out what you want or be off with you."

"My intentions are peaceful," Max called back. "I'm a federal marshal."

"Then come on along, but keep yer hands in plain sight," the man called again.

Max walked into view, holding Buck's reins in his left hand while keeping his right hand free and close to his side and the ever-present holstered Colt.

"Evening, folks," Max said as he entered the small clearing.

There was an uneasy silence for a moment. The man, who was holding a Sharps carbine in both hands, and the woman exchanged nervous glances until she finally said, "Good evening, sir. And welcome."

The man threw a sharp glance at the woman; but she looked disapprovingly at him in return and added, "My husband and I, with our two sons, are traveling to California. Our name is Nelson; we're from Texas – formerly from Texas, I should say – and before that from Arkansas."

Max tipped his dusty black Stetson to the woman and nodded at the man and the two boys, noticing that the smaller one had moved close to his mother while the older boy had edged a little closer to the man.

"My name's Max Blake," he said. "I'd appreciate it if you'd put down that carbine, Mister Nelson. Somebody might get hurt."

The man lowered the weapon slowly, almost sheepishly; he clearly would have been more comfortable with a shovel in his hands, and he knew it. But he was still suspicious. He put the butt of the carbine on the ground, holding the barrel with his right hand. "You said you was a United States marshal."

"That's right," Max said.

"Well, I don't see no badge nowheres."

"A badge can be an invitation for some folks in these parts to shoot first and ask no questions later," Max said simply. "I carry

76

my badge under the collar of my shirt."

"Well, I'd feel a whole sight better if'n I could see that badge right now, mister."

Max peeled back his coat and turned the collar of his shirt outward, exposing the tin star. The older boy whistled as his father edged forward to get a closer look and then nodded, first at Max and then at his wife.

Max smiled at the boy as he saw him admiring the big chestnut. "His name's Buck, son," he said. "He's a good old horse." The boy didn't say anything; he just whistled again.

"That tin star looks all right to me," the man said after a minute. "My name's Larry Nelson, marshal. My wife here's called Sally; I'm right proud of her, too. She used to be a school teacher back in the East, up in Pennsylvania, before moving down to Arkansas and marrying up with me. And these two sprouts here are our boys, Josh and Jason."

Sally Nelson added: "We don't have much, but you are welcome to spend the night at our fire, Marshal ... Blake, was it?"

"Call me Max. It's a pleasure, ma'am, to find an educated woman in these parts – a rare thing."

Sally Nelson blushed a little and said, smiling: "You will join us for supper, Marshal Blake? I was just about to cook some stew when you surprised us."

"I'd be pleased to stay the night nearby. I don't want to put you to any trouble," Max said. "Mind if I ask a question or two?"

Larry Nelson grunted, and Max said: "I don't imagine you've seen three tough-looking men: an ugly, heavyset man on a big horse and two others who might well look like brothers?"

The Nelsons exchanged glances and shook their heads. "Why do you want to know?" the man questioned.

"Well, that accounts for the fact that you are all still alive, I guess," Max said, almost talking to himself.

"I beg your pardon?" the woman asked.

"I've been tracking three outlaws out of a village west of here in the foothills," Max said more loudly this time, taking in the surroundings of the camp as he spoke. "Their trail leads this way. Had you crossed their path, you'd likely be begging Hoss Johnson's pardon."

"We ain't seen no one in two days and wouldn't mean 'em no harm if'n we did," Larry Nelson said.

His wife added, "We are heading for California, marshal. Times were hard back in Texas and harder in Arkansas. We want to start fresh and hear that California is the place to make your fortune."

"The gold rush is long over, folks," Max said as he moved away from the fire.

"It's land we're after, marshal," Larry Nelson said, setting the carbine against a branch near the fire and walking after Max. "We're farmers, not miners; we're after good land, not gold."

"What was wrong with the land in Texas?" Max asked. "There's plenty enough of it."

"The ground just gave out on us in Texas – and in Arkansas, too," Nelson said. "And we run into some shootin' trouble on our Texas stake, first with ranchers who didn't like the fencin' we done and then with no-account Mexican bandits. So we are striking out a'new."

"California's a long way off," Max said.

"We hear tell that the ground's so rich in California, a man just might strain himself harvesting what he plants. Least, that's what we've heard tell," Nelson said.

Max smiled a little at the man's enthusiasm and walked over to where he had tied Buck. He quickly stripped the saddle off, pulled a horse brush from the saddlebags, and started running it over Buck's flanks and legs; then he looked across at Larry Nelson.

"If you want to reach California," he said, "you'd best start to build a smaller fire. There's enough flame there to attract every horse thief and outlaw between here and the border. And there are likely to be a few close by."

"Marshal Blake, there is no need to scare my children – or, for that matter, my husband or myself," Sally Nelson said from a distance.

"I'm not trying to scare you, ma'am," Max said. "I'm trying to warn you. A smaller camp fire can mean the difference between living and dying in this country."

Max finished rubbing Buck and added: "Traveling across country's not the same as farming in Texas or Arkansas. If you've been on the trail this long without trouble, you've been lucky."

He reached again into the saddlebags and pulled out a canvas sack filled with oats. He strapped that around Buck's head, patted the horse a couple of times, and then walked back to the fire.

"You mind helping me?" he asked Larry Nelson, starting to kick some of the branches away from the edge of the fire. "We could take most of this away and still have plenty of flames to cook and see by."

"We always build us a big fire. It helps to see in the night and to keep people away," Larry Nelson said, reluctantly kicking at the outer edge of the flames with his booted toe.

"A big fire like this keeps you from seeing at all," Max said. "You start to staring into it, and pretty soon you look away and all you can see are flames dancing.

"Keep the fire small and the sparks down. You can still cook, it helps chase away the cold, and it won't expose you to much extra danger."

The older boy joined in helping the two men, and soon the fire was reduced to a safe size. Max glanced with satisfaction at the flames and turned to Sally Nelson. "You can cook on that fire now, ma'am, and still have some success," he said.

"I'll just get out some things..."

"Now don't be silly, Marshal Blake," she said. "You've offered to help us here tonight. The least we can do is offer you some of our food. We haven't had much to eat along the way, but Larry got lucky today and shot a deer."

"Luck had nothin' to do with it," Larry Nelson said.

Max muttered a simple thanks and walked over to where Buck was standing. He removed the oat bag, stroked the horse's neck a few times, and tied him up to a small scrub pine. He then made his way back near the fire and sat down.

"You take good care of that horse of yours, marshal," the oldest Nelson boy said.

"I'm partial to my horse, son," Max said. "We've covered a lot of ground together. I depend on old Buck there to take me..."

He was suddenly interrupted by the boy, who could no longer refrain from asking the question he really wanted to know and blurted out, "Do you really shoot outlaws?"

"Josh," his mother scolded, looking up from where she was adding shriveled hunks of dried onions into the stew pot. "I declare, where are your manners, young man?"

But Max smiled and looked at the boy. "It's all right, son." And to his mother Max added: "That's all right, ma'am. I'm sure he meant no harm. It's only natural that the boy would be curious about what a marshal does."

"Being curious is one thing, marshal. Being polite is another," she said. "There's a time and a place for both in this world."

"Sometimes life doesn't leave us much time," Max said.

"You are certainly right in that, marshal," the woman said. "We have seen our share of senseless killing these past two years."

"Oh?"

"These outlaws you're chasin' after," Larry Nelson said, quickly cutting into Max's discussion with his wife. "A tough bunch, I take it?" His voice trailed off as though he already knew the answer but didn't care, so long as he was included in the conversation and it didn't go any further into the family's past.

Max sat silently for a moment longer, poking a corner of the fire with a stick where he had added a small triangle of good-sized stones to hold the stew pot, while at the same time avoiding looking directly into the flames. He wondered what combination of events or deeds or misfortunes had driven the Nelsons out of both Arkansas and Texas. And he was curious about the woman and her education and background. But he also knew that as long as Larry Nelson was around, no one would volunteer to supply the answers.

The fire had settled to a nice, steady glow. "It's just about ready for your stew, ma'am," he said to Sally Nelson and then turned to her husband.

"The men I'm after are killers. They passed this way, close by, within the past day and a half. They probably moved south of here a ways."

"Why south?" Nelson asked.

"North would take them back into the mountains, and it's been snowing up there. So I suspect that they are heading toward one of the border towns."

"What did they do, marshal?" the older boy asked.

"Within the past week alone, they robbed the same bank twice, shot up a saloon, and killed upwards of nine people – and that's all I know of so far."

80

Sally Nelson stopped in her tracks, surprised by Max's words. She was struggling under the weight of the large pot of stew as she carried it with both hands toward the fire – more from the size and heft of the pot than from what was in it – and she took several deep breaths before she continued forward.

"We were lucky then," she said softly.

"Here, let me help you," Max said, taking the stew pot and carefully placing it over the stones. Then he added, "Yes, I would say that you were lucky."

"Still, we wouldn't pose them any threat," she said. "I mean, what would a family of simple farmers heading west to California..."

"Shhhhhhh."

Max put his hand out to punctuate the sudden signal that he had given and turned quickly, looking over to where Buck was standing. The horse's ears were turned forward, and he was looking out into the darkness in the same direction that he and Max had traveled less than an hour before.

"Really, marshal, if this is your idea of a..."

"Quiet," Max ordered in a crisp whisper, catching Sally Nelson by surprise with the sharp tone of his voice. He already had his gun drawn and was moving off away from the fire in a low crouch. "Something's moving out there. Get under your wagon and huddle there until I can check it out."

The Nelsons were so caught off guard that Max looked over his shoulder as they continued to stare blankly back at him from their seats by the fire.

"Move," he commanded. "Now!"

Then he ducked off into the night.

Chapter Eight
Two New Allies

Sally Nelson and her two boys were huddled under their wagon, straining hard to hear or see any signs of trouble and waiting anxiously for Max Blake's return from the darkness surrounding their camp.

Larry Nelson stood in front of the wagon, clutching the Sharps carbine that he had forgotten minutes before in his haste to leave the fire and help his family to safety – a fact that annoyed him a great deal. He had been forced to crawl along the ground to retrieve the Sharps once he remembered where he had left it, which sent shivers of fear through his wife.

And even though he made an easy target standing by the front wagon wheel, the carbine held awkwardly in both hands, he felt considerably better there than he had while lying on the ground like a helpless fool.

The two boys were quiet but afraid, scarcely breathing, when they heard Max Blake call out, "Coming back in!" He appeared slowly and cautiously out of the darkness by the fringe of some pines a moment later, leading two boys who, as they came into view, were obviously both as frightened and as nervous as were the family of migrating farmers.

"It's all right," Max said to the Nelsons, still holding his Colt. "Near as I can tell, these two have been on my trail since I left Indian Wells. They came to help."

"Si. That is right, senor," one of the boys said in halting English. Then he spoke quickly in a dialect that Max puzzled with for a time, asking questions in both Spanish and the little Apache he knew, before turning toward the Nelsons again.

"You can come out from under there now," Max said to Sally Nelson and her boys.

"It seems these two left the village to help because the others there, the men in Indian Wells, were afraid."

"Los hombres muertos — amigos; friends," the other boy added for emphasis.

"The dead men in their village were their friends," Max translated aloud.

Max waited for the woman and two boys to crawl out from beneath the wagon and for her husband to put the stock of his carbine on the ground before he holstered his Colt again. But Nelson kept wrapping his fingers around the barrel of the big Sharps and frowning at the two boys; there was a sudden bitterness in the man's eyes – a sullen look that Max had not noticed before.

Max looked at the two boys again; he saw nothing unusual, shrugged slightly, and then turned toward Sally Nelson.

"There's not much to do now except add two more for dinner – if that's all right with you, ma'am," he said.

The woman was about to answer when Larry Nelson jumped in. "These two are pure Mex or 'breeds, by the look of 'em," he said. "I ain't gonna share my food with a couple of –"

"Larry Nelson, how could you?" his wife countered without letting him finish the sentence. "You know very well that these two boys were not responsible for our troubles back in –"

"Hold your tongue, woman," he said, cutting her off sharply in return. "I'll not stop till I've had my say. And I say there ain't no need for us to share our food with these two Mexican half-breeds."

His wife gave him such a disapproving look at this point that he added, "Well, dammit, they are; and there's no denying it, anyway, even if they didn't..." But his voice trailed off for a moment as a confused look spread across his face and he searched for the right words.

One of the boys spoke again in the odd dialect, liberally mixing his Spanish and Apache phrases; it was apparent that the two understood much of what Larry Nelson was saying. Max again translated as best he could. "The boy here suggests that the two of them leave now and catch up with me in the morning," he said.

"Nonsense," Sally Nelson said, turning to the boys. "You are both welcome here."

"Dammit, woman, I don't like this," her husband barked. "I'm trying to say somethin' here —"

"What is it exactly that you are trying to say that is worth hearing, Larry?" she asked.

Nelson shook his head, exasperated at his inability to easily communicate his thoughts, at his confusion with the situation, and at what he took as a razor-sharp rebuke of him in front of strangers as well as his own two sons.

Things were different away from his farm and out on the trail, and he didn't like the feel of it. He had neither heard of nor set eyes on Max Blake until an hour or so earlier, and already he was taking orders from the man — orders that helped to protect himself and his family, it was true, but orders nonetheless. Nelson thought of himself as a man who issued the orders; and now, out on the trail in the darkness and a long way from either Texas and Arkansas, a new set of rules seemingly applied.

"It's just that, if we was back on the farm..." He stopped again, sputtering.

"But we are not back on the farm, Larry," his wife said. "These boys did not force us from our land, try to run us out, start the shootings, or even cause it to stop raining and dry up our crops. They are merely boys.

"And to hear you speak the words 'half-breed' like a curse chills me; it's almost as if I don't know the man I married. I just don't understand it."

"Well, neither do I," he said. "It's not just these here two kids; don't you see that? It's ... it's him" – pointing a thick, soiled finger at Max Blake.

Max had watched the give and take of the Nelsons' conversation with mild interest, his arms folded as he leaned against the wagon, saying nothing. Even Larry Nelson's sudden turnabout had no visible effect on him; his face was unchanged in the dim light away from the camp fire.

"What has the marshal done that would cause you to say that?" Sally Nelson asked. "If anything, he has offered us some help this night from —"

"But that's just it," her husband broke in. "That's my job. That's what I'm supposed to do, dammit. The three of you have been scar't to death out here, ever since we left Texas. And you all were again tonight, right up till the point this man here showed up. Well, he may be a federal marshal and all, but that don't make him no better a'man than me.

"I know how to build a fire. I'm good with a gun," he added, almost pleading now. "I can protect you."

"I understand what Mr. Nelson here is getting at," Max said, breaking his silence. "I also happen to agree with him. It is a man's job to protect his family, and I've pushed myself on you folks tonight.

"I'll just move my camp over a ways and take these two boys here with me."

"We wouldn't think of it, marshal," Sally Nelson said.

"No, ma'am, I insist," Max said. "I've already put you folks through enough, worrying you about outlaws and sending you scattering under your wagon."

"Marshal, I – I mean we..."

"There's no need to say anything," Max said. "You can tell me why you left Pennsylvania for Arkansas some other time, perhaps."

Max nodded as Sally Nelson's face turned from exasperated with her husband to puzzled at the marshal's surprising statement, and he walked away to gather his gear. Even though he wanted to say a few things to Larry Nelson, he figured that the man would find out soon enough in this country – if he managed to stay alive long enough.

Max spoke softly in Spanish to the village boys, mixing in a few words of both English and Apache, and the two slipped away and returned with their horses to join him just as he finished tightening the cinches on Buck. He climbed aboard the big horse and turned to face the Nelsons and their sons.

"I'd still like to have the three of you stay for supper," Sally Nelson said. "It's late, our food already is cooked, and you all must be very hungry."

"That's generous of you, ma'am, but I've already taken enough of your time and caused you enough trouble."

Max turned Buck toward the trail heading east and then added over his shoulder: "We'll be down the way a bit. If you need something, just fire that gun a time or two."

"Not likely," Larry Nelson muttered half aloud as Max and the two Indian Wells boys disappeared into the pines.

The Nelsons could hear the hooves of the horses and the light murmur of voices for another minute or so. And then all was quiet around them.

"That wasn't right, pa," the older Nelson boy said at last. "I mean, I felt good having the marshal around."

But Larry Nelson said nothing as he stomped back toward the fire.

That night in Twisted Junction, a tall, reed-thin man with dark sideburns and two large Remington revolvers rode up to the edge of town and stopped at the livery stable.

A small lantern burned outside the building; but the man could find no one around, so he mounted again and rode around behind the main street. He tied his horse close to where the noise of an out-of-tune piano alerted him to the fact that he was behind a tiny saloon.

The man got off his horse, brushed some of the dirt and dust off his clothing with his hat, and moved up to the back door, pushed it back slowly, and looked cautiously inside. The door opened into a large storage area stocked with bottles of tequila, mescale, whiskey, and beer that were stacked in open wooden crates. On the opposite wall to his left were two swinging doors that opened into the saloon itself.

Just as he was about to enter the room, one of the bartenders pushed his way through the doors and started rummaging around in the crates. The tall man silently pulled out one of his long revolvers, crept up behind the man, and put the gun into the small of the bartender's back.

"Don't turn. Don't shout," he said. "Do what you're told and you'll live a little longer."

"Sure thing, mister," the bartender replied. "If you're looking for a bottle of something..."

"I'm looking for a man," the tall man said in return. "He should have been through here during the past couple'a days, or maybe even as late as today. He's a federal marshal. Goes by the name of Blake."

"If you're talking about Max Blake, I've heard the name – like most everybody else in these parts," the bartender said, so nervous from the cold feel of the gun at his neck that he couldn't stop talking. "But that's as far as I can help you, mister. I just came on call a few minutes ago – I've been out of town all day, over to my brother's spread five miles or so from here, helping him with some new mounts – and I haven't heard a word about Max Blake being in town. That's something a man wouldn't likely miss. But like I said, I've been out of town. He might have been here, all right.

"You tried over at the stables?"

"No one's there," the tall man said.

"Tim Weller runs the stables, but he likes to stop by and chat with the deputy now and again after dark," the bartender said, figuring that continuing to talk might keep the man's finger off the trigger of his big revolver. "He and Tom Bolton are friends. You might try on over at the sheriff's office.

"What's this all about anyway, mister? I mean, why are you looking for Max Blake – not that I'm overly curious, mind you?"

"I'm just looking up an old friend. Here, let me leave you my calling card," the man named Grant said before he suddenly clubbed the bartender over the head with the butt of his gun.

An evil smile came over Grant's face as he saw the bartender lying on the ground, a trickle of blood running down the back of his neck. Grant then holstered the big Remington, bent down and grabbed the arms of the prone bartender where he had slumped, and dragged him out through the door and into the inky blackness behind the saloon.

A few minutes later, Grant walked boldly through the doors of the sheriff's office and nodded to the two men who were playing cards across one of the two desks in the place.

"Howdy," one of the men said, a big grin stuck on his face. "Sheriff Clark's not here. Something I can help you with? I'm his deputy."

"Your name Bolton?" Grant asked.

The deputy smiled even wider and nodded.

"And you? Your name Weller, from over at the stables?"

"That's right, mister. How'd you know that?" Weller asked.

"A man over at the saloon told me," he said.

The two men exchanged glances, Bolton's face never losing its annoying smile, as Grant continued: "I'm looking for a U.S. Marshal by the name of Blake; he should've passed through here sometime..."

"Marshal Blake was in here late morning yesterday," the deputy said, interrupting in a friendly manner.

"He's gone then?" Grant asked.

"Gone not more'n an hour after he rode in," Bolton said, the spurs on his boots jingling as he raised them up and placed them on the edge of the desk. "A downright serious man – a real rough customer, the marshal is. Who wants to know, anyway?"

"My name's Grant. You might remember that."

"Grant? All right, Mr. Grant, I'll remember your name if you like," Bolton said, his grin growing even wider. "Now what is it you want to know again?"

"I want you to tell me where Max Blake is heading."

"So why do you want to know that, Mr. Grant?" Bolton asked.

"That's not your concern," Grant said, annoyed at the delay. "Just tell me where Max Blake is heading.

"Tell me now."

"Well now, why are you so all-fired anxious to find that out?" Bolton asked, his suspicions only beginning to rise. "It don't seem to me like it's anybody's business but..."

The sudden appearance of a large Remington revolver in Grant's right hand stopped Tom Bolton short; the big grin slowly drained from his face.

"Stand up, you grinnin' skunk," Grant said, pointing the gun at the deputy. "Drop your gunbelt slowly – left hand only." Bolton was the only one wearing a gun, and he cautiously did as he was told. "Kick it over here and sit back down.

"Now then," Grant continued as the gun skidded to a stop near his boots and Bolton slowly sank back into his chair, "one or the other of you is gonna tell me where Max Blake went."

Tim Weller began stammering that he didn't know, but Grant moved with surprising suddenness and kicked the chair out from under him, sending the stable owner crashing to the floor.

"There's no need for that, mister," Bolton said, starting to rise from his chair again. But Grant snapped back the hammer on the Remington.

"You got something I want to hear, you'd best say it now. Otherwise" – Grant turned to where Weller was still on the floor and kicked the man so hard in the stomach that he began to gasp for air – "otherwise you'll watch yer friend here get stomped to within an inch of his life."

"Blake is on his way to a village called Indian Wells; it's southeast of here," Bolton blurted out.

"Why's he going there?"

"There was trouble there a few days ago that looked like it might have been caused by the three men Blake's chasing," Bolton said. "That's as much as I can tell you. I don't know anything else."

Grant looked at the deputy and then turned and gave Weller another hard kick, sending him sprawling and moaning across the floor once more.

"He don't know nothing. And I don't know any more'n what I just told you. Honest!" Bolton yelled.

"I believe you," Grant said, the same evil grin starting to spread across his narrow face again. "After all, you've got nothing to hide, right?"

Grant pulled some rawhide strips from his pocket and then ripped the sleeves off Weller's shirt; he directed the deputy to tie Weller and gag him with one of the shirt sleeves. He then pushed Weller into an open jail cell, locked it with Bolton's keys, and pushed Bolton into the cell next to it, following him inside.

"What's this all about, anyway?" the deputy asked as Grant tied his hands behind his back. "What do you want with Max Blake?"

"I've got a message for him – a message from my brother."

Grant spun the deputy around so that his back was to the cell door. Then he hit Bolton with the side of his gun across the back of the head. He kicked him once, just to make sure that he wasn't going anywhere, and then knelt down and gagged the deputy, using the other sleeve from Weller's shirt. When he finished, he walked out and locked the cell.

Grant turned toward Weller, who was still groaning for air on the floor of the jail cell, and said: "Tell him it's a message that Max Blake won't want to hear. And then tell him I don't cotton to his damn stupid grin."

With that, Grant slipped out of the jail and into the shadows of Twisted Junction's murky streets.

An hour after they had pitched camp and eaten a bit, Max Blake was still trying to explain to the two boys who had joined him in the hunt for Hoss Johnson and the Morgan brothers that he didn't want or need their help.

He wasn't having much luck.

Max had learned that one of the boys was named Hector and the other was named Martin; he also had given them his own name and Buck's. But when he tried to explain the dangers of chasing Hoss Johnson and the fact that he only worked alone, the two indicated with shrugs and puzzled looks that they didn't understand.

That may have been the truth; and perhaps it wasn't – perhaps they were just playing dumb. Max simply couldn't tell. To most everything that Max had said since the three had heated some beans for dinner and ate them with some of the corn biscuits that Max had packed, they had said little or nothing; they merely continued to smile broadly or to nod or shrug their shoulders frequently.

"I know that you want to get even for your friends," Max said at last in a mixture of Spanish, Apache, and English, carefully choosing words from each language. "But the fact is that you might end up as dead as them – and you might take me with you.

"The first part of that would be bad enough," he added in English. "The second part ... well, I wouldn't like that much at all."

The two boys smiled at Max and then at one another, but they shrugged and said nothing, leaving Max to again suspect that they understood more than they let on.

"The two of you don't even have guns, for God's sake," he said in desperation after another minute of awkward silence had passed, again lapsing into English. "How do you expect to kill someone if you don't carry a gun?

"You know? Guns?" Max pointed to his Colt for emphasis, more out of frustration than anything else.

"Oh, but we have guns in the pouches on our horses," Hector said slowly and carefully, giving Max time to translate the dialect.

He turned then and spoke rapidly to his friend.

"Si," the other boy added, also talking slowly for Max's benefit. "When we find these bad men, we will take out our guns from our pouches and kill them."

"And you expect them to wait for you to do this?" Max asked incredulously, speaking in English again once the boy's words had registered. "Do you actually think that Hoss Johnson will wait while you go to your horses and find your guns? Do you think that he'll stand by while you take the time to shoot him?"

The two only smiled and nodded again, saying nothing.

Max walked over and took a bedroll from where he had stashed his saddle and gear. He looked at the two boys again, shook his head, and spread the bedroll out on the ground.

"We'll take this up again in the morning," he said. "Tomorrow." And with that, he started to laugh at the situation he suddenly found himself in.

It was the first time that Max Blake had laughed in a long time.

Chapter Nine
The Compass Points South

Max Blake was up before the sun. He went to the stream, a hundred yards from where he had put down his bedroll, and washed his face and hands in the chilled mountain water. He hadn't slept much during the night – he never did on the trail – and the water served as a keen refresher.

Shaking off the numbing cold, he gathered a few dried branches that would burn with little smoke and quickly struck a small fire.

Max had just put a tin of coffee over the flames, using a small pot he carried with his other trail supplies, when the snapping of some twigs behind him brought his Colt Peacemaker into his hands as he silently slipped into the trees.

A moment later, the figure of Larry Nelson appeared in the small clearing and edged close to where Max's bedroll was still pitched on the ground, away from the fire.

"Marshal Blake?" Nelson whispered. "Hey, Marshal Blake – you in there?"

Max stepped out from behind the tree, still holding the Colt.

"Morning, Nelson," he said casually. "Like some coffee?"

Larry Nelson swung around, surprised to see that Max was not bedded down. He was even more surprised to see that the marshal's gun was drawn and that he had been watched from the moment he stepped out of the woods.

"Thought maybe I'd surprise you some this mornin'," he mumbled. Then he cleared his throat a little, coughed, and cleared his throat again.

"Listen, I ah, want to ... sure, I'd — I'd appreciate some of yer coffee," Nelson sputtered. "Thanks.

92

"Listen, marshal. I came over here to ... I guess maybe I ought to say a few words 'bout what got said..."

"Hope you like it hot and black," Max interrupted.

"...last night," Nelson finished. "Sure, hot and black's jest fine.

"Like I said – like I was saying, marshal. Well, my wife – I mean, well, I guess I owe you an apology..."

"You don't owe me anything," Max broke in again, not wanting to hear Nelson's struggling explanations a second time. "You might want to consider one to those two kids sleeping over yonder" – he pointed to where Hector and Martin were sprawled out, wrapped in Indian blankets on the ground, still asleep – "but you don't owe me a thing."

Nelson looked down at his feet and sheepishly kicked at the ground.

"I made a fool outta myself last night, and that's a hard thing for me to admit," he said. "But like my wife says, what happened to us back in Texas don't matter a whit out here on the trail. You see, there was some claim-jumpers after our land, and most all of 'em was Mexicans. When I seen them two kids last night – well, it just sorta brought it all to mind is all, and I thought..."

Nelson stopped for a minute, hoping that Max would say something, but then he continued as Max looked on but didn't interrupt.

"I just don't know what got into me's all. I'd like to make it up to you somehow, marshal, but I don't rightly know what I'd do exactly. You don't really need anything from me, I know. It's jest. It's jest..." And he let the words drift into the air.

Max shook his head. "You like the coffee all right?" he asked.

"Oh, yeah. It's good. Jest fine, in fact," Nelson replied expectantly, as if waiting for Max to tell him what to say or do next.

"I'll tell you what: There's something I do need from you," Max said after another couple of minutes of silence.

"You're traveling west – and the village where these boys are from isn't much out of your way as the crow flies. You can help me out by making sure that they get back to Indian Wells all right."

Max looked hard at Nelson, expecting an argument that didn't come. Larry Nelson said nothing.

"There's no way I can take them with me," Max said after a minute, "and I don't have the time to make sure they get back all right."

Nelson shook his head slowly up and down in resigned agreement.

"I had a feeling you might ask me somethin' along that line," he said at last. "The missus knew them boys would jest be in your way; she – I should say me – well, I mean we..." He paused, flustered again, and then said: "It's the same thought I had, marshal. Me and the wife'll be happy to see them two kids get back safe. The wife says they look like good-enough kids, and she don't want to see 'em get hurt none."

Max nodded. "That's good of you both," he said.

"Lemme jest do this," Nelson said. "I'll scoot on back to the missus and tell her 'bout this. You might want to tell them two boys that you'll be packin' 'em along with us. You expecting they'll make much of a fuss?'

"They might," Max said. "I'll tell them they need to keep you safe on the trail. That might be enough to work. If that doesn't work – well, there are other ways."

"Anything else I kin do?" Nelson asked.

"When you get to the village, find an old man named Ruiz and explain what happened. He's the town's trail boss, I'd guess you could call him."

"Mind tellin' me why you want me to do some explainin'?"

"The folks in Indian Wells might not know that this was the kids' idea," Max said. "Besides, after what happened in their village, the men are likely to be skittish."

"That makes sense enough," Nelson said. "Anything else?"

"Just steer clear of Hoss Johnson and the Morgans," Max said. "I doubt they are in these parts now, unless they've doubled back on me in the night. But those three do surprise."

Nelson finished his coffee and put the cup down by the fire.

"I'll wait for the kids on over by my camp," he said. "You send 'em by when yer ready, marshal, and we'll feed 'em along with ours. That suit ya all right?"

"Just fine," Max said.

Larry Nelson looked up and then put out his hand. The two shook wordlessly.

94

As Nelson turned to leave, Max was tempted to ask him if his wife had insisted that he come to apologize, even though he well knew the answer. Max smiled to himself as he pictured an indignant Sally Nelson righteously kicking her husband out of their wagon and into the night until he had agreed to go to Max's camp at first light and say that he was sorry for acting like such a fool. But he let the moment pass.

Nelson might be all right after all, Max thought. *The man just might make it, though I can't imagine why that woman would leave a school job in Pennsylvania to go to Arkansas – Arkansas of all places – and marry him. And I guess I'll never know.*

Nelson stopped at the edge of the woods and turned. He waved his rough hand once but said nothing.

Max nodded his head slightly, watching as Nelson turned and moved into the woods.

Then he went over to where the two boys were sleeping and gently shook them awake.

Minutes after Max Blake had packed the two reluctant boys from Indian Wells off with the Nelsons, he resumed his methodical search for the elusive trail of Hoss Johnson and Freeman and Weasel Morgan. He moved Buck slowly and carefully across both sides of the stream, looking for a telltale sign or a hoof print that would point him in the right direction.

He found the lone print 15 minutes later: a deep indentation made by a large horse that was carrying a great weight. It had been left in a small patch of mud at the edge of the stream five miles or so away from where Max had camped the night before with Hector and Martin. It appeared as though other tracks along the river crossing had been brushed away.

Max moved slowly in the direction that the print pointed — southeast — until he picked up another set of tracks and then a second and third set.

"Good job, Buck," Max said aloud, patting the horse on the side of the neck.

After two hours of patient tracking through a thinly forested area where the stream fell away from the mountains and slowed to little more than a trickle, Max broke into a clearing that stretched away for as far as he could see. The pine needles had given way to packed hardpan and then to loose sand and sagebrush, with the land cresting in brown and purple swales that rose and fell in the sunlight, casting enormous shadows across the earth.

Max studied the area for a minute, mentally picturing where he had come from and projecting that landscape against where the trail led into the desert. Then he smiled as the geography and the images of his memory clicked into place.

"That's it," he said aloud to Buck. "They're headed for Aguante – as sure as hell itself."

Max urged Buck forward in an easy gait, looking for the certain trail that he knew would take them for two days along the edge of the desert and into Aguante, a dusty but deadly dangerous border town.

Max recalled what he had heard from a variety of conversations with other marshals and lawmen about Aguante, although he had never been there himself. A Spanish word meaning endurance, he knew that Aguante was well-named, for a man had to endure just to get there from anywhere else.

It was the kind of place that honest lawmen swapped information about; telling details about a place like Aguante could mean the difference between life and death, and Max Blake had a wonderful memory for telling details.

He remembered hearing that the town consisted of a small and hard-shelled collection of ramshackle buildings that supported a variety of shady characters and criminal pursuits.

Like most border towns, Aguante had a reputation for harboring murderers, bandits, cutthroats, thieves, rustlers, and assorted other outlaws, along with the women those men required.

The only law in town was crooked: A man who could pay the going rate was either afforded protection from the legitimate law in the territory or at least was tolerated with a shrug of indifference. A man who could not pay the going rate was either run out of town or killed outright by the town's sheriff and his group of hand-picked deputies; Max knew that they amounted to no more than killers with badges.

Max had heard that the town had one enormously popular saloon and at least three bordellos – possibly more. All of the establishments spawned frequent gunplay that spilled out of the bar and the bedrooms and onto the streets.

He recalled being told that there was a blacksmith shop connected to the livery stables, a general store of modest size, and some sort of hotel. He also knew that a well-stocked gun shop offered a wide selection of revolvers and long rifles. Most of these had been stolen from towns to the north and brought to Aguante for sale, or they had simply been taken from the men killed in gunfights on the streets, with the profits going to the sheriff and his men.

"Aguante's a good place to cut clear of, Buck old boy," Max said aloud.

At the very least, he knew that it would be foolish to race across the desert in hard pursuit of Hoss Johnson and the Morgans now. They weren't likely to be merely passing through the town, Max reasoned; they would get to Aguante and stay for a time – certainly long enough to rest their mounts, throw down a few drinks, find a woman or two, and get into whatever trouble they could find without getting run out or caught in a cross fire of deputies.

"Anyway, Buck, there's no need for us to hurry. A man shouldn't be in a hurry to ride straight into hell."

A good day's ride ahead of Max Blake, Hoss Johnson and the two Morgans had just the opposite feeling; they had been moving ahead as hard as they dared without running their horses into the ground.

"Some drinks and a card game; that's what I want most. Hell, I ain't had a good card game in days – you sure can't count the one with them dead Mexicans back in that little pile of shacks," Hoss Johnson said.

"I want me a woman," Weasel Morgan replied. "Been a long time since I peeled down the dress of a pretty young thing." A big smile creased the outlaw's narrow face, his grin exposing the large gaps in his stained teeth.

"You ain't never peeled down the dress of any young thing less'n you put some hard cash money in her hand first, and no coins, neither, with a face like you got," Hoss laughed. "Haw. Haw.

You think yer carrying enough money there, Weasel, to buy you a woman in Aguante? I don't know if they done yet made enough money for you to buy yerself a good woman there. You jest might need a second horse to carry the amount of money you'd need. Haw haw haw."

"You never mind that, Hoss," Weasel said. "You jest watch me go when we git there, 'cause you won't see me again till we's ready to leave."

"That being the case, there's no need for you to hurry along with us then, Weasel," Hoss said. "It's time we covered our backside here a bit, I'd say."

"What are you driving at, Hoss?" Freeman Morgan asked.

Hoss pulled back on the reins of his big horse, slowing the animal down to little more than a walk. "I'm thinkin' 'bout some of the messages we been leavin' behind us," he said. "Them two visits we made to Twisted Junction weren't left unminded, I wager. And that little Mex village – what the hell was the name of that dump again, anyways?"

"Indian Wells," Freeman said.

"Yeah, Indian Wells. Well, we left our mark there, too. Those things don't go unminded, like I said. I think it's about time we watched fer what jest might be followin' along our trail."

"Well, I guess that makes some sense," Freeman said after a minute of thinking about Hoss's words. "So, what yer thinkin'..."

"What I'm thinkin'," Hoss said, "is that the Weasel here hang back for a spell and see if there's any dust bein' kicked up behind us."

"Dammit, Hoss, why's it got to be me?" Weasel protested.

"Because I say so," Hoss snapped back. "That's all the reason you need."

"What if I don't like it and don't do it?"

"Then I kill you here and now and prop your carcass up to watch our backside. Makes no never mind to me one way or t'other."

"You hold on there, Hoss," Freeman said. "You ain't killin' my brother without me havin' somethin' to say about it first."

"Then you'd best say it fast, Free Morgan, because it'll be the last thing you ever say," Hoss said quickly through teeth locked tight together and a free hand hovering near his holstered revolver.

Weasel Morgan looked at Hoss Johnson and then at his brother. He figured for a few seconds that he might try to draw on Hoss, knowing that the big man probably couldn't get both him and his brother. But tough as he was, back-shooting was more his style; the percentages said to wait for a better chance and then get Hoss when his back was turned, if need be.

Understanding the percentages helped keep the Weasel alive.

"I wanna git into town and git me a woman," Weasel whined aloud, not wanting Hoss to know what he was really thinking. "I don't wanna wait out here fer nothin'. There ain't nothin' and no one out here chasin' us now, Hoss. I don't think there's anythin' chasin' us a'tall. Hell, you kin see fer yerself if'n you jest take a look behind us."

"I told you before, Weasel, that you ain't here to think. That's my job. And I think you need to hang back a day or so and see what's on our tail. Might be nothin'. Might be somethin'. In either case, I wanna know. You git my meanin'?"

Hoss brought his horse to a stop and carefully, deliberately, looked at both of the Morgan brothers. "I've thought on this, and I've got my mind set to it," he said after a minute of uncomfortable silence. "Anyone thinkin' of arguin' the point, you'd best git prepared for the sound of my gun."

Freeman held his horse up short and looked first at Hoss and then at his brother.

"Hoss is right, Weasel," he said finally, not wanting to risk a shooting war with Hoss Johnson. "We got to be careful – and that needs doin' before we git into Aguante. There's not a better man to do the job than you, brother. Besides, Hoss here seems to have his mind made up on it, and I ain't anxious to push him on that score. You understand what I'm saying?"

"All right, dammit," Weasel said. "I don't like it none a'tall, and I ain't gonna be happy 'bout it tomorrow, neither. But I'll do it if'n you say so, Free."

"Now you're talkin' sense, Weasel," Hoss said. "But mind now, you keep a sharp eye out. I don't want nobody sneakin' up on me in the middle of the night in Aguante. That place is well disagreeable enough."

"You jest mind it ain't the middle of the night with my woman in Aguante, damn you to hell, Hoss Johnson," Weasel said.

But Hoss just laughed as he watched Freeman sling an extra canteen of water across to his brother. "Here, you'll likely need that out here," Freeman said.

"We'll see you in town, Weasel. You watch yerself out here now."

"I still don't see why it's gotta be me..."

"Jest keep yer head low and yer mouth shut, Weasel," Hoss said, cutting him off before he could finish the complaint. "And keep yer damned eyes open. You give it a full day before you head on in to town, ya hear? I'll know it if you don't."

"Then I'll see you boys in a day – and to hell with the both of you."

Hoss and Freeman started off and had gotten several hundred yards away when Weasel called after them.

"I said to hell with the both of you," he yelled, but neither man turned or acknowledged his shout.

"Bastards," he muttered aloud. "The two of them – jest bastards. And one of them's my own brother. Dammit to hell.

"You'd best watch yer backside, Hoss Johnson."

Then Weasel Morgan dismounted and started to walk his horse slowly along the trail, looking for a place where he could find some shade and watch in all directions for any signs of dust being kicked up by a horse or riders following from behind.

Larry Nelson had taken his family and the two boys from Indian Wells seven hours or more away from their morning campsite and brief good-byes with Max Blake when he first spied the figure: a solitary man riding a horse, a good mile or more away across the upward slope of the foothills.

He pointed and said to his wife, "There's a man up there, ridin' toward us. You can see him there." Sally Nelson nodded, and her husband continued: "Wonder what he wants. God only knows out in this here country. But after what the marshal told us, we'd best be careful."

The two of them continued to watch as the figure grew gradually nearer.

"I want you to slip down in the back of the wagon there with the two boys," Nelson said to his wife. "I'm sure there's no need to be worryin' none, but there's no reason to take no chances out here, neither. Jest grab the rifle when you git back in there, git a shell into the chamber, and keep a watch on out fer trouble."

"You know I don't like guns, Larry," she said.

"Jest git it done, woman," her husband said, cutting her off abruptly. "We got no time to argue here. Got no audience this time, neither."

Nelson called out to Hector and Martin as they rode ahead of the wagon, ignoring the glare from his wife, and he pointed up at the rider when they turned back to look. Then he motioned for them to come closer.

A few minutes later, they could make out a tall, thin man in his mid-forties with a leathery, sunburned face and long sideburns. Nelson heard Martin say something that sounded like "grande pistoleros" and knew what the boy was talking about: He, too, could now see that the man carried two enormous revolvers at his sides.

"Let me do the talkin' here," he said to his family and then called out, "Hullo, there. We ain't seen too many people out this way, no sir."

The lone rider drew closer to the wagon and stopped. He nodded at Nelson, looked at the two boys on horseback for a second or two, and then looked back at the farmer.

"The name's Grant," he said, leaning forward a little in his saddle as he spoke.

"Mine's Nelson."

"And I'll wager them two are from that little Mex and Indian village up the trail a'ways," Grant said.

"That's right," Nelson said, caught off guard. "How'd ya know that? How'd ya know 'bout these here kids anyways?"

"Just came through there and heard that a couple'a boys was missin'," Grant said. "These two appear to fit the bill. They've also got more nerve than the rest of the men in the town, apparently. How'd you happen to come by 'em?"

"We ran into 'em down by the stream a good ride back," Nelson said. "You been out looking for 'em, have you?"

"Not them," Grant said. "I was told that these two lit out after a man named Max Blake. You seen him hereabouts?"

"Sure have, mister," Nelson replied, feeling easy for the first time since the tall man came into view. "We left him down at the same stream not more'n five, maybe six, hours back.

"Might'a been longer, though – hard to tell out here on the trail. He was in an all-fired hurry chasing after three tough outlaws. He asked me to see after these kids here."

Grant looked past Nelson and into the wagon for a minute; Nelson figured that he was either naturally curious or that he had caught a glimpse of something or someone moving inside.

"My, ah, family's back there," Nelson said without elaborating.

Grant grunted and made a point of looking into the wagon a moment longer.

"Can you tell me where Blake was headin' when you left him?" he asked at last.

"No idea a'tall," Nelson answered, "although I 'spect that you kin find him easy enough; he sure don't seem to hide from no one, near as I kin say. What ya lookin' for the marshal fer, anyway?"

"I need to deliver a message to him," Grant said, a slow and twisted smile passing across his long face. "It's from my brother."

He started to ride on and then stopped and tipped his hat toward the wagon. "Hope you ain't gonna shoot me in the back with that big-bore rifle there, pretty lady," he said.

Nelson swung around, surprised, and saw his wife blushing as she looked out from behind the canvas covers that were stretched in a big bow over the top of the wagon. She was holding the Sharps carbine in both hands.

Grant laughed loudly and started down the trail, following the wagon tracks.

"Hey, mister," Nelson called after him. "Did you come across a fella named Ruiz in that village? We need to find him. He's the boss of the place – or somethin' like that."

"Not no more he ain't," Grant called back over his shoulder without turning to look. "Not no more."

Nelson turned to his wife as she crawled out from the back of the wagon.

"I wonder what he meant by that?" he asked.

Sally Nelson sat back down on the wagon seat next to her husband and breathed deeply. "I don't know what he meant. But I do know that I didn't like the looks of that man at all, Larry," she said. "And I'm glad he's gone away. I surely am."

Chapter Ten
A One-Sided Conversation

Weasel Morgan was talking to himself. He frequently talked to himself when he was angry, and Weasel was an angry man.

He had been out in the sun of the day and the cold of the night and a new day's heat for hours now; and he was so damned mad at the moment that he could chew nails.

The more he thought about the bad hand that Hoss Johnson and his brother had dealt him, in fact, the madder he got and the more he talked to himself.

Weasel had located an outcropping of rocks that topped the back side of a small hill a couple of hundred yards off the trail. He could keep his horse out of sight, but he couldn't do much about keeping the two of them out of the constant sun.

Weasel also could see for miles in every direction, provided that he climbed around the rocks to the top of the hill and peered out into the distance. But the heat made the rocks and the scrub brush and the dust and the desert sand shimmer and move eerily about, and that made Weasel angry.

Whenever Weasel crawled up to look, each time seeing nothing but the same shimmering, shifting heat, the more angry and frustrated he became. And so he started to carry on a two-way conversation as though he were two different men inside the same tormented body; but each one of them was uniquely Weasel Morgan.

"Now why do you suppose that horse's ass of a Hoss Johnson up and left me out here in this damn heat and all this damn sand?" he said aloud.

"I'll tell ya why, Weasel Morgan," he answered himself, barely waiting to draw a breath to reply. "He left you out here to die 'cause he wants all the women in Aguante. He ain't thinkin' 'bout leavin' none fer you. He wants you to die in this heat so's he kin have all of them pretty things for hisself."

And then he replied to himself again: "Yer right. He wants you dead so's he can git hisself every whore in the territory. He's a bastard – a right ornery bastard's what he is. And he's jealous 'cause he knows the Weasel kin git all the whores he wants."

The second Weasel paused only to catch his breath.

"He's a bastard all right, dammit. And that no-account brother of yours is another no-good bastard."

And so it went for more than an hour, with Weasel answering Weasel and carrying on both ends of the discussion with enthusiasm, even if the choice of words from both sides was limited in imagination and vocabulary.

By the time he was a half-hour or so into this dual tirade, he had stopped climbing around the rocks to look back into the distance; he had forgotten, in fact, that he was there to watch the trail over which he and his brother and Hoss Johnson had traveled only hours before.

By the time that more than a full hour of conversation had passed, he had pulled out his revolver and started shooting at rocks and other targets, real or imagined, across the way.

"There's no one back there. Might as well keep yer shootin' eye sharp, Weasel," he said.

"I don't even care if there is someone back there," he answered himself. "Let 'em hear, anyway. What they gonna do anyhow – sneak up on me? Git me from behind? Wait till it's dark and then plug me? Ha! That's a laugh, all right. It sure as hell is now. Ha ha."

Weasel carried a big .44-caliber double-action Starr with an eight-inch barrel. He used combustible paper cartridges because they were easier and faster to load than loose powder and ball, although the gun could be used either way – even if the paper shells weren't quite as accurate. He liked the feel of the gun, though: the way it kicked back in his hand as he pulled the trigger and the way the long barrel gave him the feel of something solid and dependable.

The Union Army had ordered 37,000 Starrs during the Civil War, and Weasel Morgan and a lot of men like him were the fortunate recipients of the Army's generosity.

In Weasel's case, however, he didn't have to wear a uniform to get the Starr. Weasel and his brother had tried for a time to use the war as an opportunity to make some easy money. They followed the battle lines for a few days, quickly scavenging the dead after the fighting had stopped and before the stretcher-bearers moved in to carry off the wounded and bury the corpses.

Weasel had merely picked his prized Starr off the body of a dead Union officer after one of the battles – he could no longer remember which one, or even where it was – along with the man's pocket watch, leather wallet with folding money, and a wedding ring. He had long since thrown the wallet away and used the ring and watch for drink money or to buy a woman for the night — he couldn't remember that, either – but he had kept the Starr through a lot of hard years.

"Them was good times all right," he said aloud as his mind drifted back. "Too bad all them people were as like to kill me and Free, even if we weren't up fer fightin' their war."

And then he answered himself, with only a slight pause, "Yeah, we could have made a fortune if people had jest left us alone to do our collectin' and such instead of shootin' at us. No-account bastards is what they was."

Weasel fired three rounds in rapid succession to punctuate his conversation and then stopped to load his revolver again as the shots echoed across the landscape.

"There," he called out. "Let 'em hear that. Let every bastard within a hundred miles hear it."

But the only person within earshot of the Starr's peculiar high-pitched wail was Max Blake, who had been tracking the outlaws along the trail and was now close enough to where Weasel Morgan had packed himself among the rocks that he could hear the shots before the echoes rolled across the miles of empty space.

Max was off Buck's back in seconds and quickly moved the big horse away from the trail before pulling hard on the reins, taking Buck down on his side in a maneuver that man and horse had worked many times before. Max already had pulled his Colt, and he flopped flat behind the horse, scanning the area ahead of him with just his hat and his eyes showing above Buck's great chestnut expanse.

Max knew that if a man was watching him from the rocks on top of the hill ahead, the move he had just made might invite gunfire that could kill or wound Buck. At the same time, the horse was the only protection he had at the moment, and he didn't hesitate to protect himself. As much as he treasured Buck, he could always get another horse.

Max couldn't see a thing, so he waited. Then the sound of a revolver cracked across the open spaces a moment later, and Max focused on where the shots were coming from – most likely the other side of the small rise, which was 500 yards or so ahead and just off to the right of the trail.

"You stay down here, Buck, until I whistle," Max said quietly to the horse and then sprinted to the base of the rocky hill, keeping as low to the ground as he could. He stopped at the edge of the hill as two more shots rang out.

It almost sounds like someone is plinking – target practicing, Max thought. *But who in hell would be shooting at targets out in the middle of nowhere? That sure doesn't make much sense.*

Max slowly made his way up to the crest of the hill, careful not to dislodge a rock or make any sounds along the way, and he slowly peeked over the other side as yet another shot rang out and then another.

What Max finally saw made him smile.

A man was talking to himself as he paced back and forth, every now and then turning to fire his gun at nothing but the empty countryside. As Max watched and listened to the strange comedy unfold, he could see that the man was filthy and disgusting, with missing teeth and tattered clothing that had seen more hard trail than soft water.

If I didn't know better, I'd think that was one of the Morgans, Max thought to himself. *That man's ugly enough to be the devil himself — and not too bright by the looks of him, either.*

The man had stopped to reload his revolver once more, and Max listened closely so that he could pick up on his strange conversation.

"Can't take much more of this waitin' now," the man said aloud, unaware of Max's presence. "Can't stand fer much more'a this.

Don't see no reason fer it. Don't see why I'm still out here and them bastards ain't."

"You're right, Weasel Morgan," the man said back to himself. "The time's come to move and move fast outta here. Ain't no reason a'tall to wait for no ghosts."

So that's Weasel Morgan, Max thought to himself. *Wonder where his friends are.*

Max was cautious now. He could easily shoot Weasel where he stood, asking no questions, with no questions being necessary. But he had no idea where the other two outlaws, Hoss Johnson and Freeman Morgan, were – and he wasn't anxious to make a move until he could be certain that he wasn't among those who would be surprised.

Besides, Max had Judge Thomas R. Radford to think about.

Weasel had reloaded his gun again and tucked it back into his holster. Without looking around, he moved over to where his horse was tied and started to gather his bedroll and the few other odds and ends that he had spread across the ground.

Max looked carefully around in all directions. The only other living thing he saw besides Weasel Morgan and his horse was Buck, still waiting several hundred yards behind him.

He'll be on his horse in another minute, Max thought. *Time to act; no other choice.*

With that, he crept quickly but silently up behind Weasel and put his gun into the outlaw's ribs before the man knew what had happened or had time to react.

At the same time, Max lifted Weasel's gun from his holster and tossed it well out of the way on the ground.

"Easy now – no sudden moves," Max said. "Get those arms up and keep them up."

Weasel did as he was told, so surprised that he at first said nothing.

But the heat and his sudden capture and the way that Hoss Johnson and his brother had treated him by leaving him behind all combined to make Weasel mad and reckless – and talkative.

"Who the hell are you? What'cha want with the likes of me?" he finally sputtered without yet attempting to turn around.

"Twisted Junction and Indian Wells," Max replied evenly and without elaboration.

"Yeah? Well, what of 'em!" Weasel said, spitting out the words as a taunt instead of a question. "Nobody's business but mine, it ain't."

"It's my business now," Max said. "Murder's a crime in this territory, and you've done your share of it."

"What makes ya think yer man enough y'kin handle me, mister?" Weasel snarled.

"You doubt that, it's your last doubt," Max said. "Make no mistake."

"Jest who in hell are you, anyways?" Weasel asked, starting to turn around.

But Max pushed the Colt harder into Weasel's ribs and said, "Don't chance it."

"All right – take it easy, mister," Weasel said through clenched teeth, trying to control himself. "Jest what'cha plannin' to do with me, anyways?"

"I'm planning to take you back to Twin Forks to hang," Max responded.

"Are you the law or somethin'?"

"I'm the law, Weasel Morgan."

"How do'ya know my name?" Weasel whined, genuine surprise now registering in his voice. "It ain't fair you know my name and you won't even tell me yers."

"Life's not fair," Max said, stepping back from Weasel so that he could keep a careful watch for any sudden movement. Max turned toward the top of the hill and whistled for Buck, all the while keeping his gun trained on the outlaw. The big horse stirred when he heard the sound and started to move at a brisk pace toward Max.

"I don't like this a bit, mister," Weasel said. "I don't cotton to it none, and I ain't gonna stand fer it neither."

"You've got no choice – unless you want to die right here. Your call," Max said.

"Well, then it is my choice," Weasel said.

He turned quickly and made a dive for the rocks to his right, figuring that it was his only out. Max was surprised at the outlaw's quick move and lack of caution, but he responded with a snap shot from the Colt that tore into Weasel's right boot as he flew through the air. Max hit what he wanted to hit; he figured that a hole in the outlaw's foot would be more than enough to slow Weasel down.

"Gawd a'mighty, mister," Weasel yelled as he hit the ground and rolled over, grabbing at his boot. He looked down and said, "You shot me clean through the foot." Then he hobbled back up and started coming at Max, a murderous look of rage and hatred in his eyes.

"I don't take kindly to gettin' shot, dammit," he said. "You done shoot me, you get kilt in turn."

"That's close enough," Max said.

Weasel stopped momentarily, 20 feet or so away. He looked Max over for a second or two and then spit on the ground near his own boots, one of which had a gaping hole ripped through it and was beginning to show blood on the leather. He snarled aloud and bent down to pick up a large rock. Max fired a shot in the air as a warning, but Weasel clutched the rock and started forward again. Max fired a third bullet, this time hitting the outlaw in the hand that held the rock.

Weasel yelled out again and grabbed his right hand, clutching it to his stomach and bending over at the same time. The rock had shattered into pieces as the bullet struck it dead on, spraying sharp fragments in all directions. But he stood upright almost immediately and started limping toward Max once more, his face now twisted in pain and fury.

"I'll tear yer heart clean out with my bare hands, damn you to hell," Weasel said, his voice tight in a futile effort to control the pain.

Max fired a fourth time, whistling a bullet past the outlaw's ear. But Weasel Morgan was 10 feet away now and still coming, although each step was an effort.

"I'll kill ya here 'n now. You cain't stop me none," Weasel hissed. His left hand snaked down into his left boot and pulled out a knife with a six-inch blade. Weasel drew the knife back to throw it, and Max fired a fifth time, knocking the knife from Weasel's hand.

Even then, Weasel Morgan wouldn't stop. Limping badly now and with both hands bleeding, he pressed forward again.

"Enough," Max said.

Five feet.

"I'm gonna rip yer heart out," Weasel said.

Two feet.

Max looked at the rage in the outlaw's eyes and knew that nothing short of a bullet would stop Weasel Morgan now. He fired a final time.

The bullet ripped through Weasel's chest, striking him so hard that it knocked him backward despite the force of his steady forward motion toward Max. Weasel hit the ground and crumpled backward, his chest showing an ever-expanding red stain as blood starting to pump its way out of his mouth.

Max stood over him.

"You got your death wish," he said simply.

Weasel coughed blood and looked at Max with questioning eyes.

"Who are you?" he sputtered, the blood choking him. "I got to..."

Weasel's voice trailed off as his head dropped abruptly backward; it bounced for a second on the ground and then was still.

Max shrugged. "Names aren't important," he said. "But mine's Blake."

Max did the best he could to bury Weasel Morgan's body. But he didn't have a shovel, it was as hot as hell's fire itself in the unfiltered sun, and he still had no idea where Hoss Johnson and Freeman Morgan were, or whether they might return at any moment to this spot.

He moved a few feet away from the rocky outcropping, scooped out a shallow grave with the long-bladed Bowie knife that he carried in his boot, and pulled Weasel Morgan's body into the pit. Then he covered it over with dirt and sand and piled a scattering of rocks on the top.

It's not much, he thought. *It might keep the coyotes out for a day, if that. But it's probably better than he deserves.*

The worst of it was that Max was annoyed. He had wanted to take Weasel in alive so that Judge Radford could hang the outlaw with no questions asked. Max figured that he had done his best, short of shooting Weasel in both legs or the knees to stop him, but even then he would merely watch him die from the loss of blood.

Max knew that when he was forced to leave a dead man in a shallow grave along the trail, there were always questions from the judge – regardless of the circumstances. And Max never liked the questions.

Max's efforts to wipe the sweat from his face with his hands were futile, so he went over to where Buck was waiting close to the rocks and pulled the edge of a blanket from his bedroll loose a foot or so. He used that to wipe his face again; then he took a small drink from his canteen, splashed some water across his face, and took another small drink.

He wiped his face once more with the end of the blanket and walked back to the shallow grave.

"No marker, no sermon, no prayers," Max said aloud. "But no man should die crazy like that."

He looked down at the grave for another moment, then tipped his hat slightly and walked back to where Weasel's horse was standing. He finished the job that Weasel had started when Max had surprised him, loading the gear onto the horse's back. Then Max climbed on Buck, attaching the reins of Weasel's horse to his own saddle horn and keeping his right hand free in case he needed the Colt quickly.

Max sat still for a moment and considered what had just happened.

The judge is not going to like this much, he thought. *And there'll be no easy way to explain Weasel Morgan's crazy charge; hell, I saw it and I can't get it straight myself. But the judge ought to try this work sometime himself. That would help his understanding about what can happen outside of his courtroom.*

Max started off slowly, thinking now of what was ahead, and his thoughts of Judge Radford vanished as a new concern crossed his mind.

"I don't like this much, Buck," Max said aloud. "Riding into town with this horse is a calling card for trouble. We'll have to figure something else out."

And with that, he prodded Buck back on the trail heading toward Aguante.

The willowy man with long sideburns and the two large Remington revolvers saw the tracks clearly – as though someone had drawn a map to the spot as it lead away from the trail.

He could see plainly where a man had dismounted from his horse and then had most likely pulled the horse down to the ground. That became apparent as he looked around because there was no blood in the dust, and the horse's tracks also clearly led up to the hill – the same place where the man's footprints led.

The man named Grant directed his horse up to the edge of the hill and looked over at the other side. He saw nothing but a myriad of other tracks, and he got down from his horse and walked across the rocky outcrop to take a closer look.

He studied the wide scuffle of horse and bootprints; his alert gaze detected some good-sized patches of blood in the sand; and then he picked up the signs of a man's boots being dragged, the heels downward, to a – "to a grave," he said aloud, his eyes following along to where the ground had just been disturbed.

"Don't let it be Max Blake," he blurted out as he raced to the spot to see who, or what, was inside.

A few minutes later, a large smile creased Grant's thickly stubbled face as his hands cleared the dirt and dust and sand away from the head of a man who was as dead as the rocks that had covered him, and who clearly wasn't a federal marshal named Blake.

"A damn good thing," Grant said aloud.

He sat down to catch his breath for a moment; then he brushed away the additional sand and dirt from the dead man's face and looked closer. Still not satisfied, he grabbed the man by the hair and pulled the head up, shaking it back and forth to get a better look. The dull eyes, still open, stared back at him, and he stopped.

"Is that you, Weasel Morgan?" he asked aloud, as though expecting an answer. Grant had known of Weasel and Freeman Morgan as two hard cases who worked the outside edge of the territory. He dropped the man's head, stood up, and then looked down at the exposed grave and the man inside.

"That is you, ain't it, Weasel?" he asked aloud again.

Grant shook his head slowly from side to side, as though disbelieving that Weasel Morgan could possibly be the man who was as dead as dust in a shallow grave in the middle of rocky nowhere.

That Weasel Morgan was one tough, rawboned bastard who would've took a lot of killin', Grant thought. *It don't make no sense a'tall – unless this is Max Blake's doing.*

A slow look of understanding then crossed Grant's face.

"Of course," he said aloud. "Max Blake's doing."

Grant began kicking stones and dirt back into the grave but lost interest after a minute of work. It was too hot, and the man in the hole in the ground was beyond caring.

Grant kicked a little more sand on the spot with his boot and then climbed back on his horse and picked up the tracks leading back to the trail. He noted tracks from two horses now: One was clearly heavier than the other, obviously carrying a man; the second was clearly being trailed along.

As he swung his own horse onto the path, Grant saw two different sets of tracks, smudged and a day or so older but similar to the set of three that he had spotted earlier on the trail.

That was it, all right, he thought. *Max Blake has been trackin' after this fella Hoss Johnson, just like the kid back at the stables in Twin Forks said. This Hoss Johnson character must have packed his lot in with the two crazy Morgan brothers, Freeman and Weasel.*

And then, for one reason or another, Hoss Johnson and Freeman Morgan must have split up from the other brother, and Max Blake caught up with and killed Weasel Morgan stone dead.

"That means he's tracking Hoss Johnson and Freeman Morgan into Aguante," Grant said aloud as the picture became clear in his mind.

"And that means once I find those two and tell 'em what happened, it'll be three against one."

He laughed out loud at the thought and spurred his horse ahead.

"I like them odds a lot."

Chapter Eleven
A Disturbing Revelation

Larry Nelson was in a thoughtful, almost somber, mood as he approached Indian Wells with his wife and two sons.

He had kept a detached, even reluctant, eye on the two village boys, Hector and Martin, along the way, fulfilling the promise that he made to Max Blake to return them safely home. And now that he was nearing their village, Nelson considered the debt to be paid in full, a feeling that gave him little satisfaction.

Although the distance wasn't great, a full day and a half had passed from the time that Nelson and his family had left Max by the stream bed, and a few hours had gone by since they had talked with the solitary rider on the trail – the only other living soul they had seen along the way.

A part of Nelson was angry because it had taken longer than he had anticipated to get to Indian Wells, a place that looked both rundown and out of the way to him; his team of draft horses was about worn out from the steep, uphill climb that had led into the foothills and then up again, higher still, toward the village. He knew that at least a full day of rest would be necessary before his stock could move on again – time in Larry Nelson's mind, at least, that he didn't want to waste anywhere near this ramshackle collection of adobe boxes and sheds and outhouses in the middle of nowhere.

But Nelson kept those feelings to himself and concentrated instead, during this detour into the foothills, on Max Blake: the kind of man he was, the way he could take charge in a tight situation, the way he said so little and yet packed so much into the little he said.

115

Nelson had thought a lot about the federal marshal in the past day and a half, in fact, while driving his team of horses and saying almost nothing as they had plodded along.

He finally turned to his wife as they neared the outskirts of the village and spoke: "I been thinkin'. We're gonna have to stay here a day or there'bouts, maybe more, and rest the team, much as I hate to see us lose the time."

"Whatever you think is best, Larry," Sally Nelson said.

She, too, had been mostly quiet along the way, and her husband's sudden comments after so many miles of silence had caught her off guard.

"Well, that's what I think we ought to do, even if I don't exactly cotton to the notion much myself," he said. "But the team needs the rest."

"I think that's the first time you've wanted to rest the horses since we left Texas, Larry," his wife said. "But I'm happy that you do. This has been a steeper climb than I had imagined, for them and for us."

"Yeah, well, it needs doin' – that's all. No need to make more of it 'n that."

They were both silent for a minute, and then Nelson spoke again, more loudly this time so that his two sons could overhear the conversation: "Maybe the boys'd like some time to romp around outside for a bit, 'stead of jest eatin' dust all day long. Would you two young'uns like that?"

Nelson's two sons were riding in the back of the wagon, but they had moved up to see out the front as they neared the village. "We sure would, Pa," the oldest boy said. "Do'ya mean it really?"

Nelson nodded without looking around; his wife smiled, for the first time in a long time, but she said nothing.

In her mind, however, Sally Nelson was doing a great deal of thinking about her husband.

She knew that Larry spent most of his days caught up in problems, many of them his own doing because he often wouldn't think things through. But he had a good heart and cared for his family, in his own odd way. And she loved him for that, despite his awkward manners and speech and his quick temper.

She had noticed how quiet he had been on the trail. It was something that was unusual for Larry; he liked to talk and complain and bluster loudly about. And it was unusual for him to want to let the boys play instead of constantly putting them to work at little jobs – such as gathering firewood or carrying water.

She wondered at first whether he was merely tired or perhaps was just feeling poorly. Then she found herself hoping that there had been a change in him somehow – that something had happened to him somewhere along this hard and dusty trail.

Of course, she had lived with him too long now to be too hopeful. But the thought of it, a quiet little dream, made her smile.

"You know," Nelson said, talking as much to himself as he was to his wife or sons, "I been thinkin' some 'bout that fella Max Blake. Hard man to figure. An' he sure made me mad that first night we met up."

"I liked the marshal, Pa," the oldest Nelson boy said.

"Me, too," his brother chipped in.

"Well, I can't rightly say that I liked him," their father said. "But after rollin' it 'round in my head some, much as I hate to admit it, I'm glad we met up with the man anyway, dammit."

"I wish you wouldn't say that word in front of the boys," his wife said. "You know I don't like to hear you curse that way."

"What word?" Nelson asked, trying to look innocent, although a mischievous grin had crossed his face. "What curse are you talkin' 'bout, woman?"

"You know full well what word I mean, Larry Nelson," his wife said. "Don't you try and make me say it, too."

They were pulling onto the main street now, with an excited Hector and Martin leading the way on their horses, when Nelson immediately saw that something was wrong.

The two boys, riding proudly out in front of the wagon, had spotted a small gathering of men and hailed them in a flurry of words that were largely unfamiliar to the Nelsons. The faces of the boys, only seconds before filled with the anticipation of their victorious return and a joyous reception in the village, were suddenly clouded and disturbed, even though several of the men who were gathered on the street seemed relieved to see them.

"Something's not right here," Nelson said.

Martin climbed off his horse and began to cry; he was comforted by one of the older men in the crowd as a subdued conversation took place around him.

117

Hector said something that the Nelsons couldn't hear and kicked his horse ahead, riding at a hard gallop down the street before stopping in front of a small adobe home where a second gathering of people was clustered. The Nelsons watched as the boy jumped off his horse and quickly removed his hat as he slowed from a race to a walk. He nodded solemnly to the faces standing outside the house and then walked hesitantly inside the small structure.

Larry Nelson looked at his wife questioningly and climbed down from the wagon.

"You three'd best stay put," he said without looking back. Then he walked up to the group that was circled around the quietly sobbing Martin and said, "Kin anyone here understand what I'm sayin'?"

"I am this man, senor," one of the men said, stepping away from the crowd. "Jorge Ramirez at your service, senor."

Ramirez was in his early fifties, Nelson guessed. He was dressed in a simple dirty-white shirt and loose-fitting pants and was wearing a dusty white sombrero that sat high on the top of his long, flowing hair. A gray-flecked beard, scraggly and indifferent, covered the man's face. He had sad brown eyes – eyes that had been a witness to much pain and sorrow and unhappiness in his lifetime.

"What's caused all this fuss?" Nelson asked. "What's wrong with the boy?"

"Killing has caused bad times for our village, senor," Ramirez said. "It is one of many such times we have had."

"Well, we heard tell 'bout the deaths of the four men that were kilt the other day," Nelson said. "A U.S. marshal we met on the trail told us that. What's happened here now?"

"Our village leader was shot and killed dead. There was no reason for him to die this way," the man said simply.

"Who was kilt?" Nelson asked.

"Pedro Ruiz was killed, senor. He was our leader, the village elder. He was very ancient – *viejo*, old. He was a much-respected man, senor, and the uncle of this boy here. He was killed – murdered – by a gringo who called himself Grant."

"But why?" Nelson asked, taken aback momentarily by the man's words. After all, Max Blake had told the Nelsons to find

Pedro Ruiz when they made it to Indian Wells. And now that they had arrived, the first thing they learned was that the very man they were to visit with was dead.

"We do not know why he was killed, senor; only that there was no reason for such a good man to die," Ramirez said in simple reply to Nelson's question.

"The man who did this thing rode into the village yesterday and went to the home of Pedro Ruiz after asking where he could find the leader of our village. A short time later, a single gunshot was heard. Then the man walked to the cantina and said that he had just killed an old man and would kill many others unless he found out what he wanted to know."

The man paused and Nelson nodded, although he didn't know what to say in response. Ramirez, speaking in a thick accent, continued his story.

"The man was asked who he had killed and what he wanted to know. He said he was seeking a man. Then he said he had just killed the leader of our village and would kill others here unless someone told him where to find the man he was after, the man called Max Blake.

"I know these things, senor, because I was in the cantina myself when the gringo came inside. He told us that his name was Grant; he told us that we should remember the name well. And when the gringo left and we went to the home of Pedro Ruiz, we found him shot one time. He was dead."

A surprising realization suddenly swept over Larry Nelson.

"Was this a tall man? Thin – real thin? With dark sideburns?"

"Si, senor," Ramirez replied. "You have seen such a man as this?"

"I saw 'im, all right," Nelson said. "He wore two large pistols, one strapped to either leg."

"That was the man, yes. You saw the man who killed our friend, senor."

"Well I'll be damned," Nelson muttered.

"It's starting all over again, Larry," a shaken Sally Nelson said; she had been listening to the conversation as she sat up in the wagon, and now she slowly climbed down to be with her husband.

"The killing; it just seems to follow us," she said. "There is killing everywhere we go."

119

She turned to her husband, who couldn't seem to shake the distant look on his face as he tried to make sense out of what he had just heard.

"Hold me, Larry. Just hold me tight," she said.

But Larry Nelson didn't move, didn't speak, didn't react outwardly. He continued to stare off into space, not even aware that his wife had spoken to him.

Larry Nelson's mind was on Max Blake and the tall, thin man named Grant who was on his trail.

Chapter Twelve
A View From The Top

Max Blake spent the five hours it took him to get from the outcrop where he buried Weasel Morgan to the outskirts of the seedy border town of Aguante in deep thought, all the while considering exactly what his next move should be.

It seemed clear with every passing mile and with every passing idea that his options were fewer than he would like and that his chances of any rapid-fire success became a little more bleak.

The problem, he considered with reluctance, wasn't just in handling the likes of Hoss Johnson and the remaining brother, Freeman Morgan, who rode with him. The real problem was that the rest of the men in Aguante – and that included the town's corrupt sheriff and his deputies, all of them little more than hired gunmen – wouldn't merely stand by while a federal marshal rode into town, arrested a couple of outlaws in their midst, and then sit back in silence as he rode out of town again with the outlaws either alive and in his custody or dead and strapped onto the backs of their horses.

No, Max thought, *there's got to be a better way. And the fact that Weasel Morgan's nag is trailing along behind me doesn't help the situation much, either. That would be the first thing to draw attention to me and start a flood of either questions or gunfire.*

The sun was directly overhead now, and the heat was already intense. There wasn't a cloud in any direction, making it difficult to judge the blue of the sky and the intensity of the sun. The heat made the land ahead wave and shimmer against the distant hills, which were far off to Max's left; that, in turn, made it difficult for him to figure distances.

But as the trail ahead grew wider and provided evidence of more tracks and activity, Max knew that he was drawing close to Aguante. He cut to his left, heading north for a short time so that he wouldn't ride directly into town, and moved Buck more slowly now because he didn't want to raise up a trail of dust behind him. It hadn't rained for weeks, or maybe even months, in this country, and the choking dust was easily stirred by the hooves of the two horses.

Max traveled on for three-quarters of a mile or so farther when he saw the distant buildings of Aguante, still a good two miles or more away, as near as he could tell from looking across the flatland through the shimmering desert heat.

He continued moving north for a ways and then turned back to the east again, coming around in a half-circle toward a large outcrop that overlooked the town.

Clumps of small scrub pines, a few gnarled junipers, and clusters of manzanita bushes managed to cling to the sides and the top of the outcrop, in many cases attaching their roots to the very rocks that were strewn about the landscape. He could see various depressions and thick nests of boulders on the outcrop's slopes, even from a distance away; and he knew that while it wasn't going to be perfect, the hill was at least better than the land lying around it for the job that he had to do.

There's not a lot of cover up there, Max thought. *But if a man took his time and was careful, he could at least get a look at what was happening in the town below and perhaps spot someone – or even something – that might be of some help.*

By the time Max came around the back of the outcrop and cautiously made his way up to the top, leaving the two horses tied below in the shade of a small clump of junipers, another hour had passed and the sun was still beating down on the land and every living thing on it with a brutal intensity that could slowly kill an unprepared man or horse.

Max crested the hill and, careful not to show himself against the skyline, immediately got down on his belly and slithered along the ground into a depression of dust and dirt and small rocks and a wedge of boulders that gave him a clear view of Aguante below and also offered him some protection from being spotted.

Max took his time now and concentrated on the town.

Aguante was larger than he had imagined. He could see a group of buildings directly below on either side of the dusty main street. There were some empty areas between buildings that gave him a good view of at least part of the street, and then another smaller cluster of buildings spread out toward what appeared to be a town square – *or perhaps it's a community well*, he thought.

He could see the livery stables and the blacksmith shop at the far end of town, off to his left, and what probably was the hotel; it was one of only a half-dozen two-story buildings in Aguante. Max figured that the others were saloons or sporting houses, or both.

One of the buildings on the far side of the street obviously was a saloon; he could hear tinny piano music drifting his way, even from this distance, and he could see a number of horses tied to the long hitching post in front of the establishment. The saloon, and no doubt a brothel immediately above it, also generated the only activity that he could see on this portion of the street; a number of men moved in and out, usually in groups of two or three, disappearing either into the saloon or up or down the street around it.

Once they moved onto the street, Max could follow the men for only a few yards to the east before they were cloaked by the buildings on the near side of the dusty road; but he could follow them after they left the saloon for at least a hundred yards or more when they moved to his right, which was back to the west, before the buildings at that end of town blocked their passing from his view.

After watching this activity on the street for a while, Max took the time to study his location on the outcrop, careful to ensure that he was in the best position available.

He turned first and looked directly behind him, making certain that no one could sneak up on him without being seen. He had a good view of the ground that stretched back out to the north, and he also could keep an eye on the horses and his gear.

His view to the immediate left was somewhat obscured by a large cluster of rocks and brush, and he knew that he would be vulnerable if a surprise attack came from that direction. But he could see for miles to his right, back along the same trail that he had just traveled.

Max slid along the ground to his left and tried the view from the cluster of boulders and manzanita bushes. But his overview of the town was not as good as it was in the first spot he had found, and his line of sight to the horses behind him also was blocked by a clump of small junipers fifty yards or more below. So he made his way back to the spot where he had first crested the hill, again fitting his body into the depression in the ground and checking the view again in all directions.

It's not exactly perfect, he thought, *but it's better than nothing and the best spot up here, at least.*

I'll just have to make it a watch-and-see game.

Max slowly crawled away from the edge of the hill and then got up in a crouch and scrambled down to the horses. He quickly took the saddles off Buck and Weasel Morgan's horse and spread out some feed for both animals from one of the saddle bags that Buck carried. He took a few minutes to brush Buck down and to check the horse's shoes and the hooves for stone damage as well. He also took the time to sponge some water from his canteen into the horses' mouths and nostrils, using the dull brown 'kerchief that he kept tied around his neck.

When he finished with the horses, Max took the canteen and some jerky, along with a handful of the corn biscuits that he had bought in Twin Forks, and started to make his way back up the outcrop. He took only a few steps when he stopped, turned around again, and went over to where his gear was stored. He pulled out his Winchester, took the U.S. Marshal's badge from his shirt and stored it in one of his saddlebags, and then made his way back up the hill to again watch the activity in Aguante.

Max settled back in the same depression in the earth and looked about in all directions. The comings and goings in front of the saloon had slowed momentarily, and he could detect no other movements on the streets or in the various buildings that he could see.

He took out a piece of jerky, pulled off a bite, and chewed slowly as he patiently watched and waited.

The tall, thin man named Grant was moving steadily along the trail to Aguante, following the tracks that had been left by Max Blake.

He knew that he was approaching the infamous border town because it became more difficult for him to distinguish the prints left by Max Blake's horse and the one that the marshal was trailing behind him – the horse that had no doubt belonged to a now very dead Weasel Morgan. It looked as though many men and many horses had passed this trail in previous days, and Grant had to be doubly careful to pick up the two sets of tracks that he had been following for miles.

But Grant was a good tracker – one of the best around, he liked to think.

He also was certain, however, that no U.S. marshal, no matter how tough or fast with a gun – not even a hard case like Max Blake – would ride directly into a rough-and-tumble hell-hole like Aguante and try to pull two murdering outlaws out of the midst of a town that already was full of murdering outlaws.

It wasn't just that a man wouldn't get any help, Grant knew; it wasn't even that a man would be left alone to do his work – just simply ignored.

No, Grant fully understood that for any marshal or sheriff or peace officer to ride into a town like Aguante and go after men like the two Max Blake was chasing, he would have to consider the entire town to be against him.

There simply would be just too many outlaws for a lone lawman to contend with, Grant reasoned with smug satisfaction.

And so Grant had watched the sides of the trail carefully as he rode ever closer to the town, seeing if he could find a place where the horses and the man he was intent on killing had veered off in one direction or another.

He found what he was looking for just a couple of miles outside of town: a place where two horses, one trailing the other, left the cluttered trail and headed off to the north.

He saw immediately that these were the same two horses that he had been tracking since he discovered the rigid body of Weasel Morgan, buried with no apparent ceremony in a shallow, rocky grave in the desert.

"You're doing just what I thought you would," Grant muttered aloud, the words more cursed than spoken.

"Max Blake, I can read you like a bad poker hand."

Even though he had paused for an instant or two, Grant tried not to pay obvious attention to the spot; the land rose and fell in small hills and swales toward where the tracks of the horses led, and he knew that a cautious man like a federal marshal could be hiding and watching him even now.

So Grant continued forward, staying on the trail that led into the town.

Because he was anxious to get to Aguante – some real food and an honest-to-God drink of mescal or tequila sounded almost as good as the revenge he sought – he spurred his horse forward a little faster.

Grant also wanted to size up Hoss Johnson as quickly as he could. He figured that if he could throw in with Johnson and Freeman Morgan, he could tell the two of them what he knew: who was after them, what had happened to Weasel Morgan, and even the general direction of where Max Blake was now most likely waiting and watching in the shadows outside of town.

But all the while, Grant kept a constant eye toward the north and to the northeast, wondering where the U.S. marshal had gone and under what rock he was likely hiding in the intense heat of the fading day.

Max had remained so intent on watching the activity around the saloon in Aguante that the sight of the solitary rider coming along the trail off in the distance to his right – coming, in fact, from the same direction that he had passed only short hours earlier – startled him a little.

You don't want to be caught surprised, he scolded himself. *It doesn't pay to be surprised in this line of work: A man who gets surprised doesn't live long.*

The rider – Max could see that he clearly was a tall man, even from as far away as he was – appeared to be tracking something ... or someone.

"Or someone," he said, quietly but aloud.

It's not likely, but it's possible that he's tracking me, Max thought.

He considered that possibility for a minute. He knew that Tom Culpepper, the outlaw he had killed in Pueblo Springs scant days earlier, had no known family. And he had taken care to determine that Johnny Dole, the other man he had killed in the Pueblo Springs saloon that same day, also was alone in the world as far as anyone there could determine – except, of course, for the young saloon girl who had tried without success to keep her man from drawing on a federal marshal with a reputation for speed and accuracy with a six-gun. So it was unlikely that the tall man he now saw heading toward Aguante was on his trail and seeking revenge for either the late Mr. Culpepper or the equally late Mr. Dole.

On the other hand, the sheriff in Pueblo Springs had warned him about the family of Grants who lived in Jefferson County – a band of tough, hard-riding fearless fools, the sheriff had indicated.

That's possible, too, Max thought. *It might be one of the Grants, all right.*

But he also knew that there were countless other possibilities: brothers, uncles, cousins, fathers, sons, gang members, friends – even wives and lovers and daughters of the men he had brought in for Judge Radford to hang at his convenience in Twin Forks, or the many more men he had been forced to kill in gunfights or for resisting arrest.

Max recalled the time when a young woman of 18 or so had tried to shoot him in the back only a few weeks after he had killed her lover in a fair gunfight on the streets of Twin Forks.

That had been a couple of years ago now, he considered, remembering the look of pure hatred in the girl's eye after the shot she fired at him missed; he had turned at the sound and pulled his gun in one swift motion, ready to shoot in return, as two town deputies wrestled the gun out of her hand just outside of Judge Radford's courthouse.

You can't ever tell about women or girls, he thought with a grim smile of recollection. *At least I know what happened to that one. She was pretty enough, with lots of fire...*

Max watched as the rider seemed to hesitate for a bit, looking intently down on the ground close to the spot where Max had turned north to make the half-circle around to the outcrop that overlooked

127

the town. He saw the rider start forward almost immediately, but he also saw that the man was now scanning the area in the direction where Max had traveled a short time earlier.

He's not near as interested in the road ahead as he is in this direction, Max thought. *That might be just some lonesome cowpoke riding his own way and minding his own business, but it's not likely – not the way he's looking in this direction.*

In fact, the more that Max considered the appearance of the rider, the more he was certain that the man was following his trail. For one thing, casual travelers didn't come to Aguante unless they were running from something, chasing something, or had business there; and the only business to be had in Aguante was bad business – the kind of business that spelled trouble for someone.

For another thing, Max reasoned, this man had been too interested in following a trail of some kind to be the innocent rider he was now pretending to be.

Even as Max watched, the rider's horse picked up speed and was moving along at a brisk gait as the man on it, clearly no longer interested in watching the tracks on the ground or even the general direction he was heading in, continued to look off to the north and to the northeast.

"That man is looking for me," Max said quietly.

Max began to turn the options over in his mind. And once again, he didn't like the cards that had been dealt.

His only chance to confront the man, he knew, would be to do it outside of town – well before the rider reached Aguante. But Max had no chance of doing that. The rider was closing in on the town's outskirts even now, and there was neither the time nor the cover necessary for him to scramble down the hill, get to the trail, and stop the man without being seen or heard, or without attracting some kind of unwanted attention.

The thought ran quickly through his mind that he could risk shooting the man with his rifle before the rider reached town. But he knew that a direct hit from such a distance was a chancy thing – even for someone as good with a Winchester as Max Blake. He also knew that firing a rifle from the outcrop overlooking the town would certainly attract the attention of nearly every living man and beast in Aguante.

That, in turn, would end his chances of surprising Hoss Johnson and Freeman Morgan, and he didn't like that thought.

Besides, Max considered, *I'm sworn to uphold the law, not bushwhack a man who might not be tracking me at all. How do I really know who this man is or what he wants? It's possible that he doesn't know me and isn't at all interested in where I am or what I'm doing.*

Max rolled that thought around in his mind for another minute.

But as he continued to consider the possibilities, the sounds of sudden gunfire drew his attention back to the main street of Aguante. He listened closely and counted three shots fired in rapid succession, all from the same gun. A single shot from a second gun followed. This, in turn, was answered by two shots from a gun with a different voice – a distinct whine, probably that of a carbine or rifle as opposed to a barking revolver – and then the first gun he had heard spoke again once more and then sang out still again.

Max waited, but only a gradual stillness settled across the air.

He saw no movement or activity in front of the saloon, where he suspected the shots had been fired.

And when he looked back to his right and down the trail, the lone rider he had followed with his eyes was no longer in sight.

129

Chapter Thirteen
A Note Of Discord

Hoss Johnson was drinking hard in the main saloon in the dusty, dirty border town that he and Freeman Morgan had come across so many miles of dusty, dirty trail to find.

It had seemed like a fine idea at the time. But in the hours that followed since his arrival, he had come to the conclusion that he didn't like the town, or the taste of the tequila that he was drinking, or even the looks of the men with whom he had settled into a card game.

In fact, Hoss Johnson didn't like much of anything in Aguante at this moment as he looked down in disgust at the cards that he was holding.

He didn't like the fact that even though he had robbed the same bank in Twisted Junction twice and had robbed the saloon in Indian Wells shortly afterward, he already was close to being broke.

He didn't like the fact that he was in a town where money was a necessity and where it wasn't likely that he could easily rob a bank or a saloon and get away with it: Everyone here was a thief, and the thieves in Aguante didn't openly tolerate stealing from each other.

He didn't like the fact that a deputy sheriff already had stopped by the saloon to ask him far more questions, about who he was and why he was in town, than he was used to answering for anyone under any circumstances anywhere in the territory.

He didn't like the fact that the town's sheriff had come into the saloon only minutes later, with the same deputy for company, and had looked him over a time or two before asking him even more questions – questions that were none of the sheriff's damned business anyway, as Hoss considered it.

He didn't even like the fact, now that he was here and had thought about it a bit more, that he was in a snake pit like Aguante at all. There were too many drunks lounging about the saloon, too many hard cases lurking around every corner, far too many damned deputies, and at least one sheriff too many to suit his taste.

But most of all, he didn't like the fact that he was losing at the card game he was in, even though he had been cheating at every opportunity he came across.

Hoss Johnson, in fact, was just plain angry, and he was growing angrier by the moment.

He might have been all right even after the bad taste of the first couple of shots of tequila went away and even after the deputy had come and gone. And his luck could always change at cards, especially when the same deck was used hand after hand and he began to get used to all of the edges and the distinct feel that many of the cards had.

But when that sheriff had come in with that damned deputy who had pestered him only minutes earlier and then started bothering him with all of that business about how he and his boys ran the town and how every man who entered Aguante needed to stay on the right side of the sheriff to – how was it that he had put it, to "get along without getting killed"? – well, that was enough to set Hoss Johnson over the edge and into the foulest of foul moods. And Hoss Johnson was a man who excelled at foul moods.

"Why, that sheriff is nothin' more'n a bastard crook – just like all the other bastard crooks in this town," Hoss had said to Freeman Morgan shortly after the sheriff left the saloon, apparently satisfied that he had served Hoss with proper notice.

Freeman had a big grin on his face as Hoss spoke, and he nodded. "That's right, Hoss," he said. "That's jest why we came here, remember? We wanted to meet up with a bunch of crooks. You wanted a drink and a card game, and my brother wanted a woman..."

"Shut up, Free. I know all that, dammit," Hoss snapped, interrupting Freeman's single-minded if simple discourse. "But that damn sheriff and that damn deputy of his ought to be out on the streets giving somebody else hell – sure as hell not me and not you.

"And he'd best stay off my back, if he knows what's good for him – and that's for sure. Or else he'll be one dead crooked sheriff, the sonofabitch. He'll find his way into the ground quick enough if he wants to play that game of poker with the likes of me. You get my meaning?"

The little speech to Freeman had made Hoss feel somewhat better, so he ordered a bottle – "and give me one that's worth drinking, dammit, and not this swill you've been trying to pass off on me," he growled at the bartender – and then got himself into a game of cards in an effort to get his mind off the deputy and the sheriff and the various concerns that the two had caused him.

But the more that he thought about it, and the more that he drank, the more he was angered by the words of the sheriff and by the smug, uppity nature of the deputy who had brought the damned sheriff into play right after he had bothered Hoss to begin with. It wasn't much longer before Hoss Johnson was looking for a fight – something to take his mind off the perceived insults that he already had suffered since his arrival in Aguante.

Hoss finally threw his hand down in disgust and looked up to where Freeman Morgan was now standing with his back to the bar, a short carbine by his side, nursing a beer and watching the card game with an amused look of disinterest on his face.

At least that simple-minded bastard doesn't have to worry about a thing except his simple-minded brother, Hoss thought as he eyed Freeman for a minute. *But he watches my backside, which is a damn good thing for him that he does, else I'd have shot him dead a damn long time ago.*

Hoss grinned at the thought – *I've had worse ideas*, he thought – and then looked back to the dealer.

"Hurry it up," he said. "Let's get on with the next hand so's I can make back some of my money."

"No need to be in such an all-fired hurry there, mister," the man who was dealing the cards said, a tight and twisted smile on his face. "This day's got a lot of night to it yet. There'll be plenty of time to draw cards a'fore we're through here."

"You let me be the judge of that, and hurry it up while yer at it," Hoss snapped.

He was in a game with four other men, all of them carrying some obvious long years of trail savvy and been-behind-a-gun-before smarts to them. They at least looked as if they were used to handling themselves in a card game or a fistfight – and most likely in a gunfight, too, Hoss figured, though you never could tell exactly about that until you actually braced a man and saw his response.

Still, Hoss had sized them up to be a rough and tumble lot, something that didn't put him off much because he knew that he could cheat at cards as well as most men and was no doubt better with a gun than most any other man in the saloon.

And in any event, Hoss Johnson never was much for a fair fight: He cheated at gunplay the same as he did at cards. And he was a good cheat – as good as they came, he liked to think.

Even so, he had noticed that all four of the card players at his table were packing revolvers strapped to their sides and appeared as if they knew how to use them well enough.

The man who was dealing looked as if he has spent a fair number of years on the trail. He was sun-baked and weather-beaten; his skin was as tough as old leather, and his hands had the calloused look of a man who was used to cutting his own way in the world – and to getting his own way at whatever price. Hoss had him pegged for a cattle rustler, maybe, and noted that he didn't like the man's looks at all.

The galoot to the dealer's immediate right was the only one of the four who had offered his name when Hoss joined the game: "Call me Red," he had volunteered. But Hoss only grunted, saying nothing, and the other three men ignored the self-made introduction and made no effort to follow Red's lead. Hoss figured Red for a thief of some sort; he didn't care for the way the man's eyes kept shifting from one spot to another and one person to another – as if he were trying to take everything in but never spent enough time on any one thing to remember what he had just seen.

Red was somebody else he didn't much like the looks of.

The other two card players, both of whom were better dressed than everyone else in the saloon, at least were well-acquainted with each other – even if they had never met the dealer and the man called Red before this game, as they had claimed. Hoss had been watching them closely for indications that they were passing signals across the table to each other; and even though he hadn't yet caught them at it, he was certain that they were in cahoots with each other – no doubt conspiring directly against him. These two, he was sure, were professional card players: almost dandies, but with a harder shell on them.

He also knew full well that he didn't like their looks much, either.

In fact, he didn't like any of it, but he accepted the situation as just about what you would expect to get in a card game in a town like Aguante.

The fact that he was losing didn't help his frame of mind any, of course.

The fact that the bottle he had ordered to wash the rest of the trail dust out his mouth wasn't any better than the first couple of shots, and that didn't help much, either.

And when the piano player started up fresh again after a break, Hoss had seen and heard and tasted just about enough.

"Shut that racket up over there. Can't you see I'm in a card game here?" he yelled, loud enough to be heard above most of the noises in the saloon.

The piano player, either not recognizing that Hoss Johnson was hollering at him or simply choosing to ignore the big man at the poker table, continued with his song, a kind of honky-tonk jangle that he hoped would induce the saloon's patrons to buy more drinks. His pay each night depended on the take at the bar.

"Hey, you – at the piano," Hoss yelled even louder. "I said to shut that racket up. I meant it."

The piano player looked up and smiled this time – figuring, because of the general noise in the place, that the big man was acknowledging the song that he was playing.

"Never mind," the dealer said. "Play cards and forget the damned piano."

Hoss turned his attention back to the table and looked directly at the dealer with steely eyes that betrayed only one emotion: pure meanness. "Don't you ever tell me what to do, mister," he said, "or it'll be the last damn thing you ever tell anybody. You understand me?"

"I hear what you say all right, stranger," the dealer replied evenly, comforted by the fact that he had a revolver strapped to his leg. "The point is, are we gonna play cards, or are we gonna holler at the piano player all night?"

"I don't like the piano player or the piano," Hoss said. "And I don't much care for you right now, neither.

"Hey, shut that thing up," he yelled again, turning his attention back to the piano player, in a voice loud enough this time to make everything stop in the saloon, including the sound of the piano.

The smile on the piano player's face slowly drained away, and every eye in the place was now turned directly toward the very large presence of Hoss Johnson.

"That's better," he said after a minute, his voice now a confident bellow. "I'm playin' cards here and need to fix on the game."

"That may be, but I liked the piano music."

The voice came from directly in front of Hoss. He looked up to see the face of the deputy sheriff who had asked him the questions earlier. The man was about 20 feet away and was facing Hoss with an tight smile on his face, at once hard and confident and relentless and cocky – *almost smart-assed*, Hoss thought.

"You can go to hell then, along with the piano player," Hoss replied, not impressed by the man's presence or smile or badge. He looked quickly about for a sign of the sheriff or perhaps another deputy to back the play, but it appeared that the man was alone.

"Forget it," the dealer said. "Let's just play cards."

"You stay out of this, Tom," the deputy said to the dealer, although he hadn't taken his eyes off Hoss Johnson's frame. Then, cocking his head slightly toward the piano player, he said, "Start that music up again, Harry – if you please."

The piano player hesitated, looking from the deputy to Hoss and back to the deputy again.

"Start it up now, I said," the deputy called.

Hoss glanced over at the bar, quickly noting that Freeman Morgan was stationed with his right hand on the barrel of his carbine. Satisfied, he held the deputy's stare and again said to the piano player, "Touch those keys and you'll never touch another piano."

He slowly dropped the cards in his hands onto the table.

The four men seated at the table with Hoss Johnson now got up and cautiously backed out of the way, clearing the line of fire; everyone else in the bar quickly moved away from the deputy and the large man at the card table who didn't seem to care for the piano music.

They were all expecting fireworks at any moment, although it was hard to tell where it would come from – or who would start it. Only the piano player hadn't moved. He remained at the stool in front of the piano, shifting his gaze between the deputy and Hoss Johnson, not knowing where to rest his eyes or his hands or which man to obey.

"You gonna play that piano, Harry?" the deputy asked, keeping his eyes fixed on Hoss.

"You'd better not touch the damn thing," Hoss countered.

"You tangle with me, stranger, and you tangle with the entire town," the deputy said to Hoss.

"You won't care about that none," Hoss said. "You'll be dead as old Coley's mule before anybody else gets into this thing. It's jest me and you, pardner. And I like them odds."

The deputy clearly didn't like the sound of that and tried to force the play back to his favor.

"Tom," he said without looking directly at the card dealer, who was now standing a dozen or more feet from the table behind Hoss Johnson, "you go on out and get Farley now, ya hear? Bring him back in here quick-like. If you see Ropey or Pitts, bring 'em along as well. And get me the sheriff, too."

"Don't nobody in this place move a step," Hoss barked. "This here's 'tween me and this idiot here and nobody else."

"Tom, you go and get..."

The deputy went for his gun at the same time that he had started talking again, hoping that the move would throw Hoss Johnson off balance for just an instant.

"...moving now..."

But the deputy could not have anticipated the speed with which the big man he was facing could handle a gun. The bogus lawman had his revolver's ivory grips in his hand and was starting to pull the gun out of his holster when the first shot from Hoss Johnson's own hogleg shattered the air in the saloon.

"...like I..."

The shot did more than shatter the air. It also shattered the deputy's left arm and rocked him backward.

It was followed by two additional sudden blasts from Hoss Johnson's revolver, both of which hit the man dead center in the chest as the deputy's gun kicked out a single bullet into the floor

136

of the saloon, a shot fired by reflex rather than intent. The deputy's body, slammed backward by the sudden impact of the two bullets that had struck him almost simultaneously, crashed into a table and then sprawled onto the floor, snapping one of the table's legs and sending it crashing down as well. Bottles, bar glasses, playing cards, pieces of silver – all were sent crashing to the floor as well.

Hoss, now on his feet, followed the deputy's lurching death with a humorless smile and was waiting to see if the man would move again when two sharp bullets from Freeman Morgan's carbine cracked the air behind him. Hoss whirled around and saw the card dealer, a six-gun in his hand, pitch forward and fall to the floor without firing the shot that he had no doubt been aiming at Hoss's back.

Both of Freeman's bullets had found their mark, but the man still was alive and was starting to crawl forward when Hoss snapped off two more shots and finished him off, hitting him once in the neck and once in the back. The man's head slumped to the soiled floor, and a growing pool of blood that drained from his mouth began to run down the uneven cracks and ridges and grooves of the beer-stained wood.

An eerie silence followed. Hoss looked carefully around, slowly making sure that no one else in the room was fool enough to pull a gun and continue the fight. He took care to note that the bartender hadn't moved and had his hands in the air as though the place was being robbed.

"Anyone else?" he called out. "Any other man in here want to die here and now?"

"It's all right, Hoss," Freeman said, grinning across from the edge of the bar as he sensed the resignation in the room. "Ain't no one else here dumb enough to try nothin' a'tall, I reckon. Too bad ol' Weasel weren't here to see this. Might be time we went and got him, Hoss."

"It might jest be at that," Hoss said.

He slowly turned to the piano player.

"You know, I done changed my mind," he said, looking directly at the frightened man. "It's too quiet in here now. How's about playin' some of that piano music again – jest to liven things up a bit?"

"Are, are ... mister, are you sure you want me to..."

"Play it," Hoss snapped. "Now."

Harry the piano player quickly struck up a tune that rang hollow through the saloon.

Hoss took the time to collect the money at the card table. "Any objections?" he snapped at the men who had sat at the table earlier, but they only shook their heads dumbly and said nothing.

Hoss then motioned to Freeman and started toward the bar. He looked across at the bartender and said, "You got a back door through there?" The bartender nodded and jerked his head back over his shoulder to his left; he was still holding his hands in the air. Hoss looked over and saw a small door at the far end of the bar.

"You cover me till I get there," he said to Freeman. "Then you come along."

Freeman nodded, and Hoss edged his way to the door. He waited as Freeman slowly moved along the edge of the bar and then joined him on the other side at the door, keeping a close watch on every person in the saloon and especially on the batwing doors at the front.

"Thanks for the card game," Hoss called out when Freeman was at last at his side. "We'll have to come back again sometime and finish playing."

The two men then backed out the door, which opened into a small storage area behind the saloon. They quickly ran to a second door and slipped out into the open air of the dusk outside.

"We're gonna have to be smart and quick to git outta this," Hoss said as he hunched down and made his way over toward the buildings to his left. "They're gonna have every piss-ant bastard in town who can carry a gun out to git us."

"You think we kin make it to the horses, Hoss?" Freeman asked as he ran along behind.

"You jest try to keep up, Free."

"Well, you jest try and get shut of me," Freeman replied. And the two men moved rapidly off, away from the saloon and running hard toward the stables.

Chapter Fourteen
A Sudden, Certain Halt

It didn't take Max Blake long to figure out that all hell had broken loose in the Aguante saloon, which was several hundred yards directly below where he crouched at the top of the outcrop overlooking the dusty border town.

Shortly after the gunfire ended and a piano abruptly and – to Max's ears, at least – unnaturally started to play again, two men burst through the batwing doors of the saloon and bolted down the street to Max's left; he cursed silently when he almost immediately lost sight of them behind the facing buildings.

The two were followed, however, by a handful of men who charged out of the saloon doors and ran in either direction, most of them yelling or shouting as they went.

One of the men stopped for a moment once he reached the bottom of the steps leading into the saloon and pulled a revolver, firing two quick shots into the air, startling the horses tied at the hitching post. Then he, too, scrambled down the street and out of Max's sight, still carrying the gun in his hand.

The activity ceased for a moment. But Max could almost see in his mind what was taking place, both within the saloon and at the sheriff's office, where some of the men no doubt had run. He could picture at least one body and maybe as many as four lying dead on the floor of the saloon; a group of men now were probably clustered around the body or bodies, talking and pointing and poking at them and each other. He also could picture a cursing sheriff being told that his town had just been disrupted by an ugly killing or killings down the street.

And that probably wouldn't set too well, even for a corrupt lawman who controlled a corrupt town.

Max reasoned that the Aguante sheriff wouldn't object to a murder or two. But he also knew that the man would want a killing to be done on his own terms – and perhaps by his own hand; and what had just happened in the saloon no doubt didn't fit that picture.

Within another minute or two, a tall man dressed in fawn-colored buckskin pants with a matching shirt and vest emerged in the gathering twilight and quickly led a group of four other tough-looking cowboys into the saloon.

That would be the sheriff and at least some of his deputies, Max thought. *And that's also my opportunity to have a quick scout around the town and find out if Hoss Johnson and Freeman Morgan are responsible for all of this shooting.*

Taking his rifle, Max quickly darted away from the spot where he had been hiding and bolted to his left; he ran hard and picked up the shelter of a small clumping of trees and brush. He crouched again, selecting another target to make for down the hill. And then, carefully watching the view of the town below, he raced to a cluster of rocks and knelt behind it, all the while keeping an eye on as much of the street below that he could see.

He continued to pick his way cautiously but rapidly down the hill until he hit level ground. Once there, he ran hard for the back of the buildings that he had watched from above for much of the afternoon. He ducked behind a corner, holding his rifle with both hands so that the top of the barrel was level with the bill of his hat but was pointed straight up in the air; and he kept his back to the wall as he peered down the narrow alley between the buildings toward the main street.

Seeing no one, Max crouched and moved forward again between the two buildings so that he could get a better look at what was happening at the saloon, which was now almost directly across the street from him. He flopped on his belly when he reached the front of the buildings and found some shelter behind a rain barrel; it was almost empty – it rocked when he touched it – but the barrel was squat and wide and afforded some protection from the men who might be passing on the main street.

Max briefly tried to determine what the two buildings were, but he couldn't risk sticking his head out far enough to see.

This will have to do, he thought as he stayed low to the ground and focused on the activity in the street, which was now only a few yards in front of him. Max could see that there was a constant stream of men moving in and out of the saloon. Three men also stood on the porch of a building two store-fronts down from the saloon, clearly engaged in a vigorous discussion; but he couldn't hear anything that was being said that far away.

Not more than thirty yards away, however, two angular cowboys of approximately the same height and weight were moving toward him, talking loudly enough to attract Max's attention; listening intently, Max could clearly hear their voices as they moved closer, and he focused on the conversation.

One of the men had just rolled a cigarette, and he stopped to light it – striking a match against the heel of his boot – before saying, as if in answer to a question that he had been asked before he had stopped to light the match: "Well, it sure beats the hell out of me. But one thing's for certain, and I kin tell you this much: They cain't git far away. I hear tell their horses are still tied up in the stables and are bein' watched there now."

"Reckon they cain't git far without their horses, that's fer sure," the second cowboy said.

"I'll tell you something else," the first man replied after taking a deep pull on his cigarette and blowing the smoke out into the rapidly cooling desert air. "I didn't care a good rawhide damn for that loudmouth deputy who got hisself kilt in there; he probably deserved killin', knowing the way he went after every saddle tramp and no-account who rode into this town."

The man stopped, taking another long pull on his cigarette and then picking a piece of loose tobacco off the end of his tongue, before he added, "But I got to say that old Tom Murphy in there didn't deserve to be gunned down that way – not by no man and no account, no sir."

The second man nodded. "Murphy was a card cheat with strangers and had some other faults, all right," he said. "But he could handle a cross herd on the trail like few others I seen. To be finished off in the back like that – well, that ain't no fittin' way for a man to die, even if you do pull an ace out of yer boot from time to time."

141

"That's the way I got it figgered, too," the first man said as he picked another piece of tobacco out of his mouth, took a look at the wet, rumpled end of his cigarette, then threw it down in the dirt and crushed it out with the toe of his boot. "The two bastards that done this thing deserve to die hard and long. And that big bastard – what was that big bastard's name again?"

"Hoss Johnson, somebody said."

"And that big bastard Hoss Johnson – yeah, that's it – he'll git what's comin' to him if the sheriff has any say a'tall about the matter. You kin count on that much, and I kin tell you that fer sure."

Max closed his eyes for a moment and rolled the conversation around in his head a bit. *A man shot in the back; that sure enough sounds like the work of Hoss Johnson*, he thought.

A third man suddenly appeared – Max wasn't sure exactly where he came from, which disturbed him – and said, "The sheriff wants to see the two of you over at the saloon. Right now."

The two cowboys said nothing but immediately followed the man across the street, and Max used the moment to slip away from the rain barrel and back into the deepening shadows between the two buildings that marked the alley; he didn't like the thought of being surprised from behind, and he already had experienced a start with the sudden arrival of the third man.

If I were Hoss Johnson and Freeman Morgan, he thought, *I'd do my best to get to my horses and get the hell out of town. So it sure won't hurt to make my way over to the stables and see if that's their plan; maybe I can pick them up along the way.*

With that thought, Max turned and worked his way back through the narrow alley. He took a right turn at the edge of the row of buildings, doing his best to move along in the shadows and snake his way toward the stables at the far end of town.

He had moved fewer than 500 feet, however, when the cold feel of a hard steel gun barrel was thrust into his ribs from behind, bringing Max Blake to a sudden and certain stop.

The tall, thin man named Grant was approaching the edge of Aguante when he heard gun shots coming from what sounded like the center of town, and he spurred his horse forward at the sound.

Unless I miss my guess, and that ain't likely, I've just heard from the two men I'm looking for, he thought. *The thing is, can I get there in time to do anything about it?*

Grant quickly angled his horse behind the first row of buildings that he came to, trying to get an idea of what was happening without being seen. He moved his horse almost methodically in and out of the back alleyways behind the south end of Aguante, heading in the general direction where he had heard the shots only moments before.

He wasn't quite sure what he was looking for; but he knew that in a town like this one, it wouldn't take long to find the action – or for the action to find him.

The trick, he knew, was to be ready when it came.

Then he heard two more rapid gun shots close by but a street over, probably right in the heart of the town, he considered. He got down off his horse and tied the animal to a railing near the end of a large building that he thought might have been an accommodating hotel, judging by its size and the many windows he could see that looked out to the south and the east. He pulled out one of the big Remingtons that he carried and started to cautiously work his way up between the large building and a smaller one that was immediately next door, inching his way toward the main street.

Remaining in the deep shadows, Grant could hear the commotion of comings and goings through the front door of the large building, against which he was leaning, as well as the excited voices of a group of men nearby. He quickly determined that there had been a shooting at the saloon, apparently one or two buildings over, and that the town's sheriff and his deputies already were covering the streets to find the men who were responsible and who now were on the loose somewhere on the streets of Aguante.

Three men on the porch of the building to Grant's right were engaged in a vivid and at times animated conversation about the shootings. Grant listened for a moment and could tell that one of the men had been in the saloon when the shots were fired.

"It all happened so sudden-like," the man was telling his audience of two. "The big fella kept telling the piano player to shut up the damn noise. Then that crazy deputy stepped in and challenged him. And the next thing ya know, the deputy and the old trail boss was both as dead as rocks on the floor."

"Jest like that?"

"I tell ya, it happened jest like that" – he snapped his fingers – "only even faster.

"The deputy never even cleared leather that I could tell. And the old guy tried to settle it by shooting the big fella in the back. But he never counted on the ugly one at the bar who had the rifle; never seen him a'tall. Then the big man – the one who had just plugged the deputy dead – turned around and pumped two more shots into the trail boss. But hell, he was already done fer anyways."

"And then they slipped out the back?"

"As easy as you please. Walked by no more'n a dozen steps from where I was standing by the bar at the time. Cool, they were, talking at each other like it was a Sunday in church. The boys said the big one of 'em was a fella by name of Johnson; couple of 'em seemed to recognize him – 'cause of his size, I reckon. Nobody seemed to know the git of the other one a'tall, though."

The man paused for a few seconds, thinking about what he had heard and seen only moments before. "Sort of unnerves ya, bein' that close by and not bein' able to do somethin' about it," he said at last. "But the next man to draw a gun in there was a dead man, jest like the others. That much was for sure."

The silence hung in the air for a time.

"Where do you reckon they went off to?"

"My guess is they went for their horses, but I hear tell the sheriff already sent a couple'a men down to watch the stables. Ain't a whole lot of places for a man to hide in this here town anyway, so yer guess is as good as mine right now.

"For all I know, they might be lurkin' down one of the alleys through town right now – waiting their chance to slit a throat and try to git away like that."

"What say we go find 'em?" the third man in the group said.

"Try that and you'd better hope you don't find 'em alone," the first man said. "'Cause if'n you do, that big fella would as soon shoot you full of holes as he would shoot at tin cans on a backyard fence post.

"No sir, not me; I ain't gonna chase after the likes of them two unless a whole lot a'money was ridin' on me killin' 'em. And nobody's said nothin' 'bout no reward money yet."

Even though the conversation continued, Grant had heard enough; he knew that if he wanted to find Hoss Johnson and Freeman Morgan, he would have to use his wits and think as they would – as though he were running hard from a town full of deputies and a sheriff who meant business. It was a picture that he could stick vividly into his mind, and he grinned at the thought.

Yeah, I kin find them two boys all right, he thought.

Grant moved away from the main street and retreated toward where he had left his horse, using the shadows that hung like a dark veil in the narrow space between the buildings.

He made it back to where the animal was waiting for him – contented, if not totally disinterested in his whereabouts – and put his gun away to mount up when a sharp voice from a man who clearly meant business brought him to a sudden stop.

"Hold it right there, mister. You git them hands up, and you keep 'em up there high where I kin see 'em. That clear?"

Grant slowly put both of his hands in the air, looking first to his right – where he thought he had heard the voice – and then to his left when he didn't find the man where he expected him to be.

"I hear you," Grant said at last. "What is it you want?"

"You never mind that none, mister," the voice said, and Grant could now tell that the man was almost directly behind him, perhaps eight to ten feet away. He also sensed that a gun was pointed directly at his back, a feeling that he didn't like a bit.

"What's your business here?" the voice asked.

"Thought I heard shootin'," Grant replied. "I jest rode into town and thought I'd check it out."

"You always ride toward trouble like that? Most men tend to shy away from the sound of shooting in a strange town."

"A man can't be too careful," Grant replied evenly and then continued, keeping his voice casual: "Look, I don't know who you are after or why, but it ain't me. Let me put my hands down and I'll prove it to you."

"Yeah? And how you gonna do that?"

"I'm a bounty hunter," Grant said. "I can show you. Let me put my hands down and I'll show you."

"You hold still now and keep them hands up high!

"Bein' a bounty hunter won't make you no friends here, mister," the voice said. "For all I know, you're trackin' me and most anybody else in Aguante. This town's full'a men with paper on 'em."

"I'm tracking me a federal marshal," Grant said, "not no cowboy."

"Ain't no federal marshal in this town."

"There is now," Grant said. "I tracked him here, I know who he is – even what he looks like – and I know how to get rid of him nice and clean. Nobody'll know he was even here, once I'm through."

The man with the gun thought about that for a moment. "What's a federal marshal doing in Aguante?" he asked.

"The way I hear it told, he's been sent to check things out and then clean up the whole town," Grant bluffed, thinking quickly.

The man behind him was quiet for a time, as if considering the prospect and not liking it much. "Then who in hell sent you?" he asked Grant at last.

"I've been hired by some men with an interest in this town remaining exactly the way it is," Grant said. "They want to see that the crew in charge of Aguante continues operating without – shall we say? – any federal interference."

"This sounds like something the sheriff will want to know about," the man said, stepping out of the shadows behind Grant for the first time and moving a couple of feet off to Grant's right side. "I think the sheriff'll be right interested in knowin' this, all right."

"Then let's go," Grant said. "You mind if I put my hands down now?"

"I guess not," the man said, "but you watch yourself..."

The man never finished the sentence because Grant, moving as quick as a springing cat, swung both of his upraised arms in a long arc that connected into a large fist at the end and crashed into the man's head with amazing suddenness and viciousness, knocking him senseless to the ground.

Grant quickly kicked the man's gun aside and had one of his own revolvers pulled. He knelt over the man, saw that he was still stunned, and then took the butt end of his revolver and struck the man with three successive and brutal whacks to the skull, each one harder than the previous blow.

He could feel the bone giving a little more each time, and he knew that there would be no need for a fourth.

Then he pulled the body back into the shadows and went through the man's pockets. He at once found a leather wallet with some folding money but nothing else inside. A couple of gold coins jangled inside the man's right pocket. He went to search the man's shirt pocket and saw for the first time a five-pointed star attached to the outside of the man's shirt.

That's one less of that crowd tonight, anyway, he thought.

He tossed the tin star away, took the wallet and the gold coins, and put them into his own pocket. He looked up and down the street again, then pulled the body farther into the shadows near the corner of a dark adobe ramshackle structure.

Grant went across to where he had kicked the deputy's six-gun, picked it up and shoved it into his belt, and then untied his horse and quickly mounted.

He cautiously edged the horse back into the shadows and continued heading slowly east, toward the spot where he thought that he might find the stables, the disagreeable Hoss Johnson, and the equally disagreeable Freeman Morgan.

"Them boys is gonna serve me up a full plate of Max Blake," he whispered.

Chapter Fifteen
More Curious Than Cautious

Max Blake quickly considered his predicament, and he didn't like much of anything about the situation that he now found himself in.

The man who had appeared so suddenly out of the shadows was not only holding a gun to Max's ribs, but he already had taken the Winchester and removed Max's Colt from its holster and then tossed the weapons on the ground, well out of reach.

Worse, Max hadn't seen or even sensed the man's presence until it was too late for him to react, which troubled him greatly. He also didn't see a fast or easy way out, and that bothered him even more – at least temporarily.

It concerned him that he had been surprised on more than one occasion in the past few days. He recognized that it was likely the result of too much work over too many days with too little time to rest – not that he could do much about it.

In his line of work, Max knew all too well that too little too often usually meant dead and buried.

In a normal circumstance, he could merely explain who he was and why he was there. But this was no normal circumstance.

Aguante, after all, was something short of a normal town: No one hung out the "Welcome, Federal Marshals" banner here.

Max was positive, in fact, that explaining to the deputy who he was and why he had come and what he was doing at that very moment would mean a certain trip to the town jail – and from there, no doubt, to a noose or a shooting or some other grisly form of death. Aguante was a town of bandits, murderers, and thieves

148

that was controlled by the very same bandits and murderers and thieves.

"Who are you, mister, and what's yer business here?" the man with the six-gun pointed directly at Max's heart demanded.

Considering the few options that he had, Max said nothing for a moment, trying to buy some time; all the while, he kept his hands raised high and a neutral look on his face.

"I asked you, mister, jest who the hell are you?" the man said with a great deal more emphasis this time. "What are you doing here? What are you up to?"

Max again said nothing, this time shrugging his shoulders as if he didn't understand or couldn't answer the question. He had an idea now – not much of one, but it was something to work with – and he figured that it was worth a chance to play it out, at least. Night was beginning to fall, and he might be able to use the deepening dusk and shadows to his advantage.

Max half-turned so that he could look into the man's face as he talked at him. He quickly saw that the man was wearing a deputy's badge, which wasn't much of a surprise, but he pretended not to notice anything else but the man's mouth.

"What's the matter, mister? Don't you understand plain English? You deaf or something?" the deputy growled.

At this, Max shook his head vigorously up and down several times and turned fully toward the man now, smiling and nodding all the while. Then he shrugged his shoulders again, as if to indicate that it wasn't his fault that he couldn't hear what was being said to him. He continued smiling broadly, however, doing his best to appear to be no serious threat.

"Just what the hell is this?" the deputy muttered.

The man clearly was confused. He wanted answers, but he had come across someone who apparently couldn't hear him and couldn't deliver those answers through conventional means – words that he could understand. And he also was at a loss as to how to continue the conversation so that he could determine how to deal with the situation.

"Well, what are you doing here?" he asked at last in frustration, not really expecting an answer, for he had already asked the same kind of question seconds before and received nothing more than a smile and a nod.

Max just grinned widely and shrugged his shoulders again, nodding his head up and down at the same time.

"Oh, what the hell is all this about?" the deputy said, now fully exasperated. "I'm better off talking to the wall, or to my own damned horse.

"I'd better jest take you back to the jail and let the sheriff figure this out for hisself."

Max shook his head quickly from side to side and pointed the index finger on his right hand straight up in the air, as if to indicate that he wanted the deputy to wait for a moment; he continued to keep his left hand raised over his head all the while, and he continued to smile broadly.

"Yeah, so what is it?" the deputy asked.

Max carefully took his right hand and moved it toward his mouth, taking his index and middle fingers and joining them with his thumb as though he was going to feed himself. Then he moved his hand quickly in and out in front of his mouth.

"I don't get it," the deputy said.

Max grinned as widely as he could now and moved his lips as though trying to speak, all the while keeping his left hand in the air. He curled his index finger on his right hand now and moved it back and forth as though beckoning the man to move closer so that he might be able to hear Max's voice if he got near enough.

The deputy, more curious than cautious at this point, kept his eyes on Max's fingers and mouth and leaned forward, putting himself slightly off balance.

Max used the opportunity to bring his right knee up into the man's groin with such brutal, sudden force that it took the deputy's breath away and doubled him over. Max then came down hard with his left elbow, striking the deputy across the back of the neck.

The startled deputy dropped down on his knees, and Max cocked his right arm and hit the man flush in the face as he slowly looked up, his eyes dulled in pain; the blow sent him rocking over backward, bending his legs cruelly beneath him and knocking him senseless in the process.

Max immediately pounced over the man's body while pulling out his Reid's Knuckleduster from behind his belt buckle, just in case the deputy stirred. But seeing that he was out cold, Max picked up the man's revolver from where it had fallen and then scrambled over to where his own Winchester and Colt were lying on the ground.

Max tucked the Knuckleduster away, holstered his Colt, and shoved the deputy's gun – a Merwin and Bray .38-caliber revolver that had seen better days – into his right boot.

He pulled the deputy's limp body close to the side of the building. Ducking into the darkness, he took the man's hat and quickly cut the top of it out with his Bowie knife. Working like a skilled tailor with inferior tools, Max cut the bill of the hat off in a full circle, discarding that piece after removing the drawstring that kept the hat from blowing away in the wind or while its wearer was on a horse. Max took what was left of the hat and pulled it down over the deputy's head past his ears, forcing the bulk of the front of it into the deputy's mouth as a gag. Then he took the drawstring from the hat and tied the man's hands behind his back.

That'll hold him for a little while, at least – just long enough for me to get out of here, Max thought.

He looked at the deputy one more time to determine that the man was unconscious. Then he turned and vanished into the rapidly darkening night.

He was heading for the stables, where he hoped to surprise Hoss Johnson and Freeman Morgan in a similar fashion.

Chapter Sixteen
An Uneasy Partnership

In the faraway village of Indian Wells, Larry Nelson and his wife and two sons watched as a half-dozen or so men used thick, hand-woven hemp ropes to lower the rough-hewn wooden casket containing the body of Pedro Ruiz into the ground.

Hector and Martin, the two boys who had ridden so hard and so far to find Max Blake and who had returned to Indian Wells in the company of the Nelsons, stood nearby. They were as stoic and stony-eyed as they could manage, but their ragged composure came at great effort. The women of the village, and even a few of the older men, wept softly in the background.

The tiny cemetery now contained five fresh grave sites, all dug in a straight line at the far end of a small plot of land behind the town: Pedro Ruiz, the village elder and town mayor, killed for no apparent reason by a man named Grant; he was buried next to the four men who only days earlier had been brutally gunned down for no good reason by Hoss Johnson and Weasel Morgan, while Freeman Morgan had stood by and watched with a smirk.

"All of this is so senseless," Sally Nelson murmured to herself as a village elder began to quietly intone some mumbled prayers at the head of the grave. Her husband heard her and looked into her eyes, tightly squeezing her hand to offer some comfort and reassurance.

"Yer right," he said quietly so as not to disrupt the service. "It don't seem to make much sense. That old man surely didn't know a thing useful to that gunslinger, and he sure couldn't do the man much harm. It don't seem right – don't make much sense a'tall."

"Maybe it's just that life doesn't make any sense any more," she said. "Maybe it's just as simple as that. None of these men deserved to die like this. It's this country, Larry..."

A single tear fell from Sally Nelson's eye. It caught on her cheek for a moment and then slowly drained down her face until it disappeared from sight. She made no effort to dry it or to wipe it away.

"I'm not sure I want to continue on to California," she said after awhile. "I'm not sure that I can take any more of this senseless killing and violence and cruelty. Everywhere we go there are guns and more violence. I don't want to raise our two sons in this kind of life." She shook her head slowly from side to side, holding back more tears.

Her husband looked at her for a time, saying nothing. Then he turned and watched as the elder slowly blessed the grave, moving his right hand up and down and then from side to side again and again, repeating the motions of faith from ancient and universal scripture.

It ain't like her to be put off from a dream, Nelson thought. *But she'll come around; she'll snap out of it. It just might take some time, that's all.*

But as Larry Nelson looked at his wife once more, he wasn't quite so sure that his family would ever see the golden fields of California that they had talked about for so long.

He also wasn't sure that he now even wanted to take them there.

"We can always head back to Texas," he said at last. "We can try again there. It weren't so bad, you know, outside of that one little dust-up; we could probably manage it."

"You don't understand, Larry," she said without looking at him. "It's finished. All of it. You just don't understand at all. You don't see it, do you?"

He looked at her questioningly.

"I'm not even sure that I understand it anymore," she added softly, her voice barely heard over the gentle murmur of the words of prayer that drifted by in the dusk. "It's just this country..."

Hiding in the darkness outside of the livery stable in the seedy border town of Aguante, the tall, thin man who answered to the name of Grant stayed low and listened for the telltale sounds of men or other creatures that might be carried on the still night air.

Crouched near to the ground, he could smell the horses inside the stables and could sense, more than hear, their restlessness. His eyes were gradually adjusting to the changing and fading light, and the flight of a small insect caught his attention in the dusk. He swatted at it with his left hand as it came near his face, in much the same way that he had first swatted at the old man back in the village when he had asked about Max Blake and was told nothing of value in return.

It was too bad that the old man had been so stubborn, Grant considered. It wasn't that he had wanted to kill the old man, really. It was just that he had been in a hurry to find the federal marshal who had killed his brother, and the old man had been so insistent on offering nothing to help him that he finally just lost his temper.

But it didn't matter in the end; he was just an old man, Grant rationalized. What difference did it make if one less old man woke up to the world, anyway? Who would possibly mourn his loss? Who would possibly care?

It was odd, though, the way the thought of the old man in Indian Wells continued to stay with Grant even this much later. He couldn't recall that happening to him before; he had taken the lives of more than a dozen men in all, he figured – including time spent in the war – and he wondered what it meant.

Why dwell on the past? he thought at last. *Why stop and worry about someone of so little consequence?*

The snap of a twig behind him immediately pulled Grant back to the present, and he crouched even lower to the ground. Slowly, deliberately, he pulled one of the big Remingtons that he carried and slipped his index finger on the trigger and his thumb on the hammer.

He waited, silently watching, without moving again.

"Watch what the hell yer doin', dammit," he heard a man whisper. "You are gonna git us both kilt, if'n you keep that up."

"All right, Hoss. Jest let me git to a place so's I kin see what's up ahead there."

It's them, all right, Grant thought: *Hoss Johnson and Freeman Morgan, just like I had it figured, making their way right to their horses. And it would be so easy to kill them both and be an instant hero in Aguante. There might even be some reward money on the two of them – especially after the shootin' in the saloon.*

It would all be so easy...

The two men were moving slowly not more than six feet away now, and Grant could clearly see their faces and the fact that they had their guns pulled and pointed ahead of them as they moved along in single file.

Freeman Morgan was in front, picking his way through the shadows toward the stables. The big man behind him was Hoss Johnson; there was no question at all about that, given the man's size.

This is going to be tricky, Grant thought: *A man could get killed, if he's not real careful, in a situation like this with two tough boys who'd rather shoot first and never even think about asking a question later.*

But surprise was an instrument that he could play well, and Grant carefully and silently slipped in behind Hoss Johnson as the outlaw moved past him and stuck the Remington none too gently into Hoss's ribs, cocking the hammer at the same time to let the big man know that he was serious.

"Drop 'em, both of you, or you both die," he said with authority, his voice quietly hissing the words. "Do it. Now!"

Hoss Johnson froze in mid-stride and tightened his body as if thinking about a defensive action. But Grant shoved the big Remington even harder into the outlaw's side and said, "Don't you even think about it."

Hoss dropped his gun and then snapped at his partner, "You, too, dammit. You want to see me die or something?"

"You've had worse ideas lately, Hoss, but I can't hardly remember none of 'em right off," Freeman Morgan said, watching Hoss scowl as the sarcasm slowly registered on the outlaw's face. But Freeman did as he was told and dropped his own gun onto the ground.

"We've only got a minute, so listen close to what I tell you," Grant said. "There's a man on your tail named Blake. He's a U.S.

marshal, and he's been chasin' the two of you for some time now, I suspect."

He paused for a few seconds, letting the words sink in, before he continued.

"While he's interested in killin' the both of you, I'm only interested in killin' him for what he done to my brother over in Jefferson County some days back. Max Blake kilt my brother, and I aim to make him pay fer it.

"My deal is that the two of you work with me to go get him."

"That don't sound like much of a deal to me," Hoss said. "I don't know this Max Blake. Heard of 'im, sure, but wouldn't know him if I knocked him down. And what do I care about yer brother? What if we jest say no?"

"God a'mighty, man, your head is as thick as a board," Grant said. "Ain't you heard half of what I just said? This Max Blake is huntin' the two of you down right now, in this very town. And he's good at killin' people – better at it than you want to find out.

"Look, it's real simple. You throw in with me, or I kill the two of you dead here and now, collect whatever reward I kin git, and continue on after Blake myself," Grant added simply.

"But with the three of us workin' together, it's easier – that's all. He cain't very well kill you two if we kill him first."

Freeman Morgan started to say something, but Hoss cut him off with a grunt and a poke in his ribs with a big elbow.

"I don't like it," Hoss said after a few more seconds of uncomfortable silence had passed. "I don't know anything about you, mister, and don't know nothin' a'tall 'bout a U.S. marshal chasin' around after the likes of us.

"Besides, there's three of us, not jest the two you see here now."

"That's another thing," Grant said. "Max Blake left your partner dead in the desert, buried in the ground till I dug him up just a few short hours ago and saw it for myself.

"He shot Weasel Morgan close in and dead as a stump, from the looks of it.

"Now what d'ya say about that, you dumb stupid silly bastards? Are you gonna work with me now?"

Not more than a few hundred yards away, but on the opposite side of the livery stable, Max Blake was slithering carefully along the ground. He was trying to get close to where he suspected the horses of Hoss Johnson and Freeman Morgan were tied; at the same time, he was doing his best to avoid the deputies, friends of the dead men in the saloon, and other nervous thugs with guns in their hands who were out looking for the two men who had shot up the saloon only an hour or so before.

Not an easy job, he thought to himself. *There's too much action now; too many people looking for the same two men.*

Max made his way to the base of a small juniper tree and curled around it, cautiously listening to the voices of two – no, he could hear three – deputies who were hanging around the door of the stables. Their voices drifted across the night; and while he couldn't see their faces, he could hear them talking plainly now that he had moved in close enough.

"Do you really think them two's dumb enough to come back around here and try to collect their horses? I don't believe that for less'n a minute," one of them said, a hint of nervousness in his voice despite the brave words.

"Then you tell me how in hell they's gonna git outta town if'n they don't ride out, Avery Burns? Honest to God a'mighty, but I wonder about you most times, Avery. I really do."

"You don't need to wonder 'bout me none, Toad Masters. If'n you'd think 'bout it a minute, you'd know I was right as a rainstorm."

"A rainstorm? A rainstorm in this part of the territory at this time of year? My gawd, man, but you done must've fried yer brain in the sun; I do believe that's true. What do you think about that, Jim?"

"Shut up – the both of you," the muscular deputy named Jim said. "Jest keep yer big mouths shut and watch fer sign out there. The two of you is makin' enough stupid noise to keep away the devil hisself."

"There's no one gonna show hisself here, I tell ya – the devil included."

"Jest keep yer mouth shut, else I tell the sheriff what's goin' on here. 'Cause he'll shut the two of you up fer good."

157

A noticeable hush fell over the two men, and the big deputy looked on smugly for a few seconds and then again directed his attention back to the darkness around him.

So the whispered mention of the sheriff of Aguante could shut up a passel of big-mouthed deputies, is it? Max considered: *That must be one tough, mean bastard of a sheriff.*

The stillness lingered for a minute, then two, then five or more. Max didn't move, and the three deputies didn't speak. The silence gave way at last to the sounds of the night and the insects that flitted or crawled or snaked about.

"Quiet!"

Max had just been about to move toward the far edge of the stables when the sudden command from the big deputy froze him again.

"What is it?"

"Quiet. Listen!" he hissed.

There was another long silence, and then the deputy called Jim said, "Thought I heard somethin' over by them trees across the way. Guess not."

"Want me to take a look and see fer sure?"

"Shhhhh. There it is again. Listen close now."

The three of them strained to hear what the big deputy had heard, looking off into the direction away from Max, and Max listened as well, trying to pick up some sound and trying even harder to see off into the blackness of the night.

"Prob'ly just an old hoot-owl, Jim."

"No. There's somethin' out there. Somethin' goin' on out there. I kin hear it. I kin feel it, too. Listen for it."

Max heard nothing. But he suspected that the deputy was right, and he wanted to get closer for a better look. He silently uncoiled himself from the base of the tree and, keeping low to the ground, quickly scrambled to the far edge of the stables to the right of where the three deputies were watching.

He came up to the edge of the building and abruptly pulled his back against the wooden siding, drawing in his breath and making every effort possible to remain motionless.

At the same time, he felt the thrust of a gun push hard into his ribs from around the edge of the stables.

"Don't move an inch," a voice snarled.

"Don't intend to," Max said, while at the same time thinking a deadly thought: *No. Not again.*

"Mind if I..." He started to turn around, thinking that he would play for some time and a ruse, when the dull thud of a gun whacking against the back of his head registered somewhere deep within his brain, and he couldn't finish the sentence that he had started.

Damn, he thought. *Not good...*

And then he surrendered to the closing blackness.

Chapter Seventeen
Mister Smith, or Mister Jones?

"Who are you? What are you doing here?"

The words sounded distant, jumbled – foreign somehow – and Max Blake puzzled at them for a time.

Where am I? he wondered. *And God, but how my head hurts.*

He realized after a few seconds that his eyes were open but were not focusing on anything; he concentrated, forcing his brain to think about his eyes and what must be immediately in front of him, and came to the conclusion that he was lying flat on his back, staring up at a ceiling of some sort.

He also realized for the first time that a man was looking down at him and was talking to him.

"Who are you? What's your name, mister?"

Max looked up at the man who asked the question. He saw a face with high cheekbones and narrow-set eyes with a thin mouth that couldn't hide the sneer of a cruel, even sadistic, smile. The man was wearing a buckskin shirt and vest that seemed somehow out of place in the desert, but Max knew that he had seen it before.

He looked hard at the man's face and deep into his eyes for a time and thought for just an instant that he knew this man – that he had seen him somewhere before.

There's something familiar here; something I should remember...

"I'm losing my patience, mister. Who the hell are you?"

The voice at least no longer sounded like it was distant or jumbled or foreign. And then it came back to Max with a rush: the three deputies talking by the livery stables door, his dash to the far corner of the stables to get a better view, a gun stuck hard into his

160

ribs, and then the blackness that surrounded him as a gun butt rattled off the back of his head.

He recalled in the same instant the man in the buckskin outfit who had calmly walked into the Aguante saloon after the gunshots that stirred up the town like a swarm of hornets – a big man surrounded by deputies.

Clearly he was looking up at the sheriff of Aguante.

Careful now, Max thought to himself. *This is the kind of situation that can get you in deep trouble – and you're in enough trouble already.*

Max shook his head once or twice, trying to clear away the fog that seemed to persist in his mind.

"Names don't matter much. I've had my share," he answered at last.

"What was the last one then?"

"Smith, I think," Max said. "Or maybe it was Jones; I don't remember exactly."

"All right, Mr. Smith, or Mr. Jones: Just what are you doing in my town?"

"Didn't know it was your town, mister. Just passing through," Max said simply. "I'm on my way to Mexico. I got rapped in the head back there awhile back. You know anything about that?"

"I'm askin' the questions here. And you'd best start comin' up with some answers – better ones than I'm hearing, anyway."

"I'm happy to oblige, mister. Head's just a bit off kilter, that's all," Max said.

"You never mind this mister stuff with me. You can call me either *sheriff* or *sir*. You got that?" the sheriff demanded, his voice filled with venom. He leaned in closer to Max and continued.

"I got a dead deputy with a hole shot clean through him and another who's been busted up pretty bad. That don't say nothing 'bout the saloon fight and the dead men in there not more'n an hour ago. Now you ain't the one done the shootin' in the saloon; that much is clear. But you are trying my patience sorely, and I don't have a lot of it anyways.

"So I want some answers from you, and I want them now."

"Sure thing," Max replied. "You mind telling me..."

"I'll tell you nothing – nothing at all. You're gonna tell me who you are and what you're doing in my town, or I'm gonna beat

161

you to within an inch of your life," the sheriff said, the agitation in his voice growing with each word that passed through his thin lips. "And then I'm gonna beat you to hell and gone again. Do I make myself clear?"

"Wouldn't do that right yet if I were you, sheriff – beat the hell out of me, I mean," Max said.

"No? And just why the hell not?"

"Because you wouldn't collect the reward money." He paused and then added, for effect, "Sir."

Max started to sit up on the bunk where he was stretched out, and he immediately noticed that he was in a jail cell and that the sheriff had company: Two other men wearing badges, obviously more of the sheriff's band of gun-happy deputies, were looming close by – one to his right, and the other slightly behind him.

"What money? How much money? What are you talkin' about here?"

Max had the sheriff's attention now, and he needed the slight advantage that it gave him.

He swung his legs over the side of the bunk and felt the back of his head. There was a good-sized lump that was still tender to the touch, and his fingers came away with the slight feel of blood, even through his thick black hair.

"That was a pretty good whack I took back there," Max said, trying to clear his head a little more while he further assessed the situation. He saw immediately that his Colt was gone from his holster, and his knife and the duped deputy's gun were gone from his boot, but he could feel the Knuckleduster still tucked inside his belt. That offered some degree of comfort, though he didn't like his odds any better.

The sheriff stood directly in front of him now, and the two deputies had shifted so that one was on either side of the sheriff; the deputies, in fact, had moved in close to him and had their arms folded over their chests – *like a couple of bad-looking bookends,* Max thought.

Surprised twice in the same night – and he groaned inwardly as the recollection raced through his mind. *Either I'm getting worse at what I do, or there are a damn sight too many deputies running around this town who are trying to arrest or slug or shoot the first thing they see.*

162

"Come on, mister. Quit the stallin' and talk. What reward money are you talkin' about?"

"Well now, let's see..."

Max stopped again, looking for any edge, when the sheriff broke in once more.

"You are gonna start talkin', beginning with your name." He drew his fist back and then sent it crashing into Max's jaw, rocking his head back. It wasn't the man's best shot, but it did warrant some attention. "Let's have it."

Max looked up and managed a thin smile, still trying to think of what he could say next that would buy him a little more time. "The trouble is," he muttered aloud, "well, the trouble is that my head just isn't clear enough to think straight. You'll have to give me a few minutes here. Sir."

"That's enough of this. Hold him, boys," the sheriff said.

The two deputies immediately closed in and seized Max by the arms, bending them well behind his back. Max struggled, but he was still groggy from the gun blow to the head, and the deputies were big, strapping men with powerful arms.

The sheriff took the time to pull on a pair of leather gloves that he kept looped over his belt. Then he stepped in close and, cocking his right fist, hit Max square in the jaw with a shot that rattled his teeth and almost sent him reeling into the blackness of unconsciousness again.

Max struggled to free himself and shook his head, still trying to clear it, when the sheriff hit him again – this time with a straight short right hand to his left eye. The power of the punch, even though it was thrown at close range, was incredible – the sheriff had put his entire body weight behind it – and Max could feel the eye starting to close immediately and the waves of blackness swirl around him.

He twisted hard in an effort to free himself once more, but the deputies continued to easily hold him tight.

He looked at the sheriff with his good eye and saw that there weren't going to be any more questions, at least not for a while. Max had seen that same look in other men before, in fact. It was a look of hatred. At the same time, it was a look of lust – the insatiable lust of violence.

The sheriff of Aguante obviously was a man who enjoyed what he did and gave some time and attention to his work.

"Lot of money," Max managed to spit out. "Enough for everybody."

"The time for talking's over," the sheriff said evenly, almost matter-of-factly. "You'll be lucky to end up dead by the time I'm through with you."

Cocking his fist once more, and again throwing his entire weight behind the punch, the sheriff hit Max with a solid, vicious blow. It split Max's cheek wide open and snapped his head back with a tremendous force that sent him falling into darkness for the second time in less than an hour.

Chapter Eighteen
A Respite From The Trail

Hoss Johnson and Freeman Morgan didn't like the looks of their tall, wiry, new-found partner at all, and they liked the message that he had delivered to them even less – a lot less, in fact.

The three men had moved away from the livery stable where Grant had first surprised the two outlaws with his sudden appearance and a gun and then had told them matter-of-factly about Weasel Morgan's death at the hands of the same lawman who was chasing them.

The news was not well-received; and keeping Freeman Morgan under control was becoming something of a problem.

Under the watchful eye and gun of the man called Grant, the three men continued to distance themselves from the livery and now worked their way down a quiet alley to an arroyo, which they followed beyond the outskirts of town.

Freeman was so upset when he digested the fact that his brother was dead that he was at once spitting, kicking, fighting, stomping mad – and he was losing the fight for self-control that both Grant and Hoss had demanded of him.

"What'd you say this bastard's name was?" he choked out through a rage of violent movements and gestures that alternated for the moment between kicking at the ground and picking up large rocks and throwing them as far as he could into the air in whatever direction he was facing.

"I done told you this already. His name is Max Blake. He's a federal marshal outta Twin Forks, which is all the way to hell and gone from here – and fer god's sake git control of yerself," Grant said.

He had holstered one of the big Remingtons, but he still held the other in his right hand, his finger lightly in contact with the trigger, his eyes in constant contact with the two outlaws he had picked for partners. "I'm surprised you boys ain't more knowin' 'bout Max Blake. He's got hisself quite a name in these parts."

"What fer?" Hoss asked, ignoring Freeman Morgan's bizarre antics for the moment.

"Fer killing people. What else?"

"I thought you said he was a damned federal marshal."

"He is," Grant answered while watching Freeman with a look that registered somewhere between amazement and disgust.

"Well, what's a federal marshal doing killing people? I thought federal marshals were supposed to – hell, you know, save people somehow, not kill 'em. What the hell is that?"

"He kills the likes of you and yer friend, and yer friend's brother," Grant said, growing annoyed with what he considered to be Hoss's mindless prattle and Freeman's strange and ongoing outburst at the word of his brother's death.

"Look, you boys want in or not? It ain't like you got much else going, seeing as how the sheriff hereabouts will string you up and shoot you full of holes at the same time, if he gets his hands on the both of you. So let's have it."

Hoss scowled at Grant and then abruptly kicked hard at Freeman's leg, catching him off balance and knocking him to the ground.

"Shut up a minute, Free, and let me think here," he said.

Freeman sputtered indignantly but remained on the ground, his hands clawing in the loose dirt.

Hoss went back to eyeing Grant suspiciously. He didn't like the man; there was no doubt about that. And he knew that Grant's offer of a so-called partnership, coming at the business end of a large Remington revolver, as it did, was only part of the reason that he neither liked nor trusted the man. But for the moment, at least, he knew that it was wise to play along.

"You got a first name to you, mister?" Hoss asked after a minute.

"Sure. Got one somewheres in the middle, too. But I don't use neither of 'em, and what's it to you anyhow?" Grant answered.

"Well maybe you do and maybe you don't, but I'll tell you what it is to me. If the three of us is gonna be partners, then I wanna know what to call you friendly-like," Hoss said without any effort to conceal the sarcasm in his voice.

"No need for us to be friendly-like. You jest call me Grant and leave it at that. Think of it as a first name, middle name, last name – whatever the hell you like."

"Grant, huh? Well, look here, Grant: Let's get one thing straight between us," Hoss said. "You are along for the ride on this one only 'cause I say so and only 'cause you know of this federal marshal fella and what he looks like."

"Seems to me that you ain't in a position to..." Grant said, his tone a mixture of irritation and surprise, but Hoss cut him off and kept talking.

"You shut up now and listen to me. You gotta know that I don't much like you any more'n I like this idiot over here" – he gestured at Freeman – "or liked his brother, comes to that. And I don't like the sound of this federal marshal none, whoever the hell he is and whatever the hell he wants.

"But you'd better figure out but quick that it's me gonna give the orders around here. It ain't him" – pointing a big thumb again at the still-sputtering Freeman Morgan, who had by this time gotten on his feet again – "and it sure as hell ain't gonna be you. You got that straight?"

"And what if I think different? Yer forgettin' the fact that it's me holding the gun."

The speed with which Hoss Johnson drew his own six-gun was so quick, so sudden, that even a seasoned outlaw like Grant was caught off guard. One minute he was convinced that he had been in control; in the next, however, he suddenly was looking down the chamber of Hoss Johnson's hogleg, which was cocked and pointed directly between his eyes.

"You beginning to see what I mean?" Hoss asked as he pressed the barrel of the gun into Grant's forehead.

Grant had his Remington aimed directly at the big man's midsection; his eyes, unafraid, remained fixed on Hoss.

"I track that all right," Grant said at last, taking the time to form his words plainly and distinctly so that Hoss would have no trouble understanding that he was dealing with an equal. "But it seems we got ourselves something of a standoff here," he added and tucked the barrel of his gun into the taut belly of Hoss Johnson. Both men smiled.

Freeman Morgan didn't seem to notice.

"That may be so," Hoss said at last. "If only I had me a partner who was paying attention to what the hell was going on around him –"

Grant laughed aloud.

"You'd best know right now that you ain't dealin' with no pilgrim here. You might be one tough, ornery son'bitch, but you got yer hands full dealin' with me. And that goes for the both of you."

"Let's jest kill 'im and be done with it, Hoss," Freeman said, although he was looking in the opposite direction, stooping to pick up rocks as big as his hand and then toss them high in the air. "Gonna come to that anyway, you know."

"Easy fer you to say at the moment, Free," Hoss said.

And then, to Grant, he said, "So how do we settle this?"

"I suggest that we do our business without trouble to each other and jest deal with Max Blake. After that? Well – let's just see where the cards fall after that."

Hoss carefully eased the hammer down on his gun as Grant did the same. Both men slowly holstered the weapons, their eyes locked.

They held the position with grudging respect for a full minute.

Hoss then turned to where Freeman Morgan had started to mumble and curse at the rocks that he tossed into the air.

"Shut the hell up, dammit Free," he called. "Yer gonna git half the deputies in this flea-bitten town coming down on us again, if'n you keep up with that racket."

"He kilt my brother, Hoss," Freeman said, his voice coming out in great heaves between deep breaths that he never seemed to catch. "He kilt Weasel, and now he's after us. I wanna get the bastard and kill 'im dead, Hoss. I wanna make him pay fer what he done to my brother."

Freeman kicked at the ground again with his foot. Then he did it again and again, all the while smacking his right fist into his left hand.

He looked back at Hoss with tears streaming from his eyes. "He kilt my brother, Hoss. Now why in hell'd he have to go and do that fer?"

Hoss watched Freeman for a while and then, shaking his head, turned again toward Grant.

"Tell me everything you know 'bout this marshal fella," he said. "I wanna get him, if'n fer no other reason than to shut up Freeman there." He shook his head as Freeman started to pick up rocks again and hurl them out into the brush.

"Not much to tell," Grant said, pulling out the makings from his shirt pocket so that he could roll himself a cigarette.

"Like I said, he operates out of Twin Forks; there's a mean, hard judge there named Radford, and he's hand-picked three of the toughest federal marshals in the territory. Max Blake is one of the three, and he might well be the toughest – by reputation, at least.

"He's a damn fair shot, from what I understand: Good with a gun, good with his fists, good with a knife. But there's folks about who say he's the best damn draw around – fastest and deadliest.

"One thing's fer sure: He's the lowest skunk around. I know how that idiot feels over there," and he pointed a dirty, tobacco-stained finger toward Freeman Morgan. "Max Blake kilt my brother, too. My brother was good with a gun – damn fast, he was – and Blake kilt him dead in a fight. That's why I'm on this trail, and I can't wait to finish the bastard off."

Grant paused when he finished with the cigarette and offered it to Hoss Johnson. Hoss took the smoke and stuck it into his mouth, and Grant started to roll one for himself.

"I'd heard of Max Blake off and on for a few years over in Jefferson County," he continued after a moment. "Most folks in our part of the country have. But I never expected to run into him until my brother had it out with him some weeks back. Blake killed my brother dead, and now I'm fixing to do the same to him."

"Why was he chasin' yer brother?" Hoss asked. "Or was it yer brother was chasin' after him?"

"One thing led to another and it's no one's damn business now," Grant said. "The only thing that matters is what's between me and Max Blake and nobody else."

169

He finished rolling the second cigarette and put it into his mouth. Then he pulled out a long match from his shirt pocket, struck it on the heel of his boot, and lit his own smoke before handing the match to Hoss Johnson.

"This guy being such a crack shot – fast and deadly, as you put it – then how do you suppose yer gonna beat him in a fight?" Hoss asked after he lit his cigarette and threw the match down. "You ain't got the speed to beat me."

"I'm not gonna get into any gunfight with Max Blake," Grant said. "A man would have to be a fool to do that, and that goes for you, too, good as you are with that gun of yours. All I'm gonna do is shoot the bastard good and dead – front or back, it makes no never mind to me. He'll be jest as dead, and my brother will be jest as served.

"You sure you ain't never run across Blake? Like I said, he carries a big name 'round these parts."

Hoss glanced at Freeman again when one of the big rocks that he had thrown landed within a few feet of where he and Grant were talking, but he said nothing.

"I've heard of this Blake fella a time or two, though never had the chance to see him close-up," Hoss said after a time, turning his attention back to Grant. "It's jest that I don't pay no never mind to that sorta talk, you know? I mean, who cares what federal marshal is fast on the draw? They're all worthless bastards to me."

Hoss paused for a minute, enjoying the cigarette that Grant had rolled for him. He looked over at Freeman again, shook his head in exasperation, and then continued.

"I spend a lotta my time in Mexico. When I get the itch, I come across the border and raise a little hell. Then I slip back down and across the border once more with whatever I kin carry and live high on the old hog till it's time to go and make me a few dollars more.

"So unless this guy Blake does much huntin' down in parts to the south, well, I wouldn't have much of a chance of runnin' into him a'fore this. But I've heard the name a time or two; it's something familiar-enough, I guess.

"Now this Blake fella, he didn't..."

Hoss looked up suddenly at where Freeman was starting to curse loudly again.

"Dammit, Free, you sit down and shut up before I knock you down again," he said. "That squalling' don't help none a'tall."

"He kilt 'im, Hoss," Freeman said, turning around and around in agitated circles as he spoke. "I don't like it. He kilt the Weasel good and dead. Gotta get him, Hoss. Gotta kill this Blake bastard for what he done to the Weasel."

"We'll get him, all right," Grant said, taking a final draw on his cigarette before throwing it to the ground and crushing it out with the heel of his boot in the soft sand.

He looked first at Freeman Morgan and then at Hoss Johnson, and he said again: "We'll get him; you can stack the deck on that, all right. We'll get Max Blake, one way or t'other."

"You sound all-fired certain of it, mister," Hoss said.

"You ain't?"

"Oh, I'm certain enough that this Blake fella's gonna die," Hoss said. "But I jest might be interested in making some spending money on who is gonna fire the one shot that kills him.

"Now it might be you. Then again, it might be Freeman, there" – he pointed over to where Freeman was continuing to kick at the ground – "although I wouldn't count too much on that right now. "And then, well, it might jest be me. You interested in puttin' down some hard money on that?"

"I wouldn't bet against me," Grant said, a hard edge creeping into his voice.

"Then that's noted," Hoss said. "Let's say a hundred dollars – gold money, no paper money – will cover that bet. That suit you?"

"Done."

The two men shook hands on it, and they both could feel the power in the other man's grip as their handshake tightened and then tightened again.

"Just remember, Hoss Johnson, that you've got your hands full with me," Grant said when they finally broke free from one another. "I ain't no Morgan brother for you to push around."

Hoss said nothing. His look of contempt, which quickly turned into full disgust as he saw that Freeman was back to rock-tossing, did all of his talking for the moment. He threw his cigarette away and patted the butt of his gun for reassurance.

The two men glared at each other again and then smiled.

It was dark, and Larry and Sally Nelson were talking in hushed voices so that they wouldn't wake their two sons, who were sleeping soundly in the next room.

They had been talking for more than a hour now, quietly going over their feelings and discussing again their plans and their dreams.

The Nelsons had decided to stay over in Indian Wells for a time – clearly because of the insistence of Sally Nelson – and the villagers had suggested that the family use the empty home of Pedro Ruiz so that they would be comfortable for as long as they wished to stay.

"Our friend has no need for the house now," Tomas Hernandez had explained to the Nelsons after Larry protested when the offer was first made. "You are welcome to use it for the time that you stay in our humble village. We know that Senor Ruiz would want it that way."

"It's really not necessary," Larry Nelson had said. "We only want to stay for a short time. Our stock needs rest. And my wife..." Nelson paused, not sure how to explain what his wife was thinking – or even whether he understood her feelings himself.

"We owe you all a great debt for returning Hector and Martin to the village," Hernandez had said after seeing that Nelson wasn't going to finish the sentence. "This is the least we can do to repay your kindness."

Now, a day after the simple but touching funeral ceremony of Pedro Ruiz, the Nelsons were talking once more about whether to go on to California, return to their previous home in Texas and start anew there, or to simply stay put – at least for a while longer.

"I like it here," Sally said, breaking the silence of the evening and her husband after their conversations had stopped and they both had let their minds drift deep in thought. "I think we should stay here, at least for a time."

"Why?" Larry asked. "Think about it. This place ain't right for us. We don't know anyone here, really. We have nothin' in common with these people.

"Most of them don't even speak English, and God knows I'm not going to learn Spanish – or Apache, for that matter. It's not fair

172

to you, and it's not fair to the boys, neither."

"Larry Nelson, I really don't understand you – even after all this time," his wife said. "These people are farmers. So are we. These people have been good to us, kind to us. They took us in, offered us food and shelter, helped us. Your sons are happy here; you can see it in their faces, if only you would take the time to look.

"For the first time in our lives, we are in a place where people care about us and care about each other. Doesn't that mean anything to you? Doesn't that mean anything at all?"

Nelson looked hard at her for the first time in a long time, holding her eyes. "Don't the dream of California mean anything to you anymore?" he asked in reply.

"Yes," she said simply. "It still does. And I still know in my heart that we will go on to California one day – or at least that most of us will.

"But not now, Larry. Let's just stay here for a time and enjoy this moment in our lives. That's not asking for too much, is it?

"I'm worn out from the trail and the killing and the violence and all the rest of it. I'd like to stay and share what we have and what we know with these good, simple, trusting people. I'd like to give them something back after what's been taken from them. And I'm tired, Larry. I'm just plain tired. Can you understand that?"

He considered what she had said for a moment, continuing to look at her. He loved the lines and the contours of her face, the spark in her eyes, the way her hair was brushed and pulled back, the softness of her features. And he remembered the first time that he saw her, spoke with her, held her, kissed her.

It all seemed so many miles ago.

"If that will make you happy," he said at last. "If that's what you really want."

"For now, at least, it is," she said.

"At least for right now."

Chapter Nineteen
A Flicker Of Hope

When Max Blake regained his senses again, his head ached with a dull throb that wouldn't go away, and his face – both of his eyes, his left cheek, his lips, his teeth, and his chin – felt as though it had been hammered enthusiastically, relentlessly.

He kept his eyes closed while his head slowly cleared, although he wasn't sure that he could open either one of them anyway. But if any of the sheriff's hired gunmen were nearby, Max didn't want them knowing that he had come to until he was far more ready to do something about it than he was right at the moment. And from the way he felt, it would be awhile before he would be in any shape to do much of anything – a thought that gave him almost as much pain as what he felt in his thrumming head.

He slowly and methodically began to take stock of his various body parts, and he didn't like what he felt and sensed.

He knew immediately that he had been beaten thoroughly, and by a man who knew exactly what he was doing: His face felt raw and tender, and his neck and shoulder muscles were sore as well – no doubt from trying to absorb the blows that he had suffered at the hands of the Aguante sheriff, even after he had lost consciousness.

He could sense that there were more than a few welts on his face, in addition to at least one good-sized cut on his left cheek. He concentrated hard and sensed that there might be at least one other slice in the same cheek, although it was hard to tell without looking, and he was in no position or condition to look.

He also was afraid of what he might see.

His left eye was closed tight, and it felt as though a crust of some sort had formed around it, clamping it tight to the skin. He

174

also could sense that there were a couple of hard knots on his head, both front and back.

He licked the right side of his lip and tasted dried blood; he got the same result when he tried the other side of his mouth.

Yeah, I'm a mess and I know it, even without looking in a mirror, he thought. *But at least I'm alive, which is a far sight better than a lot of men end up after they tangle with this Aguante crowd of cutthroats.*

Max listened carefully to pick up any sensation of sound or movement, but he sensed nothing and hadn't heard anything that resembled a human voice, at least, since his brain had started working again.

He figured that he had been left alone, probably in the same jail cell where he was attacked. He could sense that he was now in darkness, but he couldn't tell how much time had passed since he had been beaten or how long he had been out.

He waited for another five minutes, counting the seconds off slowly and deliberately to keep his mind off the pain, and then tried to open his eyes. The right eye fluttered a couple of times and finally popped open; it rolled around for a few seconds and eventually focused. The left eye remained shut.

Max waited while his one functioning eye adjusted slowly to the darkness. After a minute or two, he saw the thick bars of the jail cell off to his right. He turned his head slightly, winced in a wave of pain, and looked up to see a small window with thick iron bars above his head and to his left. It was nighttime, and he could vaguely see a half-dozen distant stars flickering faintly in the night sky.

Maybe there's only a single star up there and the rest of it is just my head acting up, he thought. Then he chuckled silently: *Under other circumstances, that might even be funny.*

Max slowly moved his toes, then his feet, and then his knees — just to make sure that everything was working. He started next on his hands, flexing each of his fingers, moving his wrists back and forth, and then making a fist with each hand at the same time.

He bent his arms slightly at the elbow, pulling his hands slowly toward his chest and then moving them slowly back to his sides and relaxing them again.

The pain seemed to be contained to his head and to his shoulders and upper arms. Everything else seemed to be all right and move all right, even if those movements made his head throb all the more.

Max relaxed for another few minutes, taking deep breaths, and then moved his right arm slowly across to his belt and patted at the buckle. The small, seven-shot Knuckleduster was still there, exactly where he had tucked it away.

The derringer gave him a flicker of hope.

These cutthroats never did bother to give me a good going-over – other than with their fists, he thought. *That kind of sloppiness wouldn't set well with the judge – or with me, for that matter. Maybe they're just too casual for their own good, or just too cocky.*

Well, I can do something about that, all right, given the chance.

Max moved his left hand up to his closed eye and gently felt around the edges. The skin was puffy in some spots and grossly swollen in others, and the crust that had formed beneath the eyelid grudgingly peeled away, but only with difficulty and stabs of pain that felt like thick needles were being inserted roughly into his skin.

He worked at the eye for another minute and was about to try forcing it open when he heard voices off in the distance. He quickly closed his good eye and pulled his arm down at his side again, feigning sleep, as the voices grew closer.

He could hear at least two men approaching his jail cell.

"...need to roust him, I reckon. Have a little fun with 'im along the way, while we're at it, too, maybe."

Max wasn't able to hear the first part of what the man said, but he figured that he was in for another go-round – and most likely for yet another beating. He knew, at the very least, that he would be hard-pressed to stop one, feeling the way that he did.

A second voice spoke up now as the two men opened the jail cell with a rattle of keys and then halted once they moved inside.

"The best thing for us to do is jest git him outside'a town, dump him off in some spot where the buzzards'll have him picked bone-clean by sun-up a day or so from now, and be done with it.

"As bad'a shape's that man's in, we wouldn't near even be needin' to waste a bullet on 'im. And he sure as hell wouldn't be any sport to us in the condition he's in. Let's jest dump 'im off 'cause there's no way he can make it back to town – or anywhere else, comes to that. You reckon?"

The first man spoke again, making no effort to keep his voice down.

"Naw, there's no need ta'go out that fer. We'll take 'em out a mile or so, plug 'im, and then git back here in time for sun-up drinks at the saloon. No need to make a bigger deal outta this than it's already become."

"I can't figger why we jest don't kill 'im here and now and be done with it," the second man said.

"Jest 'cause that's what the sheriff says to do, you know? If you want to cross the sheriff, be my guest."

"Well, what the hell? I don't see what one more dead cowpoke makes or means anyways to no one. Sure would save us a heap'a trouble to jest do it here and now and be done with it fer good."

"Yeah, but we'd best not cross the sheriff on somethin' stupid like this. Let's jest get this job done with, exactly like the sheriff wants it done."

The two men came up to Max now, and one of them shook him hard on the upper arm. The pain shot through his muscles, but he didn't move.

"Looks like he's still out cold, Jim."

"Damn small wonder. Look at the man's face. He's been beat up awful bad."

"Not near good enough, you ask me."

"Come on. You grab his shoulders and I'll take his feet. We'll hoist 'em out to the wagon and jest let 'em bounce along in the back for his last ride."

The two men picked Max up – one at his feet, the other lifting under his arms – grunted under his dead weight, and lugged him out through the iron bars of the jail cell, down a short but narrow hallway, and through a thick wooden door with large metal hinges that led to the back of the jail.

A wagon with two horses was hitched to a post, and the men – Max supposed them both to be Aguante deputies – heaved Max's body into the back without stopping to see if the jolt was forceful enough to bring him around. The pain that shot through his head was intense, but Max still didn't make a sound.

The two deputies had pitched him up onto the bed of the wagon so that he landed with some force on his back; but he instinctively rolled at the same time to help cushion the force, and his right arm was now cradled under his body to help support his weight.

This also meant that his hand was close to his belt buckle – and to the Knuckleduster that was still neatly tucked away.

The two men clambered aboard the wagon, and they started off with a shout at the horses; one of the men had a handful of small stones that he threw at the animals from behind to help get them moving.

They had rattled along for a minute or two when the deputy driving the team called across to his partner.

"Better git back there and check to see that all this jostlin' hasn't brought 'im around. You reckon?"

"You kin see fer yerself he ain't stirred none."

"Jest git back there and do as I says, 'fore I smack you upside the head a time or two."

Max knew that the wagon hadn't moved far enough out of town at this point for him to pull out the Knuckleduster, so he remained still and unmoving as the deputy climbed back onto the buckboard, steadied himself by holding onto the seat with one hand, and kicked at the prone marshal once, then again, with his boot in an effort to make him stir.

"Take it easy, will ya?" the man called out to his partner in the front of the wagon as he balanced himself in the jostling wagon bed. "Yer like to knock me clean off'n this rig."

"Never mind. Is he movin' or what?"

"Naw. He ain't stirred a bit. He's still out cold."

The man carefully climbed back to his seat in the front of the slowly moving wagon and sat down again, but Max could still hear their conversation plainly.

"Might be he's already dead, ya know? Wouldn't be the first time the sheriff beat somebody to death in one of the jail cells."

"Well, we'll make sure he's dead 'fore we taken off back fer town again, I kin promise you that. Last thing we want is this one turnin' back up at the sheriff's office askin' what in hell happened to him and who in hell done it. Why, the damn sheriff'd like to bust our heads fer that one."

"The sheriff's good at bustin' heads, ain't he?"

The two men started laughing at that, and Max slowly began working his right hand behind his belt buckle to get a grip on the brass handle of the Knuckleduster.

When the time comes, he thought, *I'll be ready. And these two won't know what the hell happened to them.*

At least there's some satisfaction in that.

Chapter Twenty
Diversions And Distractions

Hoss Johnson was searching for a way to get in and out of the livery stables of Aguante with his horse and with his skin, and he was having trouble figuring out how to succeed at either proposition.

He had spent the better part of twenty minutes pondering the situation, and he was no closer now to a plan than he had been when he started.

His frustration was beginning to get the better of him, in fact – made worse by the goading that Freeman Morgan served up from time to time.

"If you tell me to hurry it up one more time, dammit, I'm gonna shoot you myself and hand you over to that damned sheriff and his pack of wolves," Hoss finally snapped at Freeman, who by now had collected himself a little but was still not exactly right in the head – a problem that seemed to run in the Morgan family tree.

"It's bad enough we've got to keep dodging them deputies who're lookin' for us all over the place," he muttered in gradually mounting anger, this time addressing the mysterious stranger with the two big Remington revolvers who had forced himself into a partnership with Hoss and Freeman in his quest to hunt Max Blake.

"Look at all them bastards out there, hunting us jest like we was ordinary outlaws," Hoss complained, pointing in the general direction of the main street. "Ain't nothin' ordinary about us.

"And jest how do they expect me to figure this puzzle out when they won't even let us alone for five minutes of peace, anyhow? It ain't right."

Hoss spit at the ground for emphasis.

"Let's just go in there blastin' away and git our horses and ride," Freeman suggested, pointing to the stables.

"There's nobody man enough in this town to stop us; hell, we already proved that to 'em back in the saloon.

"Besides, I'm mad enough on account on what that bastard marshal did to my brother to feel more'n a might good about pumpin' some people full of holes jest about now."

"Shut up, Free. You're not helping the situation at all," Hoss said.

"Don't you try and get me started now, Hoss. Else I'm gonna have at –"

"You're gonna do nothin' less'n I say so," Hoss interrupted. "Now quit the jabberin' while I think about what in hell it is we need to do here, dammit."

Freeman started to respond again when Hoss quieted him once more with a raised fist and a deep-furrowed scowl; he then turned to his new-found partner, the silent Grant, who until this moment had remained distant and apart while Hoss considered the options available to them.

"I suppose you got somethin' to say there, Grant?" he hissed, more as a question than as a statement, but with a challenge in his hushed voice that he couldn't disguise and didn't want to anyway.

Grant shrugged, indicating indifference. He was keeping an uneasy vigil of watching for deputies and making sure that Freeman didn't go through any more of his bizarre anger spells that might attract attention to them.

"Naw? Nothin'? You got plenty enough to say every other time we've had any chance to talk," Hoss said, wearing the same scowl that had shut up Freeman a moment earlier.

"What do you want to know?" Grant said after a minute.

"Well, how 'bout it? You got any ideas on what we might want to do next? I'm askin' what you think here."

"What makes you think I've got an opinion?"

"Look, it's bad enough I got to carry this one around," Hoss said, pointing a meaty finger at Freeman. "Sometimes a man gits tired of doing the thinkin' for two or three others. So if you got any ideas, I'd like to hear 'em now. Else we jest might end up doin' what Free here wants to do: Go in there blastin' and git on our horses and ride the hell out of town."

181

"We need a diversion," Grant said simply.

"A what?"

"A diversion — a distraction. We need to start some commotion or ruckus that'll draw everyone's attention away from the stables. Then we can go in there, get yer mounts, and leave without no one bein' the wiser. Once we're out, we can figure out where Blake's gone to and catch up with him."

"Never mind Blake for a minute," Hoss said after a slight pause. "This diversion – distraction: like what, suppose'n? What kind of a ruckus – a distraction – are you talkin' 'bout?"

"How 'bout a fire?"

The words came from Freeman Morgan.

Hoss looked at Freeman and then at Grant. Then he looked back at Freeman once more.

"That you talkin' there, Free? You the same Free Morgan who a minute ago wanted to go in there shootin' up the place? I could swear you was the same Free Morgan who an hour ago was kickin' and pawin' at the ground like a bull with a bee in its tail end?

"Is that really you in there, Free? Come on – answer me now."

Freeman had a silly grin on his face by this time; he figured out half way through the litany of questions that Hoss was pleased with him, and that made Freeman happy – even if he did want to shoot at the first thing that moved.

"Yeah. It's me all right, Hoss. It's me, yer old pal Free Morgan."

"Well, Free Morgan, that's jest what we're gonna do. We're gonna go light us up a bonfire in this ol' town and see jest what the hell happens after that."

Grant said nothing. His mind was still on Max Blake, and all that registered with him was that a fire would serve to make it even more difficult to get to the federal marshal who had killed his brother.

Freeman's face, however, remained plastered with a grin as wide as the brim of his dirty Stetson.

There was just enough of a moon to cast a thin shadow across the dusty trail as the wagon carrying Max Blake and his two captors, deputies named Pete and Jim, lumbered out of town.

Max had managed to silently work his hand down to the inside of his belt buckle and had carefully wiggled the compact Reid's Knuckleduster free. He slipped two fingers through the hole in the handle and closed his index finger over the unguarded trigger.

The gun felt solid in his hand; it gave him a sense of security – a feeling that he could seize some control over his own fate instead of being at the mercy of the two men who were taking him out into the night to kill him and leave his body for the buzzards or the turkey vultures, or perhaps for the even worse things that lived in the desert.

But he did miss his Colt and wondered what had happened to it.

"You wanna snort?" the driver asked his partner in the front of the wagon. "I got a good whiskey jug stashed away in the boot jest for such a time as this here."

"A right friendly offer," the other man said. "Why don't you jest pull it outta there and dust it off a bit, if'n you don't mind." The two laughed at the exaggerated politeness of the conversation.

The deputy named Jim opened the small box behind the buckboard's wooden seat and found the jug. He pulled the cork as he sat back down and took a long draw, loudly smacking his lips when he finished. He took another pull and then handed the bottle across to the driver.

"That'll put another couple of hours on the day," he said as he wiped the back of his hand across his mouth.

"This stuff'll more'n chase off every mongrel and ugly woman in the territory," the driver named Pete said. He took a hard pull on the bottle and then swallowed with a gulp.

"But it sure hits the spot right now," he added. He took a second drink, wiping his mouth with his shirt, and belched loudly. "That is some powerful stuff," he said.

He passed the bottle back and then said, "How's he doin' back there?"

Jim looked behind to where Max was lying in the back of the wagon, watched him for a few seconds, and said: "Well, he ain't stirred none. I don't expect we'll have any need to share the jug with him, no sir."

They both laughed loudly at that and passed the jug back and forth once more.

The time's getting about right, Max thought, tensing himself for what he had to do.

He flexed his leg and arm muscles to make sure that they wouldn't fail him. Then, with a sudden spring, he jumped up in a smooth motion, ignoring the ringing pain in his head, and whacked the driver in the back of the head with the Knuckleduster. The blow drove the man right off the side of the wagon and onto the trail. He landed with a dull thud and remained motionless as the wagon rolled slowly past.

The second deputy looked up in surprise, still holding onto the whiskey jug, as Max rapidly stuck the gun into his face, pulling back the hammer at the same time.

"Don't move an inch," he said.

The deputy kept both hands on the jug and remained still, refusing to take his eyes off the small gun. Max was glad that he didn't move because a sudden wave of dizziness and nausea swept over him, not surprising after the beating he had taken only hours earlier and then his sudden leap from the floor of the buckboard scant seconds earlier. He steadied himself on the seat, regained control with some effort, and returned the steely gaze to his face once more.

"That's not much of a gun, mister," the deputy named Jim muttered at last as Max motioned for him to take hold of the reins from where they had fallen on the seat.

"It's plenty of gun at this range," Max said simply. "It'll kill you seven times dead. Pull us up here."

The wagon slowed to a halt, and Max quickly slipped behind the seat onto the flatbed where he had been riding. He felt better now, but he could tell that he had been worked over by an expert, and he silently vowed to settle up with the Aguante sheriff somewhere along the line – and sometime soon, if at all possible.

He reached into the deputy's holster, removing the gun there with his right hand while transferring the Knuckleduster to his left hand.

"That gun you jest pulled might seem familiar to you," Jim said. "It's your own Colt – damn nice piece, too. You can see I didn't hurt it none – didn't have it near long enough to do it no harm."

Max could tell by the feel of the Colt that it was his, all right. The engravings on the handles, which fit the curve of his right hand exactly, and the certain heft that the gun produced as he leveled it at a target were as familiar to him as his hat and his boots. He tucked the tiny Knuckleduster back into his belt and kept the Colt trained on the Aguante deputy.

"Kind of you to return it in one piece," Max said.

"Never mind that. It's a damn mean trick you pulled on us back there, mister," Jim said. "We thought you was out cold or dead, you know. And you hit ol' Pete there hard enough to kill him, I'd say."

"Let's go see," Max said. "But first take your pants off."

"Like hell I will."

"You will if you want to live," Max said. "You idiots didn't check me for a hidden gun. I'm not going to make the same mistake."

They both stepped out of the wagon, and Max waited while the deputy named Jim reluctantly unhitched his belt and dropped his filthy pants. "See, no hidden guns," the man said. "Let me pull my pants back up."

"Slowly," Max said. "Do it slowly."

He waited for the deputy to hoist his pants again and cinch up his belt before motioning for the man to walk in front of him; Max kept his gun trained on Jim as they walked a couple of hundred yards or so back to where the driver was lying in the dust off to the left of the trail.

Max quickly reached down and removed the man's gun, tucked it into his own empty holster, and then said: "Go ahead and check out your friend. Just don't make any sudden moves."

The driver was starting to come around at this point, and his loud groaning made his partner look up at Max. "Well, at least you didn't kill him," he said.

"Not yet, anyway," Max said.

Jim's eyes grew large, but he didn't say a thing.

"Help him up now, and let's get back to the wagon," Max said after a minute.

The driver, alert now, slowly realized what had happened. He looked at his partner and then at Max, and he shook his head a couple of times and tried to rub some of the trail dust out of his eyes and off his face. His partner gave the man a hand as he struggled to his feet. With a motion from the marshall's Colt, they started to walk warily in front of Max with their hands up, saying nothing.

"We really weren't gonna do you no harm, mister," Jim said, turning to look back at Max. "We're the law in these parts, you know."

"I've seen your justice first-hand," Max said. "Just keep moving. No talk."

When they got back to the wagon, Max ordered the two deputies to lie in the dirt with their hands on the backs of their heads. He climbed up on the seat of the buckboard, looked into the boot, and rummaged around for a few seconds before pulling out a good-sized coil of rope.

He tossed it to the deputy named Jim and said, "Tie him – up there on the bed of the wagon. Do it right," while nodding toward the man's partner.

The two men both climbed up onto the wagon, and Jim took the rope and slowly tied the hands of his partner behind his back. Under Max's directions, he sat Pete down and wrapped the rope around his legs a few times, tying it off in a good square knot at the base by his boots.

Max now took the rest of the rope and expertly tied Jim's hands behind his back, adept at looping the coils around with a single hand, all the while holding the big Colt hard in the man's back until he was immobilized. When he was finished, he motioned for the man to sit with his back to his partner and looped the rope around the two of them a couple of times. Then he bound Jim's feet tight, knotted the rope by Pete's boots, and tied what was left of the rope onto the wagon by wrapping it around the seat a half-dozen or so times and giving it a couple of sharp hitches.

"You ain't jest gonna leave us out here, are you, mister?" Pete asked. "Surely you ain't gonna do that."

The man was still groggy from the thumping he took a few minutes earlier, but he recognized the clear danger that he and his partner were in.

Max didn't answer immediately. Another wave of dizziness passed over him, and he was forced to pause to let it pass.

He finally took the kerchiefs that both men wore around their necks and used them as gags, knotting each one in the center and then sticking the knot into each man's mouth before tying it off tight in the back.

"You boys have been cooperative here," Max said as he unhitched one of the horses that had been pulling the wagon. "They'll find you all right in the morning, and no real harm done. But this had better be the last I see either one of you again in this life."

He reached in to where the whiskey jug had been left on the seat and took a short pull to wash some of the trail dust and remaining cobwebs away. Then he emptied the rest on the ground and set the jug back in the wagon. Max looked at the two hogtied deputies and nodded slightly, a faint smile crossing his face.

"You two might want to find a new line of work.

"Adios, and thanks for the drink," he said as he climbed onto the back of the unhitched buggy horse and headed back toward the outcrop where he had left old Buck and Weasel Morgan's horse.

Freeman Morgan moved around to the back of the saloon where he and Hoss Johnson had earlier started a shooting spree. It was a surprise move that no one in Aguante expected, and it worked brilliantly.

Freeman waited in the shadows while two deputies slowly passed by, and then he carefully stuffed the rags that he had soaked with lantern fuel minutes earlier into a small corner at the base of the tall wooden building, just as Hoss Johnson had told him to do.

"I don't need you to tell me how to start up no fire," Freeman had said. But Hoss had insisted on going over the plan in detail so that nothing could go wrong.

Freeman looked at the rags, thought about what Hoss had told him for another few seconds, and then pulled a match from his shirt pocket, struck it against the side of the building, and touched it to the rags.

That's got it, he thought. *Ol' Hoss'll be happy now.*

The cloth immediately puffed into flame and then into a crisp fire as the fuel took hold. Freeman took off his hat and fanned the flames a bit, watching carefully as the fire started to eat into the bone-dry wood on the wall of the saloon. Certain now that the flames would spread quickly, he hurried back into the shadows and continued to watch for another couple of minutes as the fire grew larger, quickly engulfing the back of the building.

"Gonna look like the gates of Hell itself here, pert quick," Freeman muttered under his breath as he crouched low to the ground and ran off back toward the stables, where Hoss and Grant were nervously waiting.

Five buildings down, he had to hold up while another couple of deputies paraded past – "no doubt lookin' for me," Freeman mumbled aloud – and then he took off again as the deputies moved out of sight and continued on until he reached the spot where Hoss and Grant were standing out of sight and in shadows.

"Well, how 'bout it?" Hoss asked as Freeman pulled to a stop by a cluster of small sheds that were gathered around a grove of short scrub pines. "I don't hear nothin' yet from down that way." He pointed in a broad gesture toward the saloon.

"You just hang on there, Hoss, 'cause all hell's gonna break loose thereabouts in a might near of a hurry," Freeman said, unable to suppress the toothy grin on his face. "I done it jest like you told me to, Hoss. You jest wait an' see."

"Well, let's be ready to move then," Grant said. "We won't have but a minute to make this work and get the hell out of here."

"Fine thing for you to talk, what with yer own horse in hand there, Grant," Hoss said. "You jest keep us covered and this thing might jest –"

The sound of excited voices carrying through the night air cut Hoss off short.

"Fire! Fire!"

They could hear the call plainly, even from where they stood a good distance off from the saloon.

An even louder voice called, "The saloon's on fire! We need help over here! Now!"

The clatter of a bell loudly banging suddenly shattered the night air, joining with the constant yelling of men's voices off in the distance. The three outlaws could see the flames shooting up into the sky now, and a glow of yellow and orange and red colors started to meld itself into the blackness of the night.

Two men emerged from the stables, both of them holding rifles. They peered around the corner of the building to where the fire was crackling in the night air and looked nervously up and down the street and then at each other. They were no doubt talking to each other, but Hoss couldn't hear anything from where he stood with Freeman and Grant. A third man came out, said something to the other two, and they ran off toward the saloon. The third man waited for a moment and then went back inside the stables, looking out at the night cautiously as he walked.

"That's jest what we've been waitin' fer," Hoss said. "Let's go."

Without a sound, Hoss and Freeman ran toward the back of the stables, keeping low to the ground with their guns pulled. Grant remained in the shadows, holding his horse's reins in one hand and one of his two large Remingtons in the other.

From the top of the outcrop, Max could see that a large fire had engulfed the entire back end of the saloon, its angry flames flicking high in the sky and the dense smell of burning lumber carrying even to where he watched.

He found Buck where the big horse had been left along with Weasel Morgan's; it was apparent that no one had come across the two animals. He stopped to pack up his things and saddle up Buck before turning the wagon horse loose; then he had climbed quickly up to the top of the outcrop for a look around and was surprised by the fire.

Max looked down at the commotion on the center street of Aguante and thought for a minute that he spotted the buckskin clothing of the sheriff down below, although he couldn't be sure because of the uncertain light.

But it was plain to see, even in the little light that existed outside of the flames that raged behind the saloon, that a bucket brigade had been formed in an effort to save the building; most of the men in the town, and doubtless some of the women, too, were passing water pails by hand along an unsteady line that streamed from a horse watering trough on the main street and then down the narrow alleyway to the back of the saloon.

There must be thirty or more people in that line, he thought.

Max watched, mesmerized by the fire for a time, and then he began to consider what might have started the blaze.

The thought came to him almost immediately:

Hoss Johnson and Freeman Morgan.

Max knew that to get out of town, Johnson and Morgan would have to get their horses. But the stables were guarded, so they would have to distract the entire town and then get their mounts and go.

Of course, Max considered. What better way than to set fire to the saloon – the one building that every single man and woman in Aguante would want to make certain was saved, at whatever cost?

Max quickly made his way back down the hill and climbed up on Buck. He had distributed some of the pack weight onto Weasel Morgan's horse, and he took the reins of the second animal in his left hand and headed out the long way around the town.

There's no question which way those boys will be heading, Max thought. *They'll be going south — straight into Mexico.*

And I'll be right behind them.

"One way or another, we'll end this thing quickly, Buck," he said aloud to the horse, patting him on the side of the head.

Chapter Twenty-One
Familiar Ground

In the sudden, almost stunning light of morning that began to bounce off every rock, Max Blake easily picked up the trail of three riders who were heading south, directly for the Mexican border.

He immediately determined that Hoss Johnson was one of the three: *a big horse with a lot of weight there*, Max thought. He also recognized the distinctive look of the horse's shoes from his earlier tracking of the outlaws across the dusty trail leading into Aguante: a single jagged nick in the rough-hewn iron on the back right side of the horse.

The other two horses doubtless belonged to Freeman Morgan and the man who had trailed him into Aguante – likely one of the disagreeable Grants from Jefferson County, Max considered, although he couldn't be certain of that.

The tracks were made by horses moving at a gallop, and Max knew that the three men had left Aguante in a hurry.

"And unless I miss my guess, Buck, we won't be alone in chasing these boys down, either," Max said aloud, talking to his big horse as he looked from side to side at the tracks.

Max knew that a handful of deputies, and perhaps even the Aguante sheriff himself, eventually would be riding hard on the trail after the three outlaws.

That would present some interesting opportunities, Max thought*, and perhaps even a chance to settle a score.*

But he knew that it also would make his job tougher in a number of ways. As much as he wanted to settle up with the sheriff of Aguante – and this was something that he most certainly wanted

191

to do – Max knew that he couldn't lose sight of the job that Judge Radford had sent him to accomplish in the first place: to bring to justice Hoss Johnson and the surviving Morgan brother, Freeman, either in the judge's courtroom or at the business end of Max's Colt Peacemaker.

But somehow he didn't think that leading a hog-tied Hoss Johnson and Freeman Morgan across the many miles to Twin Forks was a likely prospect – alive and riding, if not willingly then at least upright on their own horses – in any event. And then he had to determine who this third man was: the man he suspected of being one of the Grants from Jefferson County; perhaps it even was a brother of Jonathon Grant, the man Max had killed in a quick and bloody gunfight only weeks before. If it were a Grant, and if the man had thrown in his lot with Hoss Johnson and Freeman Morgan, that would only further complicate his job greatly, Max considered.

At the same time, he owed the Aguante sheriff a return visit; and somewhere along the line, he knew that the two of them would met again – the next time under far different circumstances, if Max had anything to do with selecting a time and a place. And he would see to that somehow; *I will willingly see to that.*

But first things first.

Even though Max had been riding for some time now and was still hurting from the beating he sustained in the jail cell, he was feeling better about things than he had when he first started out on Hoss Johnson's trail after leaving Aguante. The deep bruises, cuts, and welts that marked his face, his head and scalp, and his shoulders continued to make him ache and were sensitive to the touch, but at least he knew where he was heading and what was ahead of him.

He had stopped by a small stream and washed the cuts as best he could, taking the time to refill his canteens and to let Buck and the other horse with him, the one that only a day before had belonged to Weasel Morgan, drink a little.

But he was still in pain, and his head was off-and-on throbbing, depending on how much he was able to keep his mind off it. His left eye also remained swollen shut, although he could see well enough to ride and to follow a trail as obvious as the one that had been left by Hoss Johnson and his two traveling companions.

I'm just lucky that I don't have a mirror, Max thought. *I'm not sure I want to see how bad I look; it can't be a pretty sight.*

Max could see a small mountain peak off in the distance and another one beyond that. He knew that he was nearing the border, and he wanted to catch up with the outlaws before they left United States territory. It wasn't that he was reluctant to go into Mexico, although his jurisdiction ended at the border.

Catching these boys on the right side will simply make things easier in Judge Radford's courtroom, he thought.

And a contented Judge Radford makes my life a whole lot easier, at least during the little time I spend in Twin Forks. But the man can be hell in a minute, regardless.

The wind, which had been gusting at times, had picked up now – a little later in the day than it normally did at this time of year, Max considered. It was becoming a typical desert afternoon of searing heat and swirling hot winds, in fact. The dust was beginning to billow about in ornery gusts that stung his face and hands and any skin that was exposed, and Max was thankful that he could still follow the trail.

If the wind continued blowing as it was right now, he knew that all traces of the trail would soon be obliterated by the ever-changing and ever-shifting desert. He pulled a bandana from a saddlebag pocket and tied it behind his neck, covering as much of his face as he could.

Suddenly, for no apparent reason, the trail cut back to Max's right, heading due west, although three sets of return tracks covered the ones that he had been following, and another series of tracks cut out at a 45-degree angle back to the north.

Max rode ahead a bit and saw that a hundred yards or so beyond where the tracks turned to the west, the riders had simply turned around and followed their initial trail back to the spot where they turned away from their original course, now picking up a northwest trail.

Momentarily puzzled, Max got down off Buck's big back and scratched around in the dirt to see if he could pick up any sign of a struggle, an argument, a gunfight, perhaps – there might be a telltale cartridge lying on the ground – or even some heavy blood spots that would provide a clue as to why the three men had veered from their path toward the border and then remained on United States soil.

Finding nothing, he removed one of the canteens from the saddle horn and took a drink. Then he pulled off his already-dusty bandana, soaked it with the fresh water, and sopped it around Buck's mouth and nostrils so that the horse could taste the water without gulping and becoming sick in the heat. He repeated the action twice more and then did the same thing for Weasel Morgan's horse.

Shrugging, Max remounted Buck and continued following the new trail, keeping a careful watch for any sign of trouble. He looped the reins of Weasel Morgan's horse around the saddle horn on Buck, freeing up his gun hand so that he could be ready in the event of a sudden fight. And he cursed the fact that he had lost his rifle back in Aguante, making a mental note to include both the Winchester and the Bowie knife in his expense report for the judge when he returned to Twin Forks.

If I ever do get back home, he thought.

The land rose and fell before him in gently rolling sweeps and subtle hills, almost like the waves on a great rolling sea of desert sand. Scrub vegetation – mostly mesquite and gnarled junipers and Russian thistle – had formed in pockets here and there, but it was dwarfed by the immensity of the sand and desert that met blue sky and giant white clouds and a high yellow sun that baked the land and the men and the horses and everything else that traveled across it, or that merely sat in wait.

There weren't many opportunities to hide in such a place, but a man could stay low behind one of the rises and surprise an approaching rider – provided that the rider wasn't cautious and on the lookout for signs of trouble, Max knew.

The wind continued to blow hard, swirling about in gusts and raising little dust-devils around him, but Max still could follow the trail without difficulty. Another hour or less, though, and he knew full well that there would not be much of anything left to indicate that anyone had passed this way at all.

He pulled the still-damp bandana up to cover his nose and his mouth again, ignoring the horse smell because it helped to keep the dust out of his face. The fact that his left eye remained shut was a blessing at this point.

Max followed the tracks for what seemed like at least an hour or so – it was hard to keep track of time in the hot sun and the hard wind – continuing to head northwest, when the trail unexpectedly turned back once more to the north.

It was almost as if the three men had come to the edge of a cliff and were forced to change directions, Max considered.

The trouble is, there's no cliff here and no clear reason for them to turn like this. It's almost as if ...

"It's almost as if they want to head back to Aguante," he said aloud, surprised at the thought – and he was suddenly even more surprised that he hadn't thought of it sooner.

It made some sense, in a twisted kind of way, Max decided as he thought about the prospect. Hoss Johnson was known to spend time in Mexico between raids in the United States, and the three men Max was chasing would be expected to head directly for the border as a result. And in fact, they had done exactly that for a time before suddenly turning toward the west – no doubt hoping that the normal gusting desert winds would erase their tracks before a posse from Aguante would figure out that they were heading in any other direction except toward Mexico.

And no one was likely to look for them back in Aguante, Max knew: *Hell, every damned soul in Aguante is expecting them to be long gone and into Mexico by now.*

It's just that the wind is slow in rising today – a truly good break – and the fact that I'm on the trail sooner than the posse from Aguante could be raised and organized, he thought.

Max picked up his pace a little, anxious to cover the ground back to the town and anxious to get himself and his horse out of the wind and the constant, stifling heat.

A series of thoughts raced through his head as Buck picked his way across the desert floor, all of which kept Max's mind off the constant sharp pain that was shooting through his head:

Have Hoss Johnson and Freeman Morgan figured out that they are being pursued by a federal marshal? Is the man traveling with them really the same man I saw on the trail leading into Aguante, as I suspect? Is that man a relative of Jonathon Grant, the outlaw I killed in Jefferson County in a gunfight four weeks ago – or was it four months ago now, or even longer?

Who could keep track of such things, anyway?

Could Hoss Johnson and his gang expect to find help in Aguante if it boiled down to a fight on the streets between me and the three men I'm chasing? What will the sheriff do if he sees me again? Will he allow me to shoot it out with Johnson and Morgan and the third man? Or will he immediately go after me, forcing me to shoot it out with him and his deputies first?

What is that sheriff's name, anyway? What makes the man tick? What has turned him to the wrong side of the law, a dishonor to his badge? And what about the two men I left hog-tied to the wagon outside of town – the ones who were taking me out to kill me and then stake me as bait in the desert for the buzzards? Did they make it back to town all right? What would they tell the sheriff? And what would his reaction be? Are these two even alive now after losing me the way they did?

And still Max's mind raced on.

Does it really make sense for Hoss Johnson to head directly back into a swirling hornet's nest like Aguante? After all, he has made an enemy of every outlaw in the town by burning down the saloon: Even if a dozen deputies and the town's sheriff are tracking him through the desert at right this very instant, Hoss and his band of thugs still won't get any support from the rest of the inhabitants of Aguante – and certainly not from anybody who likes a good drink, which is probably every man and most all of the women in the town.

What do you suppose makes him want to return there, other than the element of surprise?

Then again, what if the three are not heading toward Aguante at all?

That thought took Max by surprise, and he almost dismissed it outright. But the more he considered it, the more he recognized it as a distinct possibility – for the simple reason that Hoss Johnson might have come to the same conclusions that Max had just come to.

What, Max supposed – *what if they just bypass Aguante entirely and are headed back into the north country beyond? What if they are headed toward some territory that already is familiar to them?*

The same logic applied, of course: No one would be expecting them in a place like Twisted Junction, where they already had twice robbed the bank and succeeded in shooting up the town without much trouble.

And no one would be expecting them in Indian Wells, for that matter – a place where they had shot up the saloon, killing four men in the process, and apparently just for the hell of it.

In fact, Max thought, *Indian Wells might just make an ideal spot for the Hoss Johnson gang to hole up in for a time.*

It was out of the way, for one thing – certainly off the beaten path for most anyone traveling through this country. And they would meet with no resistance there, either. The town was filled with sheep-farmers – simple people, men of the earth who were not used to the violence and gunplay that so marked the lives of Hoss Johnson and Freeman Morgan and no doubt the third man who was now traveling with the two of them.

In fact, Indian Wells just might be a perfect place to hide in for a time, Max considered. When their killing trail finally was good and cold and they could move around with some degree of freedom again – without having to look constantly over their shoulders for a posse or a federal marshal – they could head back toward Mexico and slip across the border without so much as a coyote or a rattlesnake noticing their passing.

There also would be no risk of being outrun on the way to the border by the Aguante posse, Max considered. The Aguante sheriff would not turn around at the border; nor would he stop to ask the indulgence of the Mexican authorities to continue the pursuit.

Hoss Johnson knows that; it might well be the overriding fact that has turned him around.

The more that Max thought about it, in fact, the more certain he became that Indian Wells and not Aguante would be the place where he would find Hoss Johnson, Freeman Morgan, and their new-found companion.

The thought of a showdown in Indian Wells rather than Aguante appealed to Max as well, if for no other reason than the three outlaws certainly wouldn't be expecting him to show up in that little, out-of-the-way village.

Unless, of course, they are leading me into an ambush, Max thought. But he quickly dismissed that idea: *Those boys stirred up a mess of trouble in Aguante, and they are running from it – likely right to Indian Wells.*

197

When he considered the fact that there would be no sheriff from Aguante, no dozen or more Aguante deputies, no meddling from outlaws on the streets of Aguante, Max became convinced that Indian Wells looked better and better.

It's almost perfect, he thought.

If it's true, at least.

It's just too bad that so many innocent people might get hurt in that village again.

Max thought once more about Hector and Martin, the two young boys who had ridden so bravely in pursuit of the men who had killed their friends back at the small Indian Wells saloon. He thought of Pedro Ruiz, the old man who had answered his questions so politely when he had first traveled through Indian Wells on the trail of Hoss Johnson and the Morgans. And he also thought briefly of the Nelson family: Larry and Sally and their two boys – *what were their names again? Jason and Josh*, he thought; but he was no longer certain.

There's no need to worry about them, at least. They're well on their way toward California by now, though I can trust Sally Nelson to make sure that those two village boys were returned safe to home.

It's not likely that I'll ever see those Nelson folks again.

It was just as well when it came to a gunfight, anyway. The Nelsons wouldn't be of any help in that kind of situation, even if Larry Nelson fancied himself to be something of a hard case in attitude, if not with a gun. Max knew the simple truth of the matter, of course – that Sally Nelson provided the strength in that family; and he felt more than a little sorry for her, and for her husband as well because of it.

The trail veered back to the northwest again, and Max turned Buck and stayed right on it.

You couldn't draw a line straighter on a map, he thought. *The three of them are heading right toward Indian Wells.*

And God help them, 'cause I sure as hell won't when the time comes.

As an afterthought, he mentally added: *God had better help every poor soul living in that village who gets in the way of what will come, too.*

And it will come, Max knew – *just as surely as the constant turning of the Earth around a distant sun.*

Max had traveled for another three hours or so when his one good eye spotted a large number of vultures circling slowly and easily on the currents of the desert air, a mile or more ahead and directly on the trail that he was following.

Something dead is out there, he thought. *Maybe a jackrabbit killed for the fun of it by Hoss Johnson or one of the others.*

Maybe it's something else, though.

"Let's be careful here and not end up as crow's bait ourselves," he said half aloud, aiming the remark more or less at Buck, but only because that made him feel better that he wasn't talking to himself.

Max scanned the ground ahead of him – steadily, methodically – searching for whatever had attracted the buzzards. He could see nothing out of the ordinary ahead of him, although the occasional swirling of dust-devils driven by the erratic winds, and the fact that his left eye was still closed tight from the beating he took in Aguante, didn't help his vision.

He rode on for another few minutes when he at last spotted something still and apparently lifeless ahead, lying off in the distance in a heap on the desert floor. A half-dozen or more vultures were gathered around it, and Max could now make out that it was considerably larger than a jackrabbit or most any other animal that might be naturally found in this barren, desolate country.

He pulled out his Colt and kept it ready in his right hand; but as he steadily drew closer, he could see the body of a man being picked at by the large birds – a man beyond complaining, a man beyond putting up any kind of fight.

Max kicked Buck forward and called out loudly a couple of times. When the birds refused to move, he fired two shots into the air, finally driving away the buzzards in a noisy, angry, fluttering, circling flight.

He rode hard right up to where the body was lying stiff and unattended in the sand and then quickly jumped off Buck, cocking the hammer on the Colt again as he hit the ground. Now no more than eight feet away from the body, Max crouched low and scanned the desert floor in all directions. *Someone might be out there, using the body as a diversion*, he thought.

After seeing that nothing else was moving, Max took the time to reload his gun, shucking out the two spent cartridges and adding fresh ones from the loops on his belt.

Making a mental note to replace those cartridges as well, he walked over and looked down at the lifeless body. He stared for a moment and then cursed softly under his breath, slowly shaking his head from side to side.

Despite a massive bullet wound to the head and torn flesh where the vultures had been feasting only moments before, Max recognized what was left of the face of the dead man.

"Now what in the name of hell do you suppose happened here?" he said aloud.

But Buck ignored the question, and the desert sage and sand gave up no answers.

Chapter Twenty-Two
In His Brother's Image

Freeman Morgan was beginning to lose control again; it started with a moan – a sort of low keening that annoyed Hoss Johnson to no end and that made his new partner, the man who called himself Grant, more disconcerted by the minute.

The three men had been on the trail since before sun-up, first riding hard out of Aguante while heading south, straight toward the Mexican border, before they turned due west after making little more than half an effort to disguise their tracks by doubling directly over their own trail.

Now they were heading northwest, back toward the little village of Indian Wells, where Hoss and Freeman's brother, Weasel, had shot up the saloon and "kilt us a few Mexicans or Indians or whatever the hell they grew there," as Hoss had so eloquently put it at the time. But Freeman didn't understand the roundabout way that they were traveling and the treatment that he was receiving from Hoss Johnson, and that had set him to complaining.

"All I wanna know is what we're a-doin', Hoss. Jest tell me that much," he said. "That ain't askin' too much, for gawd's sake. Is it? Jest let me know so's I kin think on it some. That's all I'm asking here. I wanna get the bastard that shot my brother, and this don't seem to be helpin' much."

"All you need to do is shut up and let me do the thinkin', dammit," Hoss had replied. "You talk too much, Freeman Morgan. And you ask too damn many questions to suit me. You always did, comes to that.

"Now I'm tired of the talk and tired of the questions. Jest keep that big gob of yers shut and let me work things out. And I don't want to tell you that again – you understand?"

"You're really makin' me mad," Freeman had said in return. "First, ya git my brother kilt by this low-life federal marshal. And now, damn you, you won't let me..."

"I didn't get your brother kilt, dammit." Hoss cut Freeman off with a snarling hiss; and even in the agitated state that he was in, Freeman knew enough to stop at least momentarily when he saw Hoss's big, meaty hand swing down to where his gun was holstered. Freeman knew from experience, in fact, that Hoss Johnson moved mighty quick for a big man: mighty quick, indeed.

"Yer brother got hisself kilt," Hoss continued. "He died because he wasn't smart – like we are smart, you and me, Freeman Morgan. And we, the both of us, are smart because I do the thinkin' for this outfit and because you don't.

"So shut up, Free, and let me think, will ya? We'll get this man Blake and kill him good and dead, all right, but we'll do it my way and to my likin'. So you jest shut the hell up now and stay shut up."

But Freeman didn't shut up and couldn't shut up, even if he had stopped talking directly back to Hoss. Instead, he started to make a low moaning sound that picked up in pitch and volume and intensity as the miles plodded by under the hooves of the horses.

Freeman was thinking about his brother, dying in the desert at the hands of a stranger – a man, as he saw it, who didn't know him or his brother; a man who had no reason to dislike either one of them; a man who didn't have any good reason to kill either one of them.

But now Weasel Morgan was dead, and Freeman couldn't even find out why they were moving in this crazy, messed-up, twisted pattern around Aguante and why, even worse, they were headed back to that stinking little village of sheep-farmers called Indian Wells.

Freeman didn't like Indian Wells, and he didn't like the fact that his brother was dead, and he didn't like the uneasy partnership that had been formed without much say-so from him with this Grant character, either.

The more that he thought about Grant and about his dead brother and about Hoss Johnson's nasty words and harsh treatment of him and his brother during the past several weeks, in fact, the more that Freeman Morgan moaned and mumbled and wailed aloud and generally lost control of himself, without even realizing that he was doing it.

Before long, he was starting to howl in low, coyote-like sounds. That unnerved Grant and also began to set off a slow burn in Hoss Johnson's brain.

"Good lord and gawd a'mighty but shut up, Free," he said at first.

But Freeman was in his own world now, and he really didn't hear much of anything that was said to him.

"Shut the hell up now, I tell ya," Hoss persisted. "And I mean right now."

Freeman, oblivious to Hoss, continued on as before.

"This partner of yours is pure loco," Grant said. "And you are, too, if you let him continue on like this."

"Whadd'ya want me to do?" Hoss asked. "You think I should shoot him 'cause he sounds like some lonesome mongrel howlin' at the moon?"

"That's a good end to it, you ask me," Grant said. "And the sooner, the better. He's starting to give me the spine-crawls, carryin' on like that. What's the matter with him, anyways?" Both men were looking at Freeman now, but he gave no indication that he either saw them or heard them. He continued to move his horse forward, all the while making the odd sounds of frustration and mourning and sadness and anger that had been welling up in him since hearing of his brother's death and that Hoss had previously prevented him from spilling into words.

"Well, it sure beats the hell outta me," Hoss said after watching him for a minute or so. "But he'd better cut it out plenty quick now, else I'm gonna put a stop to it for good."

"Well, if you don't, I'm gonna do it for you," Grant said.

"You'll do nothin' of the sort, mister, and that's a pure fact."

Hoss looked directly at Grant and scowled. "You raise a hand or a gun to Free Morgan, damn you, and you'll answer to me for it. Anything needs doin' here, I'll take care of it myself."

"Then take care of it," Grant snapped back. "You think yer such a fired-up trail boss, well, let's see you do something now. I'm ready to vote with that lunatic there in thinking that you don't know what yer doing – or even where yer going."

"I know exactly what I'm doin'," Hoss said evenly, his right hand once again hanging close to his holster. "And this ain't no votin' matter, neither. You kin get that straight right now."

"Then what's it all about?" Grant asked. "You tell me how heading into this little flea-bitten place of a town is gonna help us kill Max Blake any faster or any better. And tell me quick."

"This Blake fella is your concern, not mine," Hoss replied. "What makes you think I give a good damn about him, anyhow? He killed yer brother, not mine. Yer brother was nothing to me, surely.

"And if he killed Weasel Morgan, like you say he did, well, the Weasel was nothing to me, neither – jest one more gun to plan for, to think for. He was jest one more mouth to feed along the way. And that one there" – waving his arm in Freeman's direction – "is a big enough mouth at this minute to worry about right now, I'd say."

Hoss was within five yards of Freeman now, and he yelled as loud as he could: "Freeeeeemannnnn Morrrrrrgannnnnn! Shut the hell up!" But Freeman Morgan took no notice at all.

Hoss looked for another minute at Freeman as he continued to wail and moan, then curse and mumble again. Hoss noticed that Freeman would seem to break into a chant of something not quite intelligible; then he would suddenly hoot and yip, holler and shake his fist, all the while keeping his glazed eyes fastened directly forward, seemingly hearing or seeing nothing else around him.

Hoss shook his head and then moved his horse closer to Grant's and looked him square in the eye. He was concentrating hard on what he was about to say to Grant, and he managed to get his mind off Freeman, at least momentarily, for the first time in a lot of miles.

"I'll tell you why we don't ride into Mexico. We don't ride into Mexico because there ain't no money in Mexico," Hoss said. "All there is in Mexico is heat and sweat. And I've had more'n enough of both of them to last me a lifetime.

"Besides, they was expectin' us to go into Mexico – them bastards back in Aguante, I mean. No one's gonna think that we doubled back to go to Indian Wells, of all the damned places in the territory. If they do track us 'fore the wind blows out the trail, they might think we're headin' back into Aguante, just to shoot up the place again and raise some more hell there.

"But not Indian Wells; they won't expect us to head back there."

"So what? Why go to Indian Wells at all?" Grant asked. "There's no money there, neither; all there is there is heat and sweat – and you already said you've had enough of both. You know that I want Blake dead; he's the only concern I got – not money nor heat nor sweat."

"Won't do you no good to get kilt a'fore you get the chance to settle up with Blake. And that's what's comin', if'n you hang around these parts without no plan. We shake off the Aguante crowd, we loop around on Blake, and then we go and git him.

"And Indian Wells is the right place to work from, you ask me," Hoss said. "There's no one in that little piss-ant town is gonna bother us none. We can come and go as we damn well please. We can eat what we want, sleep where we want – fer gawd's sake, Free, shut up! – take us a woman if we want. We can pull some raids, pick us up a few dollars, take care of this Blake bastard, and then head back into Mexico when things are more quiet-like.

"And if anyone follows us into Indian Wells, it'll be the same damn federal marshal you seem so all-fired anxious to git shut of. So if we's lucky enough to have him chase us into that stinkin' little 'breed village, then you can kill him dead or watch me do it – it sure as hell makes no never mind to me. Now how's that fer a plan?"

They moved along in an uneasy silence for a few more minutes, both of them more and more annoyed by Freeman Morgan's wailing, while keeping a wary eye on each other. Grant wanted to say something more, but he thought better of it when he saw the look on Hoss Johnson's stern, brutish face.

Suddenly and with no warning Freeman Morgan pulled his revolver out of his holster and was cocking the hammer. He was looking directly at Hoss Johnson, but his eyes still were glazed over – almost like a doll's eyes or a dead man's eyes: staring straight ahead, all right, but lifeless and sightless at the same time.

The unmistakable metallic click of the gun being cocked was the only thing that Hoss Johnson focused on, however. Thinking quickly, he pulled his own gun while dropping low across the neck of his horse at the same instant that Freeman Morgan fired.

Freeman's shot was aimed directly at where Hoss should have been. The sudden bang of the gun startled Freeman's horse, and it lurched forward a little, bouncing the dazed and still-mumbling man back and forth like a spineless rag doll in the saddle.

Still crouched low, Hoss used the delay caused by the sudden movement of Freeman's horse to fire his own gun a single time. The bullet entered through Freeman's left ear and shattered the right side of his head, knocking his hat off at the same instant.

Freeman Morgan rolled off his horse slowly, slumping over as the startled animal quickened its pace for a second or two and then, realizing that something was wrong, slowed and came to a sudden stop.

Freeman's right foot was caught in the stirrup, and his body was now twisted on the ground so that he was lying on his back with his left arm outstretched; what was left of his head was bent in an unnatural position that scraped along the desert floor.

A large red stain already was seeping into the sand.

Freeman's eyes, still open, registered none of the horror or surprise that generally went with sudden death and that took a good undertaker's patient skills to erase. They continued to stare out, as empty and as sightless and as glazed-over as they had been just before Hoss Johnson opened them permanently with the loud crash from a solitary bullet.

Grant had one of his big Remingtons pulled at this point, but Hoss already was pointing his own gun directly at his surprised and only remaining partner and was now sitting up straight up in the saddle again, a slow smile spreading across his broad face.

"Put it away. Fun's over," he said simply.

Grant did as he was told after looking at Hoss's gun, which was pointed directly at his heart, and then he looked over at the dead body of Freeman Morgan. He said nothing as he climbed off his horse and went over to where Freeman was lying, kicking his right boot loose from the stirrup so that the body could slump free to the ground.

"I'll take the gun and the horse with me," Hoss said. "But you be real careful how you fetch ol' Free's gun up to me there now. I jest might become sentimental 'bout that piece in time."

"You gonna bother to bury him?" Grant asked.

"You bother all you want," Hoss said. "I ain't all that sentimental. All I wanna do is get outta this god-awful heat."

Grant carefully picked up Freeman's gun, which was lying in the sand by the dead man's right hand, and handed it up to Hoss after turning the barrel around. He picked up Freeman's hat, dusted the sand off it by beating it on the side of his pant leg a couple of times, and examined it for a few seconds before finally throwing it over Freeman's face.

"He looks damn near like his brother did when I found him lying in that shallow grave out in the sand," Grant said, looking up at Hoss. "Hard to tell one from the other now."

Then he took the reins of Freeman's horse, walked back to where his own horse was standing, and swung up into the saddle again.

They started off once more, and Hoss was careful not to let Grant slow his horse or get behind him.

"Well, I shut him up for you, anyways," Hoss said after they had traveled for several hundred yards in silence. "You got any more complaints?"

"You just leave Max Blake for me when the time comes, ya hear?" Grant said. "I don't care how many sun-crazed half-wits you kill. I want Blake for myself."

"Yeah? And then what, Mr. Grant? Then what do ya think yer gonna do next?"

"Then we'll see, I guess."

Hoss Johnson started to laugh – a low laugh at first that quickly increased in size and volume and became a big, horse-bellied laugh that was as large as Hoss Johnson himself.

And he laughed for a good long time.

Chapter Twenty-Three
A Sweet Little Place

Sally Nelson had just come out of the house where she and her family were staying in Indian Wells when she heard the sound of gunfire: one, two, a pause, three, and then four – no, five – five shots in all, she counted.

She was standing at the stoop in front of the small, wooden-framed door with a mesquite broom in her hand; she had been trying to get the accumulated dust and dirt – seemingly a lifetime of it, she had considered – out of the house that had until only recently belonged to the town's respected mayor and elder citizen, Pedro Ruiz.

But Ruiz had been killed for no apparent reason by some kind of outlaw: a bandit, a bounty hunter, a hired killer – no one really seemed to know for sure. Now Sally Nelson and her husband and two children had been invited by the villagers to stay in the Ruiz home for as long as they wanted to use it, and she had been enjoying the tranquility of the place.

Until now, at least.

What she heard right now chilled her to her soul.

She knew that the sound of gunshots in Indian Wells in the early morning hours could only mean one thing: that something was definitely, positively, absolutely wrong. The sharp sounds both shocked and frightened her. And she thought of one thing only: her children.

"Jason! Josh! Where are you?"

She hurried back into the house, calling loudly as she ran through the modest open living area and into the small adjoining

208

spot that the boys had been using as a bedroom. She pulled back the tattered blanket that separated the bedroom from the living room but found nothing.

Yelling even louder now – "Josh! Jason!" – she turned and ran directly into her husband, who had heard her cries and walked in from the back of the house to see what was wrong.

"Sally, what in the world?" Larry Nelson asked.

"The boys – have you see the boys?" she asked breathlessly.

"Well, yes and no. What is it? What's the matter?"

"Larry, I just heard gunshots – five gunshots – from down the street toward the saloon. Where are the boys? Where are they? We need to find them now."

"They are out back with Hector and Martin. I saw 'em not more'n twenty minutes ago, rompin' around and havin' a grand time. Mucho grande. Why get excited about a few gunshots, anyhows?"

"Think, Larry. This is Indian Wells, not Dallas – and not even El Paso. Most of the men in this town don't even own guns. When you hear gunfire here, you know that something's wrong. We need to find Jason and Josh. We need to find them right now."

"Well, I really don't think we need to git too worked up here, woman. But I'll help you find the boys if'n it'll make ya feel any better," he said.

"I was jest in the back room there, cleanin' up some of the wagon parts," he continued. "Didn't hear a thing, myself. Where'd you say you heard the shots comin' from?"

But Sally was already out the back door, calling loudly.

"Jason! Josh! Come home this instant. Both of you."

Off in the distance, she heard another gunshot.

She turned frantically to look for her husband, who was just emerging from the house. "There. Did you hear that?" she asked.

"Hear what?"

A look of panic covered her face now. "Where did you say you saw them, Larry? Where were the boys when you saw them last?"

"Jest right down there," he said, pointing to a small ravine that dropped several hundred yards behind the house and was swept up into a small grove of junipers. "I'm sure they're right down there somewhere..."

209

She didn't wait for him to finish; instead, she started running as fast as she could down the hill toward the trees. "Jason! Josh! Come back here this instant! I want you both home now!"

Larry Nelson shrugged and calmly started walking after his running wife.

In the lone saloon in Indian Wells, Hoss Johnson was seated at one of the small tables scattered around the wood-planked floor, a bottle of tequila on the table. His new partner and drinking companion, the man called Grant, was seated across the table from him, his feet stretched out on a nearby empty chair.

The appearance of Grant and Hoss Johnson in the saloon touched off a panic in the bartender and the two village patrons who were inside when the outlaws strolled in and walked casually up to the long wooden bar.

The bartender had immediately recognized Hoss as one of three men who had killed four people in the saloon only days earlier. And he knew the face of Grant immediately as well; it was a face that he had hoped to never see again. Tomas Hernandez muttered a silent prayer of some sort, crossed himself twice, and then reached under the bar for an old shotgun that he kept for occasions such as this.

"No, no, and no," Hoss said, almost good-naturedly, wagging one of his huge fingers back and forth as he saw the expression on the bartender's face and his reaction in reaching beneath the bar.

Hoss had his gun pulled a second later and fired off a shot that shattered the small mirror behind the bar. He quickly fired twice more, breaking bottles on either side of the bartender.

The noise and the flying glass caused the man to drop the shotgun on the floor and raise both of his hands in the air; the two other men in the saloon, both of whom were unarmed, did the same.

"That's better – a far-sight more friendly," Hoss said.

He pointed his gun directly at the bartender's head, carefully aimed, and then jerked his hand up a little as he fired a fourth bullet, which echoed loudly as it slammed into the thick wood paneling behind the bar. Then he fired a fifth time, again hitting the same general area, after first aiming at the bartender's head again.

"Haw haw haw." Hoss bellowed out an exaggerated laugh, a huge smile creasing his face. "I see yer glad to welcome me back, amigo. Gracias.

"And surely you didn't think I was going to kill you now, did you? Jest who else would I get to serve me a drink but my favorite bartender?"

Hoss looked around the saloon and saw the two village men cowering in the corner, both with their hands still in the air.

"You boys best run along and git yer drinks somewheres else today," Hoss said. "I'm stakin' claim on this place fer sometime to come.

"Go on – git movin'."

The two men were frozen to the spot, and Hoss pointed his gun in their general direction and then waved it toward the door.

"Go on now," he said, a rasping harshness starting to develop in his voice. "Git outta here now; you do like I tell ya. Pronto."

The bartender shouted out a sharp command in a language that neither Hoss nor Grant understood, and the two looked at him for a second and then bolted for the door. Hoss fired his last bullet into the roof of the saloon as the two men cleared the batwing doors; he was laughing loudly again as the pair scampered through and out into the narrow street.

"Now," he said as he pulled up a chair to the table nearest to him and started to reload his gun, "you can bring me a bottle of yer best tequila. And you'd best bring a couple'a clean glasses with you, too. Ya git me?"

"Si, senor," the bartender said and turned to get a bottle.

Grant flopped his long legs up across the wooden seat of a second chair and relaxed.

"You see now why I'm partial to this here little town?" Hoss asked him without looking up from his gun. He had shucked out the spent cartridges and was busy inserting fresh rounds into the cylinder.

"Yeah, this is really a sweet little place, all right," Grant said sarcastically. "It was a dump when I was here last, and it's still a dump. Let's jest hope that Max Blake does like you think and shows up. That's all I damn well care about."

"Don't you worry about that none," Hoss said, snatching the bottle out of the bartender's hands as Hernandez arrived at the table. Hoss pulled the cork, took a long pull while ignoring the glasses that the bartender had set down on the table, and looked hard at Grant.

"By this time, yer friend Blake has likely found ol' Free Morgan out there in the sand. He'll be comin', all right. He'll figger we can't make a bed in Aguante, and he knows we ain't got a lot of other options. So he'll come rollin' in here, jest as sure as dust and dirt.

"And when he does, we'll be ready for 'im. Jest you wait and see."

Grant reached across the table and took the bottle out of Hoss's meaty hands. He poured himself a drink and then set the bottle back on the table.

"You'd better be right, Hoss Johnson," he said, "or we jest came a long way to this dump fer nothing – and fer no good reason at all."

"Why, I don't think you've caught the spirit of this place quite yet, Grant ol' boy. We're gonna do jest fine here; you jest wait 'n see. This place'll be like home in no time."

Grant said nothing.

And Hoss Johnson winked and took another long pull on the tequila bottle, smacked his lips loudly, and smiled.

Max Blake was feeling better. His left eye had started to open some, especially if he thought about it and concentrated hard on focusing the eye on something, and his head wasn't pounding any longer.

Or at least it isn't pounding near as much as it was a few hours ago, which is a blessing, he thought.

Even though the wind had long since obliterated any trace of the tracks that he had been dutifully following, Max wasn't worried: He had long since passed the Aguante cutoff and was moving along at a good pace toward the Mexican-Indian village of Indian Wells, where he was certain that he would find the renegade Hoss Johnson and at least one other man traveling with him.

The identity of the second man still was a question mark to Max, but he had a good hunch. Having given it a lot of thought across the bleak desert miles, he had good reason to suspect that the man was one of the Jefferson County Grants. No doubt the man had been tracking him to exact some revenge for his brother's death and had now thrown in his lot with Hoss Johnson, Max considered.

There was no question about the identity of Freeman Morgan, the man Max had found lying dead in the desert. Max had done his best to cover the body over so that the buzzards couldn't pick the bones clean. But he didn't really have any tools – shovels and such – to do the job properly; and so he had scraped at the dirt with the blade of his small eating knife, eventually succeeding in making a lump in the sand. He had briefly looked in vain for some kind of rock or a piece of wood to mark the grave; but finding nothing other than the dead man's hat, he used that and quickly moved on.

Respect for the dead is one thing, Max thought. *But I don't want to let those two get so far ahead that they kill somebody else without me there to put a stop to it.*

As he continued to move through the desert, Max had given some thought to who might have killed Freeman Morgan – and why. There were many possibilities, each one as good as the next. In the end, however, he decided that it didn't really matter much who had killed him – *or even why he has been killed, comes to that.*

All that really mattered was the fact that Freeman Morgan was stone cold dead and wouldn't be any threat to Max – or to anyone else in the territory – ever again. And there was some comfort in that thought.

The heat was intense, and Max did his best to take it easy on the two horses: Buck, his own gelding, and the one that had belonged to Weasel Morgan, the very dead Freeman Morgan's own very dead brother. Max had stopped a couple of times to sponge out the horses' mouths, taking a drink himself at the same time. He also would get down and walk for a ways from time to time to help his big horse cope with the heat.

At one point, Max had even tried to spell Buck for a time by taking a turn on Weasel Morgan's horse. But Buck didn't seem to care much for the inactivity, and Max only stayed with it for an hour or so before switching once again.

He was drawing closer to the mountains now. The scrub brush and small but thick clumps of juniper and pine were less spotty and greener here, and the ground started to become firmer. He could now see the thin outline of snow-capped mountains rising sharply off in the distance and a long line of trees a few miles ahead, probably marking the stream where he had first met up with the Nelson family and then the village boys, Hector and Martin.

The Nelsons, he believed, would be long gone and of no concern in a fight with Hoss Johnson and his partner.

I hope those two boys are all right, Max thought.

I just need to get to that village in time.

Jason and Josh Nelson, along with their mother and the two village boys, Hector and Martin, were huddled in the small adobe home that was being used by the wayfaring Nelson family, formerly of Texas and other parts east.

Sally Nelson's frantic search for her children had worried her husband, and he was happy to go out to their wagon and pull a rifle and a revolver from the boot after the boys finally answered her call and came out from the trees where they had been playing and hiding from each other.

Sally still has a concerned look on her face, but she's some better now, Larry thought.

"You gonna be all right?" he asked.

"I'm not sure," she said. "I have this feeling that something bad has happened again, or perhaps is just about to happen. I can't really say for certain."

"Are you jest wishin' that we had headed off to California like I wanted to some days back?" he asked, unable to disguise both the frustration and smugness in his voice.

"Wishing won't help us or can't help us, and never has," Sally said. "Wishing we were in California right now can't make it so. But I do wish that I knew what caused those gunshots down the street a few minutes ago."

She paused, looking at the faces of the four children who were gathered on the floor around her, staring back at her with large, quizzical eyes but saying nothing – only listening.

"Then again, maybe I really don't want to know."

"Well, I think I'll jest head on down the street and find out," her husband said. "Can't be much to it, and it'll make you feel a sight better once you know there's nothing a'tall to be concerned about."

"I don't want you leaving this house, Larry Nelson," Sally said firmly.

But he ignored the command and said, "Here, I'll leave you the rifle. That should make you feel some better till I get back."

"Larry, you're not listening to me," she said. "I don't want you to leave here now." Her voice was firm, sharp, commanding. But her husband paid it little mind.

"It'll be all right," he said, stopping for a moment at the door. "I won't be long. And when I get back, you kin fix us all a good meal. I'm just startin' to notice how hungry I am."

"Larry Nelson, I really ..."

But he was already through the door and moving down the street.

"God help me, Larry Nelson, but I just don't understand you," she sighed, listening to the fall of his bootsteps on the hard-packed dirt path outside. "And I don't think I ever have."

She was quiet until she could hear nothing but her own breathing and the muted sounds of the children. Then she looked up, forced a thin smile at them, and said, "All right, young men of mine, let's play a game."

"What should we play?" Jason asked.

"Let's pretend that bad men are coming to look for us," she said. "So what we need to do is look for the best hiding places that we can possibly find. Does that sound like fun?"

"Can Hector and Martin play, too?"

"Yes, I want Hector and Martin to play, too," she said. "I want us all to find hiding places. Good hiding places."

"Ma, you don't think that anything will, you know, happen to Pa, do you?" her oldest son asked. "You seem awful worried."

"Let's just play the game, boys," she said. "Let's concentrate on that and nothing else right now, all right?"

215

Max crossed the stream, stopping only long enough for the horses to drink while he refilled the canteens and splashed some water on his face and over his head.

I need a good shave and a bath – a nice, hot bath, he thought.

Wouldn't hurt to have some pretty young thing wash my back, either.

The picture that entered Max's mind made him smile, and he got up slowly from the bank and dusted off his shirt and denim pants with his hat.

Wouldn't mind having a wife sometime, he thought. *Wouldn't mind raising up a couple of good, tall boys, either – like young Joey Gray back in Twin Forks. Or like those two Nelson lads: They seemed nice enough, too, though on the quiet side.*

Heck, even the two village boys, Hector and Martin, were good kids – brave ones, too: the kind who would make any father proud.

But being a federal marshal was no job for a man with children, Max considered.

No, as long as I'm hunting a killing trail, there'll be no wife and no children in my plans.

And I don't see myself changing – not for a long time off, anyway.

Max swung his lean body back up on Buck and started off again, trailing Weasel Morgan's horse behind him.

"With any luck at all, Buck, we'll be in Indian Wells by sundown," he said aloud.

Larry Nelson didn't figure to be gone longer than ten minutes. The way he had it planned, he would take a slow walk down to the center of town, check at the saloon to see if anyone there had seen or heard any gunshots or anything else out of the ordinary, and then he would casually stroll on back to the house and sit down to a good, home-cooked meal.

There were many reasons to enjoy the pleasure and companionship of his wife, but chief among them was her cooking; at least that was what he thought every time he was hungry – and he was hungry right now.

The street was quiet; it was deserted, in fact, with not a soul around. *That's a little unusual,* he thought. *Even if this is nothing more than a small, poor village, I'd still expect to see someone – anyone – on the street at this time of day.*

He came to the front of the saloon and, hearing no activity inside, shrugged his shoulders and made his way through the batwing doors, comforted by the fact that his revolver was tucked into the front of his pants behind his belt buckle.

It took a moment for his eyes to adjust to the dim light within the saloon; the contrast from the bright glare outside to the relative darkness within was extreme, and a slight swirling gust of wind had kicked up some sand in his eyes as he walked down the street moments earlier.

He slowly made his way up the front of the bar, rubbing his eyes with his fists a couple of times when they started to cloud over. Then he blinked a half-dozen times, finally got his bearings, and looked at the grim-faced bartender who was standing behind the long, wooden counter.

Nelson nodded a greeting and said, "You speak English there, amigo?"

The man nodded but said nothing, nervously looking off to his left.

But Nelson didn't notice and said: "My wife thought that she might'a heard some gunshots from down this way earlier. I told her that she was most likely hearin' things – you know how women are – but promised her I'd check it on out. So tell me, you didn't see or hear anything, did ya?"

The bartender, now looking even more nervous, said nothing.

"Well, hah hah hah."

The mocking, booming, exaggerated laughter that came from behind Nelson made him turn around with a start, flushing with anger at the sound.

Two men were seated at a nearby table; evidently he had walked right past them on the way up to the bar – *probably missed them both while I was rubbing the dust out of my eyes*, he thought.

217

"What's so funny?" be blurted out.

"Why, you are, mister," Hoss Johnson said as a large smile started to work its way across his broad face. "Yer a damned sight funny, I'd say."

Nelson turned a little redder and looked carefully at Hoss Johnson; then he shifted his gaze to the man seated next to him. Nelson was startled as he recognized the face; it was the same man who had passed him and his family on the trail a few days earlier while they were making their way toward Indian Wells with the two village youngsters.

"Hey, I know you," Nelson said, although the sound of his voice, in a high and nervous pitch, surprised him.

"Is that a fact?" Hoss Johnson asked, turning his attention to Grant. "Jest where'd ya run into this galoot before, Grant ol' boy?"

"Yer the one had the right pretty wife with the big rifle in the back of the wagon, ain't ya?" Grant said to Nelson, ignoring Hoss Johnson for the moment. "Might pretty woman, as I recall – a fine looking thing. And jest where might she be right about now?"

"That's none of yer damn business," Nelson sputtered, his face hot and flushed once more.

Grant casually reached his right hand down to his holster and pulled out one of the long Remington percussion revolvers that he carried. His manner suggested that he had all the time in the world. He pointed the Remington directly at Nelson, deliberately cocking the hammer in a slow, assured manner, all the while looking Larry Nelson directly in the eye.

"Let's suppose I make it my business," he said. "Starting about right now."

And Hoss Johnson, who had watched this exchange with the eager delight of a child, started to laugh even louder.

Chapter Twenty-Four
The Trick Of Survival

The sudden snap from a single gunshot that echoed through the Indian Wells saloon carried out into the street and the open air beyond and was heard by Tomas Hernandez, by the parents and grandparents of the village boys Hector and Martin – by most all of the inhabitants of the sleepy village, in fact.

It certainly was heard by the outlaws Hoss Johnson and his partner, a vile man named Grant.

No one in the village stirred. In fact, there was little that anyone could do: The sheep ranchers and simple farmers who lived in Indian Wells were not gunfighters, nor were they even hunters. The few men who owned guns were, for the most part, uncomfortable with their use and certainly not capable of confronting dangerous outlaws such as the two who were now holed up and amusing themselves in the village's unassuming cantina.

And so the residents of the tiny community remained inside their houses, just as they had days before when gunfire erupted within the saloon and four village men were later buried in consecutive plots in the Indian Wells cemetery at the back edge of the community; just as they had when the village's respected mayor, Pedro Ruiz, was gunned down in his home and was laid to rest in the same small cemetery.

The dull noise from a gunshot on this sunny day also was heard by Sally Nelson. She shivered at the sound, somehow expecting the worst, and she wondered what had happened.

"Dear God, don't let it be Larry," she muttered.

"What was that, Ma?" her oldest boy, Jason, asked.

"Nothing. It's all right," she said, mustering her courage and trying to manage a smile and a firm, steady voice; but she recognized that she was failing in the attempt, and she added: "It's going to be all right – don't you worry now."

She knew that it was vital to shield her boys from the gloom that she felt. But she also was certain that something bad already had happened and that it was only the beginning of still more bad things to come. She could feel the tug-of-war going on inside her, eating at her, making her want to run and hide.

"Remember our little game of hide and seek?" she asked at last. "Let's play it again – right now. I want to see if you still know where your secret hiding places are, all right?

"Run off now and try to find them again – all of you. Go! Scoot! Let me see how long it takes you."

Her own two boys, along with Hector and Martin, the village youngsters who had befriended the Nelson family, all ran in different directions, laughing all the while as they scurried about. Even though Hector and Martin understood little English, they were having fun playing a game that required no language skills at all: As soon as the running started, they knew exactly what to do.

It's just a game to them, Sally Nelson thought. *They don't know that this is for real. They don't know that this might even be life and death. And I can't tell them; or at least not yet I can't.*

She waited a moment and then called out: "All right, I'm coming to find you now. Let's see how well you are hidden and how quiet you can be."

The muffled sound of a second gunshot echoed faintly in the distance, again coming from the direction of the village's lone saloon, and Sally Nelson involuntarily shuddered once more. She felt alone and exposed and uneasy in a way that she had never experienced before.

Even so, she tried to cheer herself up.

It's not Larry; it's going to be all right. It's only my imagination that's somehow playing tricks on me, she thought.

But she couldn't shake the feeling. And she was expecting trouble to walk through the small door of the adobe home at any moment.

She heard one of her boys call out: "Where are you, Ma? Are you still trying to find us?"

"Hush now," she called. "Don't make a sound. Yes, I'm trying to find you. I'm coming along right now. Just stay still and wait, and be quiet – all of you."

But Sally Nelson remained frozen, making no effort to move.

Max Blake, meanwhile, was making progress across the harsh and unforgiving land. Spelling Buck with Weasel Morgan's horse, even for a short period, had saved him valuable time. And now that he had crossed the wide stream and was traveling once more across higher country, the horses didn't have to slug and pick and slog their way through the slippery desert sand and were able to move much faster and far more efficiently.

Following tracks wasn't necessary, either. Max knew exactly where Hoss Johnson and his new partner had been headed, and he knew exactly how to get there – and exactly what needed to be done once he arrived.

The only issue that Max faced now was to figure out how to best deal with Hoss Johnson and his traveling companion, and he worked on a plan as he rode steadily and inexorably on.

Max knew that the last time Hoss Johnson had been in Indian Wells, only days before, the big outlaw had killed four men in the village saloon, robbing them of the little money they had before moving on with the Morgan brothers. It only made sense that Johnson would go back to the saloon again. The villagers would remember him and remain afraid of him; they wouldn't dare try to stop him or make a move against him: It was not in their nature to fight, and they possessed neither the skills nor the tools to cope with the guns and violence that followed the big outlaw's every move.

If I can work my way in behind the saloon and find a back entrance, Max thought, *I just might be able to surprise the two of them. And if I can get the drop on Johnson and his friend, then there won't be any more trouble – no one else in the village will get hurt.*

The trick would be to circle around to the back of the saloon without being seen by anyone: not by Hoss Johnson, not by his partner, not even by any of the village's few inhabitants.

It wasn't much of a plan, Max knew as he pushed Buck across the broad slope of the mountain ridge that hid Indian Wells, only three miles away now to the northwest. It relied too much on Hoss Johnson being predictable, on his actually being in the saloon when Max arrived, on the saloon being relatively empty of people, on the fact that few people would expect a federal marshal like Max Blake to return to the village and walk through the saloon's back door.

That's a lot to ask.

And what about the mystery partner? Max considered. God only knew who the man really was, what his real intentions were, what he would be doing in Indian Wells, what his reactions would be when Max stole silently through the back entrance of the saloon, or whether the man was even still traveling with Hoss Johnson.

It might be that Hoss's partner killed Freeman Morgan, and then Hoss killed the man in return and is only leading in the horse, Max thought suddenly. *Maybe I've already passed his body, lying in some creek bed off to the side of the trail somewhere, and won't even have to worry about the man.*

"But I doubt it, Buck," he said aloud. "I expect that we'll find the two of them when we ride into Indian Wells, and they won't be happy to see us."

Max also suspected, although he wished it were otherwise, that the two outlaws somehow wouldn't be surprised, either.

"What'd ya kill him for?" Grant asked Hoss Johnson, looking down at the slumped and oddly twisted body of Larry Nelson on the rough-hewn planks of the saloon floor. "He might'a been worth something to us."

"Him? Of what use was that sod-buster to us? He didn't have no money, and he wouldn't tell us nothin' – he proved that well enough when I put that first bullet into his damn leg. What's the difference to you if'n he's dead or not?"

"Well, he might'a at least told us where his woman was hiding, if you hadn't kilt him off so damn fast," Grant said.

"Hiding? What makes you think the woman is hiding a'tall? Hell, she ain't bound to be hiding from nothin' or no one," Hoss said. "What's she got to hide from? She don't know we're in this stinkin' little village. And she surely don't know that we might want to find us a pretty little white woman for a little night's entertainment, no sir."

He bellowed out his exaggerated laugh for a brief moment, then added: "Hell, she don't even know yet that she's become a widow."

That thought made him laugh out loud again.

"Haw haw haw. And I jest now had me a really funny thought. Maybe now that she's a new widow-woman, she'll take more kindly to seein' us once we tell her what's happened to her, ah, late husband," Hoss said. "Haw haw haw."

"I wouldn't make a bet on that," Grant said. Then, pointing at Larry Nelson's lifeless body, he asked, "What do we do with him, anyway?"

Hoss looked down and shrugged.

"Him? What do I care? You wanna move him outta here, Mr. Grant, you go right ahead. Me? I got better things to worry 'bout than cleaning up after dead bodies."

Grant looked over at the bartender, who had continued to stand with his hands on the bar since the two men had entered the saloon, frozen and with an ongoing look of unconcealed terror on his face. He had watched helplessly as Larry Nelson had entered the bar a half-hour earlier and then had been clubbed, shot once in the leg, and ultimately murdered – a bullet eventually fired straight into his chest from no more than five feet away.

"You," Grant barked, pulling the man's eyes off Hoss Johnson. "Hey, barkeep. Drag this body out the back door. You understand?"

Tomas Hernandez rapidly shook his head up and down and moved quickly around the long counter; he continued to hold both of his hands in the air as he hurriedly walked over to where Larry Nelson had fallen.

"Move it along now," Grant said. "We need some fresh air in here, and we ain't got all day and night to git it."

"Yer right about that," Hoss said. "But I think it's time we got the hell outta here anyways and went huntin' up that newfound widow-woman, don't you?"

"And jest where do you expect we're gonna find her?" Grant asked, keeping his eyes on the bartender as the old man slowly dragged the dead body of Larry Nelson, late of Texas and Arkansas, across the floor toward the small door that led out back.

"How much of a chore can that be?" Hoss asked. "All we gotta do is start knockin' on some doors. And there ain't a hell of a lot of doors to knock on in this piss-ant little place, in case you hadn't noticed such. That's part of the charm."

Grant nodded as he swung his long legs over the top of the bar and grabbed a full bottle of tequila from the shelf behind.

"The thought of that fine-lookin' woman makes me think yer right. I had a mind to have some fun with her the first time I laid eyes on her, and I would have done jest that if she hadn't a'had a long gun trained directly on me at the time.

"Besides, it'll help me think about something until Max Blake shows up," he said. "But let's jest make sure we're ready when he does. We likely won't get a second chance with that bastard."

"Max Blake's gotta be a long way behind us – if there even is a Max Blake, which I'm beginning to doubt," Hoss said.

"You know, the more I think on it, I don't think we're gonna ever see anything of this Max Blake fella a'tall. I think it's jest you and me and these sheep herders – and, of course, that new widow-woman. Haw haw haw."

"What about him?" Grant asked, pointing at the bartender, who was still struggling with the weight of Larry Nelson's lifeless corpse at the rear of the saloon.

"He's nothing to me. Go ahead an' shoot him," Hoss said and started for the door, at the same time shucking two fresh cartridges into his revolver.

Grant looked with deadly eyes at Hoss and called after him, stopping the big man at the door. "You do it, you want him dead so bad."

"What's the matter?" Hoss sneered as he turned around to face Grant, his gun hand dangling close to his revolver. "You yellow or something? Cain't do it yerself?"

The two men stared hard at one another for a moment.

"This is about Max Blake; remember that," Grant finally said.

Then he shrugged and turned to where Tomas Hernandez had stopped abruptly at the back door when the argument about his own life had ensued and was now warily watching the two men.

A single shot from a big Remington revolver boomed throughout the saloon, putting another big smile on the thick face of Hoss Johnson.

"This is turnin' out to be more fun than I thought," he said. "Haw haw haw."

Max Blake heard the shot from a single revolver off in the distance and knew that he was close.

Very close, in fact.

He could see the small cluster of adobe buildings immediately ahead now: a few houses in a row, the small church, the general store, the saloon, a few more houses and ramshackle storage sheds and outbuildings. Max veered off the trail that lead directly into the village and climbed down off Buck. He crouched to take his bearings near a small cluster of scraggly pines that had been bent into odd shapes by the wind that constantly blew down from the high mountain peaks off in the distance and swept across the edge of the hills and into the very heart of the little village.

Dusk was beginning to settle, and the deep shadows that fell across the land were exaggerated by the hills and the trees and the mountains that all helped to block out the sinking sun.

There were no other sounds: no gun shots, no shouting, no indications of movement or excitement.

Max tied Buck and Weasel Morgan's horse behind the clump of trees so that they would be out of sight from riders approaching in either direction along the trail. He took the time, because he heard no other immediate shots, to strip off the saddles and pull out an oat bag from the gear that was strapped onto the backs of the horses. He tied the oat bag around Buck's broad neck and then spread some feed out on the ground for Weasel Morgan's horse.

Then he pulled out his Colt, quickly checked to see that the gun was fully loaded, and slipped away into the shadows.

Chapter Twenty-Five
A Sudden Resolution

Max Blake found the back door to the Indian Wells saloon with no trouble.

He was moving quickly and keeping low to the ground in a running crouch, his Colt Peacemaker held tightly and comfortably in his right hand. He circled the edges of buildings that ran along the village's only street and stayed in the deepening shadows as he made his way back to where the saloon was situated, immediately alongside the general store.

A low moan drew his attention to the darkened area near the door, and he crept closer, his index finger firmly curled on the trigger of the Colt.

Max was close enough now to see the shapes of two men lying just outside the door. One was lifeless; the other was trying to crawl, but the effort was too much and the man suddenly slumped down, still and unmoving on the ground.

Max thought that he might be dead, but the man stirred again and began to moan softly once more.

Max moved in close and put his left hand on the man's shoulder.

"Lie still," he said.

The man stirred and tried to look up.

"No, don't move," Max said. Then, realizing that the man might not speak English, he said, "Do you understand me all right?"

"Yes, senor. Bartender," the man said, struggling to talk as he gasped for breath.

"Shot me. Shot him. After the woman now."

"Who? What woman?" Max asked.

"Two men. Gone now. After the woman. Ruiz house. At Ruiz house."

"Who is at the Ruiz house?" Max asked. "What woman?"

But the bartender's head had slumped to the ground once more, and Max could hear the rattle – a low, distended gurgling – in the man's throat that continued for several seconds and then suddenly, abruptly, stopped.

Nothing more to be done for him now, he thought.

Max looked over for the first time at the body that was lying just behind the bartender's. A glint of recognition crossed his face, and he moved closer to get a better look in the darkness.

Max Blake was not a man easily surprised. But he was surprised now to see the lifeless eyes of Larry Nelson staring back at him.

"Well I'll be damned," he muttered.

And then it made sense.

Hoss Johnson and his partner had killed Larry Nelson and Tomas Hernandez, the Indian Wells bartender, and now they were after Nelson's wife, Sally.

And she must be at the house of Pedro Ruiz, just down the street – the same house I was in the last time I was here, searching for Hoss Johnson and the two Morgan brothers.

There's no time, Max thought: *No time to figure out what the Nelson family is still doing in Indian Wells and how Larry Nelson has wound up dead in this saloon and how Hoss Johnson even knows of the existence of Sally Nelson.*

Max knew that he had to move, and he had to move right now.

"Gimme a slug of that tequila," Hoss said as he and Grant moved down the lone narrow street of Indian Wells.

Grant passed the bottle over, and Hoss took a long pull, stopping in the street while he drank. He finished a large gulp, looked down at the bottle, and then put it back up to his huge mouth once more and swallowed another three large gulps before handing the bottle back to Grant and moving ahead again down the dusty street.

"I'll give them sheep-herdin' bastards their due," he said as he wiped his mouth with the back of his hand. "Some of 'em sure can make a hell of a good bottle of tequila."

"Let's jest get on with this," Grant said, taking the bottle and moving off toward one of the small adobe shacks that sat back off the street. "I sure as hell don't want to get caught with my pants around my ankles when Max Blake gets here."

"If Max Blake gets here," Hoss Johnson said. "If, if, if, I tell ya. You worry too much, Grant. There's too many ifs in yer life. And I don't much like a man who worries too much."

Hoss looked over at Grant, who was moving along the street now with a sullen stare. "You got somethin' you wanna say to me?" he asked. Grant's return look was a challenge; but the two men had come up to the front of a small adobe structure now, and Hoss banged loudly on the door instead.

"Hey in there," he called out, still looking at Grant. He clubbed at the door again, his big left hand closed in a sizable fist that thumped against the wood three, four, five consecutive times, and he called out loudly once more. "I'm talkin' to you in there."

Hoss pulled out his revolver and kicked hard at the front of the door with his right foot, breaking the thick wood off its flimsy hinges and pushing it inside the house. An older man and woman were huddled in the center of the room in the darkness, holding onto each other, saying nothing. But the terror in their eyes betrayed their emotions and expectations.

"Where's the pretty white lady?" Hoss shouted.

The man shrugged, trembling, and pushed his wife behind him.

"Where is she, damn you? Talk to me."

Hoss pulled back the hammer on his revolver and aimed it directly at the man's head, but the frightened villager still said nothing.

Then Hoss pulled the trigger, at the last instant lifting the gun up so that the bullet crashed into the ceiling overhead. The man dropped to his knees, sobbing, and the woman wept loudly and also dropped to the dirt floor, clutching her husband's shoulders from behind and mumbling in a language that neither Grant nor Hoss understood nor cared to know.

"We're wastin' our time here," Grant said. "These people don't know nothin' and understand even less than that."

But Hoss went over and grabbed the woman's arm. Cruelly jerking her up on her feet, he pushed her ahead of him and out through the shattered door.

"Show me!" he demanded.

Still crying loudly, the woman pointed to a small house down the street on the opposite side from where she was standing with Hoss Johnson.

"Wasting our time, eh?" Hoss said.

He shoved the woman back into the house and then pulled the tequila bottle out of Grant's hand, ignoring the sounds of the woman's sobs as she fell to the floor and then immediately crawled over to where her husband was still on his knees, mumbling what might have been a fervent prayer.

"These people are just like the sheep they live with," Hoss said after taking a second pull from the bottle.

"Now let's go and have us a little fun."

"How do we handle this?" Grant asked.

"Why? You expectin' trouble or somethin'?" Hoss asked, laughing. "You think this lady here's gonna give us a hard time? Haw haw haw. All right, Mr. Grant, I'll tell ya how we're gonna handle this. We're gonna walk right through that door down the street and introduce ourselves nice and polite like – that's what we're gonna do.

"That bein' all right with you, of course. It is, now, ain't it? All right, I mean?"

Grant said nothing. He looked long and hard into Hoss Johnson's eyes, never liking what he saw but knowing better than to risk an open fight now in the street.

There'll be time for that later – after Max Blake is dead, he thought. *But it'll most definitely come to that – and this big man will take a heap of killin.'*

Grant merely shrugged his shoulders instead.

"Yeah. That's jest fine with me. Let's go," he said.

"Good. That's more like it."

Hoss and Grant started up the street, walking side by side. Neither man spoke; but Hoss, who was still holding the tequila bottle in his left hand, took two more enormous swigs, almost draining the bottle, and then smacked his lips loudly as he finished.

"Gonna have me a little fun," Hoss said. "Might jest have me a lotta fun. Yes sir."

The two outlaws were just turning toward the small house when they saw that a lone man was standing in the door frame, his arms at his sides. Only the low cast of the moon provided any light on the face of the night, and the shadows around the darkened house made it impossible to see the man's face.

"What in hell is that?" Hoss muttered.

"Hold it right there, you two. You're both under arrest," Max Blake said matter-of-factly.

"It's Blake," Grant said and bolted to his right, grabbing for a big Remington revolver as he moved.

Two shots from the Colt Peacemaker of Max Blake barked out in the night air.

The first shattered the lower bone in Grant's left leg, and he crumpled to the ground, screaming in pain.

The second shattered the near-empty tequila bottle in Hoss Johnson's left hand.

"What the –"

Wondering how things had turned so quickly, Hoss dropped the stem of the bottle from his hand and reached for his gun. He crouched down at the same time, cleared the holster, and snapped off two shots at the door frame where he had first spotted Max Blake.

But the federal marshal was no longer there, and the shots from Hoss's revolver slammed harmlessly into the thick bark of the wooden door.

Hoss quickly scanned around the front of the house but failed to spot any movement. His attention was drawn back to where Grant was moaning on the ground, holding his left leg in both hands.

"The bastard got me good," Grant said through gritted teeth as Hoss inched over to where his partner was struggling. "Knew we should've been waiting for him instead of trying to get us ..."

"Shut up," Hoss said. "You see where he went?"

"He must've ducked back in the house," Grant wheezed loudly. "I really didn't..."

"Wrong."

Hoss looked up again and saw the darkened outline of Max Blake standing thirty yards or so in front of him, near the edge of the Ruiz house. Hoss quickly snapped off another shot, but Max

230

had ducked out of the way and disappeared into the darkness once more.

"Keep yer eyes open," Hoss said to Grant. "I'm goin' after him."

Hoss started to move forward when he saw a shadow run out from the corner of the house toward a small tree. Hoss fired two more shots and waited; then he saw the form of Max Blake calmly step out from behind the tree.

Caught off guard by the boldness of the move and by the fact that the man facing him had his gun in his holster at his side, Hoss Johnson blinked a couple of times and waited, without moving, for something to happen.

"You're under arrest, mister. Drop that gun. Real slow."

"Like hell I am. And I won't drop the gun."

"You're going back to Twin Forks one way or another, Foster Johnson," Max said. "You can either ride your horse back, or you can get slung over the back; the choice is yours."

"You got some nerve for a man with a gun pointed square at his heart," Hoss said, a slow smile creeping fully across his face. "I think I'm gonna kill you jest for the fun of it and then head inside and have me a time with that widow-woman."

"Think again," Max said.

Hoss Johnson didn't like the assured coolness in the man facing him, and he was tired of the game. He let his muscles sag, relaxed, for an instant – almost as if he had given up. Then he fired his revolver a final time at Max Blake's chest.

The hammer clicked on an empty cartridge – the same one that he had fired only minutes before into the ceiling of the old man and woman's house – as Max's own Colt cleared the holster with surprising suddenness and barked out into the night.

Hoss Johnson dropped his gun and clutched at his chest with both hands, a look of amazement on his face. He sank to his knees and looked down at the blood pouring through his fingers. Then he looked slowly into the face of Max Blake, his eyes still wide open, as the realization of what had happened sunk in. The shocked expression on his face deepened.

"I had... You..."

Hoss Johnson never finished the sentence. He pitched forward and fell face down in the dirt, his oily hat spinning crazily around in oddly arched circles as the brim hit the ground and popped off his head.

Max started to move forward when the loud crash of a rifle shattered the silence of the night once more.

He instantly crouched down and leveled his Colt for another shot; but he froze at the sight of Sally Nelson standing in the narrow door of the house, a long rifle still at her shoulder, its barrel still pointed out into the night toward the street.

Max swung around and saw the unmoving form of a man pitched headlong into the dust, a big Remington revolver still clutched in his hand.

"He was going to shoot you in the back, marshal," she said simply, quietly, calmly. "I couldn't let him shoot you in the back."

Max watched as Sally Nelson slowly lowered the rifle and then slumped against the frame of the door. He looked at her for a moment, not knowing what to expect or even what to say. Then, when she didn't move or look up, he walked cautiously over to where Grant's long, thin body was lying in the dirt. Max kicked the man's big Remington away and bent down, holding two fingers to the side of Grant's pale neck for a few seconds.

Satisfied that the man was dead, Max stood up and walked slowly over to where Hoss Johnson's lifeless body was sprawled. But there was no need to check for signs of life.

Max knew exactly where his final bullet had struck.

He looked down at the body for a long time – unmoving, saying nothing.

When he finally looked up to where Sally Nelson had stood in the doorway, she was gone.

"Thanks, ma'am," Max said quietly and tipped his hat.

Then he walked off into the night.

Epilogue
A Brief Return Home

Max Blake rode his big chestnut gelding slowly toward the outskirts of Twin Forks, with the horses of four dead men strung out in single file behind him.

It's almost like a funeral procession, Max thought, and he couldn't help but suppress a slight smile – but only for the briefest of moments.

Some funeral procession, he thought.

Some funeral.

Hoss Johnson and his partner, the man Max suspected of being a member of a family of killers from Jefferson County, had been buried only a few days before in small, unmarked graves outside of the rickety white fence that defined the Indian Wells cemetery.

Larry Nelson and Tomas Hernandez, the Indian Wells bartender who died with him, were buried within the cemetery, their places marked with small white crosses, aligned with the graves of Pedro Ruiz and the other village men who had died violently and senselessly in the tiny settlement during the course of a few days.

A few days out of our lives, Max thought. *Not much difference to the old Earth as it turns night into day and back to night again, but it sure does matter to the rest of us down here.*

Max had resolved in his own mind, at least, the events of the past three weeks during the long ride back to Twin Forks. He took some comfort in knowing that Hoss Johnson, the two Morgan brothers, and the man who used the big Remington revolvers were never going to harm another person in the territory – or in this lifetime – again.

But it didn't make much sense that so many innocent people in Indian Wells had died so senselessly: the four men in the saloon,

Pedro Ruiz, the bartender, Larry Nelson. And there were other men from other towns who had died just as senselessly and just as violently in the span of few short days at the hands of these same killers: *What of them and of their families?* Max wondered.

What of them, indeed.

It was too bad about Nelson, Max considered as he moved relentlessly across the long miles of trail heading toward home. Larry Nelson, at least, would never see California. And it was doubtful now that his family would ever get there, either.

The promised land wasn't promised to everyone, I guess, Max said in a kind of half-whisper, stopping just short of uttering the words aloud.

And when Max had walked up to Sally Nelson after the short funeral, just before he had left the village, he found himself unable to say anything to her at all. He had looked at her as she stood silently beside the grave of her husband, with her own two sons and the village boys, Hector and Martin, gathered about her. Finally, feeling foolish as he shifted uncomfortably while she stared at him, returning his gaze but betraying no emotion at all, Max finally touched his fingers to the brim of his hat, nodded his head slightly, and then turned and started to slowly walk away.

She had called after him then.

"Marshal Blake," she said softly. "Can you explain any of this to me – or to my sons or to these two boys here? Can you tell me what to tell them?"

Max had stopped and turned, and he looked into Sally Nelson's eyes, now wet with tears, and waited.

"It's pointless, you know," she said after a time. "None of this means a thing in the long run. All of these little settlements strung out on the map through the desert on the way to California: A hundred years from now, do you still think that these places will even be here, nurturing life, filled with people who have hopes and dreams? Do you think that anyone will even remember the names or find them on a map? I can't see it, marshal; I don't believe it. All I can see here is sadness and death and destruction.

"It just doesn't mean anything."

There was a great deal that Max Blake had wanted to say to Sally Nelson and to her sons. But even now, days and miles later, he still couldn't find the right words.

234

At least now he knew enough to stop looking.

Hector and Martin had followed him as he moved intently away from the cemetery, and Max shook their hands and urged them to grow tall and to become both strong and wise. They had managed to smile bravely; but they, too, had looked sad and lonely and troubled as he left.

Too much death, he thought.

Max had stopped off in Whiskey Bend for a few hours on the trip home. He met briefly with the sheriff there and sent a wire ahead to Judge Radford. He also had a decent meal in the hotel, the first he had tasted in weeks, which allowed him to rest old Buck for a bit before he pressed on, eager to put an end to the trip at last.

Despite the wire, he knew that Judge Thomas Radford would be anxious to talk with him and to hear his report first-hand. The judge, in fact, would want all of the salient details.

He figured that the judge would not be happy. He would pretend, at least, not to understand the deadly heat and the necessity to bury the bodies instead of packing them on the backs of their horses.

Max also knew full well that the judge didn't like to be kept waiting.

I wonder what fiction the old man will want to hear this time, Max thought to himself. *I wonder how much he'll want me to stretch the truth so that the law fits his idea of justice.*

"Hey, Max!"

It was Joey Gray, hollering loudly and running along the expansive right flank of Buck as Max pulled into the livery stable at Twin Forks. The boy's sudden appearance was a surprise; the miles had slipped by faster than the pensive federal marshal had noticed.

"That's some shiner you got there, Max, but you look good otherwise. Buck does, too," Joey said, a big smile spread across his face. "And you got four horses with you this time. Must have been good hunting, eh, Max?"

"Hey, Joey. I guess you could say that."

"Did you get the fella you was after, Max? Did you get that Johnson fella all right?"

"I got him all right, Joey," Max said, swinging down from Buck; the feel of solid earth under his feet was a sudden pleasure.

"And was he quick, Max? Was he quick on the draw like they said he was?"

Max looked down at Joey, his tired eyes no longer able to suppress a slight smile. "He was quick all right, Joey. Mr. Hoss Johnson was a fast man with a gun. He left a lot of good men dead behind him to prove it."

"I see you met up with that fella named Grant," Joey said.

"How's that?" Max asked, surprised at Joey's words.

"This here's his horse, Max. This fella came riding into town not long after you headed out after that Hoss Johnson. He was tall and skinny and carried two big guns. Said he was looking for you; said his name was Grant, and he told me to be sure and remember it. I ran over and told the judge about it.

"Well, he must've caught up with you 'cause here's his horse, all right. Guess you didn't like him much, huh Max?"

Then I was right, Max thought.

"You take good care of Buck now, Joey," Max said at last, putting the thought of Hoss Johnson and Grant and the two Morgan brothers out of his mind, at least temporarily.

Lon Barbers came out from the livery, and Max nodded to him as he handed over the horse's reins to Joey. "He's been on the trail a long time, and I don't expect that he'll have much chance to rest up now, either," Max said.

"Hey — you ain't gonna head out again right away," Joey said, calling after Max as the marshal started to walk down the street toward the courthouse.

"I've got some unfinished business with a sheriff down by the border," Max said over his shoulder. "I don't expect to be staying around town for long. I might come back with something for Bones, though."

"Wait, Max," Joey called. "You're to come over to dinner with Ma and me. I asked her if it was all right when you got back to town."

Max stopped and turned slowly around. The boy stared back at him with a hopeful look on his face.

"You just do the best you can with Buck and the other horses, Joey. We'll see if there's time for dinner. I'll check back with you in awhile – after I've talked with the judge."

Max started to walk away again and then halted his steps once more and turned around.

"I didn't think your mother liked me much, Joey," he said.

But Joey Gray just flashed Max the biggest smile he could manage.

"I'll tell Ma you're home, Max," he said. "Right after I take care of Buck and these other brutes."

Joey started to whistle as he led Max's horse into the livery. Max could hear him clearly as he walked down the dusty street toward the courthouse.

It was the first time that he had felt at home in years, and he knew that it wouldn't be easy to leave.

Watch for the next
installment of the
Max Blake, Federal Marshal
Western series,
"Trail of Revenge"
Visit www.dallypress.com
for details